THE PEST

A Despondent Veteranarian Trilogy
- Book Three

THE PEST

A Despondent Vet Trilogy Novel - Book Three

Casey Campbell

This one is for Baden. The biggest, strongest Campbell and a generally nice guy.

To all those who deal with nightmares, I feel you.

Once again, a huge thank you to all those that helped with my endless questions. All mistakes are mine, or poetic license.

THE PEST

This veterinarian isn't just fighting for animals, now she's fighting for her future.

Months after being betrayed, used as bait to bring in a rogue cop, Sophie finds herself alone in a new town with a newborn baby. But who is the father and what will he do when he discovers his son?

Lonely and directionless, Jake Rowland arrives on her doorstep, now free of his past, he wants Sophie back.

Amid the emotional turmoil Sophie discovers native eggs are going missing, a peculiar belt alerting her to a smuggling ring that is decimating an already fragile ecosystem. At the same time a rodeo is being planned, the resulting confrontation bringing Sophie and Jake to the attention of a woman who will do anything to get her way. And what's going on with her sister? And who is the mystery woman attached to Louis? A woman who claims to be his wife. A woman obsessed with animals.

Sophie is forced into helping her new town while juggling her son and contemplating a life with Jake. Then enigmatic Louis Martinez returns, like usual, undermining all her morals.

THE PEST

CHAPTER ONE

I went into labor in the middle of the day at the small supermarket in the center of my new hometown of Grafton. Pregnancy had been grueling, I had felt terrible the entire time, exhausted and was looking forward to getting past this part of the process. But my waters breaking in the middle of the small supermarket was much too much. Thankfully I was standing with a wall of pickles (because I couldn't get enough of them) and in a panic dropped the huge jar I was holding on the ground where it smashed. Apologizing, overwhelmed with embarrassment, I prayed that no one would be outraged or worse, feel sorry for me. A lovely store worker found a mop and smilingly offered to clean it while I stood there not sure what to do next. I had saved her dog after it had eaten a sock, one of those huge fluffy slipper ones that had almost exploded the poor old Corgi's intestines. I left the store without pickles. Eating was the last thing on my mind now.

I had planned for this, knew to call my midwife and when the contractions got bad to go into the birthing clinic. There was no one else to contact because I was all alone.

Let me explain. I'm a vet who a few months ago had fled Auckland in the North Island of New Zealand to escape my father and two other men who were determined to ruin my life. One was an ex-police dog handler who pulled me in then cut me loose because he was told to, the other was an ex-undercover cop who seduced me (or I had seduced him, the details are foggy), then had tried to kill me because my father was an ass-hole who ruined everything.

Things had been sorted out, well, I wasn't dead but I didn't trust either of those ex-cops since one had gotten me pregnant and there was no way I was saying who. That they would have a greater hold over my life was intolerable. So I had run away to the South Island for a new job, a different life. I was doing well. Honestly. Except being pregnant is bullshit. I wasn't glowing, I was fading away with morning sickness that hadn't ended when it was supposed to. I liken it to a hangover without the fun party to blame it on.

Anyway, Grafton is a small, clean, pretty, and quiet part of the South Island, people are friendly and helpful. No one had been judgmental about my burgeoning belly and I was eternally grateful. I was still renting, had yet to buy my own place, even though I had the money, since nothing felt right and I had been so focused on my disinterested palate or when I could climb back into bed. I was living in a small house near the center of town. I had planned to buy an older property with land so I could renovate my own slice of paradise, but a new job and feeling awful most of the time meant I probably wouldn't be moving anytime soon. It was fine. Winter here was cold and the almost new home was clean and warm in a decent part of town. It was three bedrooms and one bathroom with a garage that opened onto the road, meaning I could pull right in and enter the house from the internal doorway, after Auckland I was security conscious. I only worked twenty hours a week and so walked to the shops for food most days just to meet people and get some fresh air. I always felt better after that. There was a log fire but I had not organized wood yet. It was on my to do list when I got my shit together and stopped crying every day. It was summer anyway and I couldn't see past this pregnancy. Christmas was almost on me and I was busy telling my sister back in Auckland that I couldn't come home because I had too many plans for the day.

So far, I was surviving.

I don't know if I glowed during pregnancy, no one knew me before.

My sister hadn't visited yet since she now had four kids, the youngest a baby only a few months old. It had been my decision to leave but I was lonelier than I anticipated.

My new workplace was interesting, attempting to find ethical means of eradicating introduced possums, rats and stoats by spreading chemicals to make them infertile (without wiping out every other species) instead of dropping 1080 poison that took six to eighteen hours of misery for the animal to die. I agree that pest control measures are incredibly important to our fragile ecosystems and unique species, but a quick kill is always better. The owners of the small farm were kind about the pregnancy. I only needed to work part time since life was much cheaper than Auckland. They were happy enough with my work to keep me on, delighted when I offered to bring my baby with me to work. Few careers offered that flexibility but this one did. Woman had been having children since the beginning of time. I would just spit this kid out and get back to work. Simple.

Then I had him.

Welcome to the world Jax Louis Carter. He weighed in at a healthy eight pound and was hungry from the moment he yelled his way into the world. I had an epidural and any other drug they offered, after all, I'm not an animal, neither am I a martyr. I wouldn't have a root canal without drugs so why expel a human without them? That was my theory after the event, at the time I had hoped to have a higher threshold for pain.

I had met plenty of people who welcomed me into their world yet when I left the birthing center three days later I was alone and completely out of my element.

My sister Jenny couldn't help because of her own baby, another little girl to go with her eldest daughter and two boys. She didn't have time to walk me through the trauma of a newborn. I was still jealous that she had a husband. Finn was a twaddle but he was stable and would do anything his wife asked.

Breast feeding was harder than expected, the emotions

and hormones something no one could have prepared me for but it was getting easier every day.

I was six weeks into this mothering lark when I started to feel unwell. It came on fast at three in the morning, the worst time, the loneliest time for a new parent, especially a solo one with no family. By daybreak it was obvious I had an infection that only antibiotics would fix. I needed to get it sorted quickly or I would only get worse.

I had an hour to make it to the appointment, feeling overwhelmed and exhausted. I needed to feed the little kunekune piglet and the baby goat that I was fostering from the local SPCA before I left. I was contemplating a shower, worrying that the doctor would think I wasn't coping, when someone pounded on my door and woke Jax.

Furious, I picked him up and stormed to the door ready to yell at whoever would bang like that. I wasn't deaf.

With Jax propped in my elbow so he could see who was tap, tap, tapping at our entryway, I threw the door wide and couldn't have been more surprised by our visitor, my stomach swooping like I was on a speeding camel.

Jake Rowland stood there looking all annoying and delicious, in tight jeans and a black t-shirt that highlighted his ridiculous body. He knew I couldn't resist those jeans.

He took one look from me to the baby, said, "What the fuck?" Then fainted.

"Terrific." I sighed and smiled at the baby. Jake was a big man and he took up plenty of space on my doorstep. "What now? Should we just close the door?" I was making cooing sounds and the baby stopped his ceaseless yowling to stare at me, his little face creased in concentration. I had read that at around six weeks he would begin smiling for real. I needed that. So far, a newborn was a thankless task.

Feeling strange and confused to why Jake would be here, and how he had found me, I put Jax into the bassinet in the living room (where I spent most of my day) and returned to pat Jake on the cheeks. I will admit right here that I took a moment to enjoy the sight of him, slumped in my doorway, all handsome face and bulging muscles, then reality returned with the worry that followed me around since having Jax.

He came around slowly, confused then embarrassed.

"You better not be sick." Were my first words.

"Gristle." He said, standing and leaning into me as I led him to the big old sofa I had bought second hand. He dropped into its huge hug and leaned forward, his hands clasped as his gaze flicked to the bassinet.

"Whose baby is that?"

"That's my baby, Jake. Don't ask for more because it's none of your business. How did you find me? What do you want?"

"You had a baby and I never heard?" When I shrugged, he stood, towering over me and making me sweat. "Is it mine?"

This made me roll my eyes. "How bad are you at math's? Of course he's not yours. You don't have to worry I'll take you for any money."

"I wouldn't think that." He snapped, taking the final steps to peer into the bassinet.

"Holy fucking shit." He gasped, "That is clearly Louis' baby. I didn't know you two were still together."

"We're not together, you jerk. We had a one-night stand and stupid, dumb, idiot Louis didn't know how to work a condom properly. I told you about it. Remember, it was a thoughtless mistake and you hated me for it even though you had dumped me." I burst into tears, gasping, "Not that I don't want him. I love him so much but sometimes I hate being a mother, especially at three in the morning."

Jake surprised me then by wrapping those big arms around me. I expected he would make a quick excuse and leave. I clung to him as he made soothing sounds, rocking me gently, my face stuffed into his shoulder, his glorious scent making me feel worse.

"I'm sick." I sniffled, gently pushing away from him and mopping my red eyes and nose with a handful of tissues. "I've got to get to the doctors so can you just go away and leave me alone. I can't deal with anything at all right now."

Jake's eyes were wide and damp and he ran shaking hands through his hair. "I'll take you to the doctors." He said, "You shouldn't be doing this alone."

"I'm not alone." I said then cried again, Jake only patting my back this time.

"Do you want me to feed him? I think I can remember how to make up a bottle."

"I'm breastfeeding." I adjusted the uncomfortable bra.

His gaze flicked to my chest, a slow smile lighting his face as he said, "Yeah, you are."

"What do you want?"

Instead of answering, he said, "Toby and Sarge are in the car. Can they come in?"

Peering out the window in a rush, I said, "Of course. They were out there while you're here fainting like Meryl Streep."

He took his eyes off Jax to say, "Why didn't you tell me you were pregnant?"

"To someone else. Why would you want to know that?"

"I don't know. Because we're friends."

"No, we are not friends."

"Does Louis even know about the baby?"

"Why would he? It's none of his business." The hurt and confusion in Jake's gaze was unmistakable and I couldn't deal with it while feeling so awful. So I said, "Go and get Toby and Sarge, please."

Jake left the house and Toby soon returned alone, saying, "Hi, Sophie. Dad's taking Sarge to the bathroom."

"Toby, how nice to see you." I couldn't help hugging him. It finally felt like I wasn't alone and I hoped he didn't notice how terrible I looked and felt. I plastered a grin on my face and said, "I've got someone for you to meet."

I left my arm draped over his shoulders. Toby must be ten or eleven now and I was surprised how much like Jake he was, the same fair hair and upright bearing. He was a shy and quiet boy, and knowing his mother made me feel sorry for him.

Toby investigated the bassinet on a frown to find Jax peering up at him. Both boys went still. It was weird.

"You had a baby?" Toby said and I figured he had better coping skills than his father since he didn't faint.

"Yeah, his name is Jax and he is six weeks old today. Are you surprised I've kept him alive? I'm a little bit surprised myself."

Toby laughed, reaching down and touching that black hair, running a finger over one cheek. "He's so little and soft."

"I'm trying to imagine him as a spotty teenager and can't do it."

Toby laughed again and I was fascinated at how much Jax loved Toby's voice. Then without warning Jax broke into a weird and lopsided smile. It took me a moment to realize what it was since I had seen a few gassy grimaces that looked similar.

I gasped and Toby turned to me, worried. "Did I do something wrong?"

"Toby, you little dreamboat. That's his first proper smile. I think he's in love with you. Do you want to hold him?"

Grinning, Toby said, "Yes, please."

Jake entered then. "Can Sarge come in?" He said, already knowing the answer and dropping the lead so the big dog could enter the house in full work mode, his snout to the ground for a quick perimeter check. Only when he was satisfied all was well did Sarge settle on the mat in front of the fireplace I was yet to use.

With his lips pressed together, Jake watched his son cradling the tiny baby. Toby and I were on the sofa, my arm around Toby, both of us cooing down at Jax in Toby's arms, the baby still smiling and staring adoringly into the older boy's eyes.

"I think Jax is angling for a new protector. He's a wily little guy." I said, noticing Jake still frozen at the door. "Are you coming in? It's raining out there."

Shaking himself as if out of a dream, Jake said, "There's a little piglet and a tiny goat out here. Are they all right in the rain?"

Standing, I said, "Thanks for reminding me. Are you okay for minute, Toby?" The boy nodded, still in awe of his little bundle. I thrust some animal pellets and a bowl of scraps at Jake, "Can you just toss this onto the patch of grass. They are getting picked up in the next few days. I've been looking after them since the SPCA is full. A farmer is taking the little pig and the goat is going to the local school to help the caretaker with weed control. You should see the local school, pretty with only a few classrooms but it's got a big playground and they like to grow vegetables." I was just nattering because I didn't get to talk as much as I used to back in Auckland. "They thought a goat might be good for the weeds and for the kids who don't have pets. I've agreed to take him back if he's too much but the caretaker lives next door to the school and he's happy to take him home each night. It's a perfect scenario."

"This place, it sounds like you really enjoy being here." Jake said, holding the container of pellets and the food scraps with white knuckles.

"Toby, your dad sounds weird."

"He is weird." But Toby was still grinning at Jax.

"What's going on?" I asked. "Why are you both here? Shouldn't you be at school?"

"I've got time off since something is going on with Mum that Dad doesn't want to talk about."

My glance at Jake only resulted in a guilty gaze at the ground, but I figured it had something to do with Michelle burning my clinic down months ago. I had given up talking to my brother in law (and co-clinic owner) Finn about it since he was still unstable about the whole incident and the ongoing court case.

"How long have you been travelling?" I asked, seeing Jake wouldn't fill in the gaps in Toby's story.

"We've stopped lots." Toby enthused. "I can show you photos." I returned to sitting beside him and he handed Jax back to rummage in his jeans pocket for a mobile phone.

"That's better than mine." I said as he tapped away like a pro.

"Mum got it." He said, not meeting my eye.

Something was going on. "Your mother was happy for you to come all this way?"

Jake spoke up then. "Michelle's been . . . busy since what happened to your clinic."

"I know what happened, Dad." Toby said, "You don't have to talk about it in code. Mum burned down Sophie's vet clinic and almost hurt the cat. She went to jail for it and Grandad had to pay off all the debt so she didn't stay in jail longer."

It hurt hearing this boy saying it out loud. "It was messed up." I agreed and Jake grumbled, "Sophie."

After a few photos and stories, I said, "Can I see the rest at the doctor's clinic?" I found my shoes and hauled on a hooded sweatshirt that covered any wet patches. Since having Jax I had lived in a uniform of trackpants, baggy t-shirts and running shoes, not yet willing to know if I could fit into my jeans. I felt fragile enough that I didn't want to acknowledge what damage had been done. I would deal with the expected changes to my body when I was a little more stable.

"Is Jax sick?" Toby asked, his gaze flicking to the baby who would need feeding soon. I was getting better but was still uncomfortable around others. I knew it was a weird topic of interest, and I had heard how much scorn some women got for doing the most natural thing in the world. I wasn't ready to deal with someone being offended by me. That was someone else's battle to wage, I had enough of my own.

"Not Jax. I've been feeling a little off. I'm just going to get some antibiotics and in a few days I'll be ready for action again." I hoped that was true. "Will we have to take Sarge?" I asked Jake who was still being strangely quiet. He had never been a man of many words but this was awkward, even for him.

"He'll be fine here alone for an hour." Jake said. "I'll take him for a run when later. I need to stretch."

"It can't be easy finding somewhere to stay with Sarge."

As if he knew we were talking about him the dog stood and padded over to me, resting his big head on my lap and staring up at me with those beautiful big eyes. Sarge was an ex-police dog and didn't often let his softer side show, just like his owner. I pat his head, not looking at Jake who was doing wonky things to me.

He said, "We've been booking dog friendly B&B's. It's been no problem. Toby needed a break from Auckland and there's so much of our fine country he hadn't seen. A boys road trip was just what we all needed." Jake moved to ruffle his son's hair and Toby smiled brightly and at ease. I hadn't seen this in him when I had met him with his mother, but then that had been a fraught meeting when Michelle had staked her claim on Jake who I was to discover was not officially divorced. Yuck, that still sounds awful. I'll explain it as we go if you haven't heard already.

"Where are you staying tonight?" I gathered car keys then strapped Jax into his car seat. I was still all fumble fingers at the baby gadgets and equipment, same with his stroller. I would feed him as soon as we got to the doctors which was only a couple of minutes away, another bonus of a small town.

Jake took my keys and lifted Jax in his car capsule before saying, "Got any spare rooms?" His smile was uncertain and I thought to argue but Toby was embarrassed so I dropped a hand to his shoulder.

When he glanced at me, I said, "I'd love you to stay. I've got a couple of spare rooms although only one of them has a bed. It's a double so you'll have to share. Is that okay?"

Toby nodded, relieved, "Dad can cook. He needs all the practice he can get."

As my nerves jangled at the sight of Jax being carried by a big hunk with bulging muscles, the man who had broken my heart, who I had been sure I would never see again, I wondered what he was here for, what he needed from me this time, and said, "Deal."

Relief and joy ran through Toby, and understanding how he felt, I leaned over and hugged him. "It's so nice of you to come see me. When we get back I'll take you out back and introduce you to Kuni the piglet and Billy the Kid, he's the little goat. They are both insane and really cute. You can help me look after them."

Holding the door open, Jake said, "While I look after you."

He was staring at Jax but I wasn't sure if he was talking to me or Toby.

As I followed Toby outside, Jake stopped me with a gentle hand to my arm, husking, "Thanks for letting us stay."

"You know you're not supposed to come near me." I whispered in reply, "There's a protection order."

"Call the cops if you want too. Just say the word, Gristle and I'll go. You have all the power here."

Whatever the heck that meant.

CHAPTER TWO

I t was days later that I felt energy returning. Jake had been great, helpful but quiet, and it was nice hearing people in the house. My routine was the same, I changed and fed Jax, ate and slept when I could, although several times in the past few days I had woken to find Jake had wheeled Jax from my bedroom in his bassinet to change him and let me sleep a little longer. It was enough to break my battered heart, but I refused to go back there with Jake, there was too much damage done, and we were yet to discuss why he was here or what he wanted. It was probably to do with Louis Martinez but I was not mentioning him unless Jake did first. I refused to let either man think I still cared.

I was relieved to feel like my old self, and while the baby slept I slid from the bed for a quick shower, my greasy, lank hair better than a shield against Jake and his unusual silence and long looks. When I returned Jax was not in his bassinet beside my bed. The house was silent but that wasn't unusual, Toby liked taking Sarge for walks or sitting on the large back lawn with the piglet and the kid. A cat had taken to sitting on the fence watching them and Toby was working hard to gain the tabby's trust.

I entered the living room to find Jake pacing, Jax propped in his forearms. He was dressed in jeans and an old white tee, his feet were bare and stubble was showing on his usually clean-shaven face. They were staring at each other and Jake had yet to notice me. Jax had taken to grinning and was using it as his weapon as much as possible, sucking us all in. He was using it now to its full potential and Jake was delighted in return.

A tear slid down my cheek at this lovely image of Jake and Jax together. I thought it would stay with me always. Jake turned around just as I swiped the tear away.

"I've enrolled Toby in the local school, the one that's getting the goat. I don't care what you say. You need us and we're staying."

"But what about Auckland, your friends. What about your job?"

"I quit contracting. I couldn't go back overseas when Michelle's in jail. I'm not going away again. No I'm not." He cooed at Jax. "There's nothing left in Auckland for me. I've got full custody of Toby and I want him to have stability. He won't get that with Michelle coming and going."

"Is she out of jail?"

"She was barely in there but the idea of going almost blew her mind. She believed her father would get her out of trouble like he's done every other time. She was sedated for most of her jailtime and was out in a few weeks because of all the time she spent in and out before the court case. She probably would have gotten home detention except your clinic was totally destroyed and she had priors?"

This gave me a jolt. "Priors for what?"

"Assault when she was younger, catfighting with her friends, while they were drunk mostly. Couple of drink driving and speeding issues. She also paid to have an ex-boyfriend beaten up years ago. She had the best lawyers because her dad covers all the bills so his mighty name isn't sullied. He paid off your insurance company so she could keep the house. She's shifted her boyfriend in and I don't want Toby around all that bullshit anymore."

"Who is she seeing?" I expected him to say it was Louis so was surprised when he said, "She's back with Mike. He's not that bad but they are volatile together. Michelle likes pretty toys but can't handle that every woman that Mike encounters hits on him. They scream and yell a lot and neighbors have been complaining again. I think they enjoy that type of relationship."

"Did you have that type of relationship with her?" I prodded, taking Jax off him and sitting down to feed him. Jake automatically poured me a glass of water. How would I ever get rid of him when he was being so damn helpful?

"No, as you know, I'm not the type to argue. I tend to just walk away."

"That's because you're broody. I'm not sure if that's worse."

"Screaming is worse for kids."

I looked down at Jax who was soon passing out in his usual milk coma. "Yeah, I imagine it is."

He sat down on the wooden coffee table in front of me, our knees touching just as Toby entered with Sarge clacking behind him on the entry tiles. I expected Jake to move away, instead he watched his son, that glint of adoration always there.

Not noticing any tension, Toby asked, "Dad, can I send Mum some photo's?"

"Of course. She'd love to see what you've been doing." Toby wandered to the bedroom, Sarge still on his heels. To me, Jake added, "She'll hate to see what we've been doing but I'm not going to be *that* parent."

"You are so mature. It's turning me on." I said this as a joke but Jake was Jake and his smile lit up the room.

"You know, you should really make sure everything is in working order after a baby. When you're ready, I'm willing to help you out."

"You really think I would go through that again? The event might be fun but the outcome is not swayed in my favor. Anyway, I think it's permanently broken down there."

Jake reached out and took Jax to burp, saying, "I don't know, Sophie. You're pretty good at this baby bullshit so far."

"Thanks, Jake." I took a long breath and Jake watched me like he knew I was about to say something he wouldn't like. "I'm not sure if you staying here is a good idea. I don't want Toby getting ideas about me and you being together, and I'm sure Michelle will have objections. She burnt down my clinic last time, and you hadn't spoken to me in ten months, not that I was counting. What will happen when she finds out you and Toby are here with me and Jax. What if Louis follows you? You know what he's like if he can't find you and I don't want him knowing about Jax."

"He needs to know, Sophie. This is not something you should hide from anyone."

Jax had fallen asleep, I knew not to get my hopes up, it wouldn't last long but it was nice to get a few minutes peace so I indicated that Jake should put him in his daybed bassinet. Jake and I were dressed like twins. Jake had barely gotten out of his own trackpants and t-shirt in the past few days. He changed into shorts when he went on his daily runs, but then would shower and return to his fat pants unless they were in the wash. I wondered if he was wearing them to make me feel better, after all, I did not want to see him in those tight jeans I liked so much, not now, not ever. The baggy ones he had on today were bad enough. Who knew what could happen? And I was certain I would never have sex ever again. Seriously. Jake was just looking big and buff while holding a little baby. Who wouldn't be touched?

We did have fun together once but I wondered if that would ever happen again. It didn't feel like it, not with all the bad blood running between us, add a boy and a baby and two unstable ex's and our lives were messy and complicated. But Jax couldn't stay a baby forever, even though it felt like this part of my life might last an eternity.

"Louis really has no idea about this baby?" Jake asked and I nodded.

"It has nothing to do with him. Like I told you, it was a stupid mistake that turned into the best thing."

"When are you going to tell him? I mean, Jax will ask about his father one day and hiding things can make them more alluring."

The way he said that was off. "Is something happening

with Louis?"

His sigh was long and tired and he ran a hand behind his neck as if to loosen tense muscles before saying, "He's singing like a bird, Sophie. After all this time in jail, staying silent, his name being dragged through the media, being treated as some antihero, he's finally talking and he's giving everyone up. I don't know what's changed but he wants out. I was suspicious he was with you already. If he does come for you and find you with his son, what do you think will happen?"

I shrugged, "I have no idea."

Sighing, Jake said, "I talked to him in prison, just once. I fucking hate being in there. He's different. He's done. He talked about what you said at the house, when you told him about the day his father died and how sick you were. It stopped him."

There was nothing to add. Jake had been there too, he had made me bait for a trap to capture Louis. I didn't want to hash through that mess.

"Is my father still in there? Maybe Louis doesn't want to stay if he can't get Elias?"

"No, your father isn't there. He's been moved to Waikeria prison, out of Auckland. I think Louis has lost his interest in Elias, and when his interest is over it rarely comes back."

"What does that mean?"

"It means, that if he wants you, he won't stop."

"You sound like you know something I don't."

"Usually." But he smiled at my frown. "I don't know for sure but I've heard rumor he's been looking for someone. For a vet."

"It might not be wise for Louis to come for me, Jake. I'm not feeling myself."

He sat beside me, dropping a big hand to my leg.

"Is it okay that me and Toby are here? If you're really unhappy we'll go."

Peering at my lap I thought about lying, about telling him to get out and leave me alone, anything to protect my heart from Jake. But I was too grateful to lie. "I wish I had the strength to tell you to get lost Jake. But I like having you here. The extra sets of hands are nice. Toby is lovely and I'm not sure how I would cope without you both now. It's not good for Jax to grow up with only a crotchety ex-vet. He'll get older and move away and I'll really be all alone. It was bound to happen."

Rolling his eyes at me, Jake said, "Jax is cute. I missed out on too much of Toby being tiny like this because I was working too hard, then there was the problems associated with the paternity test and Michelle suffered from post-natal depression."

"I didn't know that. I'm sorry. Do you think I've got that? Sometimes I cry for no reason. Usually because Jax does something new and I'm scared I'll forget it all, or that I want him to grow up faster, then I know I'll be sad when he's run off with some girlfriend."

Rubbing my hair, Jake said, "No, you're just hormonal. It's nice that you're not trying to beat on some pet owner for a while."

"I'm not really leaving the house that much."

"You walk every day. That's usually plenty of time for you to get into trouble."

"Then perhaps the pet gods are giving me a break. Time off."

"Maybe, you sure deserve it. Michelle was doing fine for the first few days after having Toby then she went home and expected to be straight back into her skinny jeans. She couldn't breast feed because she was starving herself and she quickly moved back home with her folks who paid for a night nurse. They blamed everything on me."

"I'm sorry you and Toby had to go through that. Having a baby is sure different than I thought it would be, and unlike Michelle I was never particularly concerned about my looks. I have found you being around soothing. I don't feel so frantic or alone."

"I've got your back." He pulled me closer and I leaned into him.

"Why do I have the feeling that you want more out of

this Jake? Which is flattering considering I'm fat and leaking and never going to have sex ever again."

"You will, and it'll be as good as you remember. We are very good together, Gristle. When it's just us we work well and that's what I want back. We didn't get a fair shot before. Louis was always in the way."

My breath hitched because it always frightened me when Jake got intense. He didn't like emotion and didn't like to express his feelings so when he did he meant it.

But our history was a mess and my trust was beyond fractured.

"That's all nice talk, Jake but I have a son that is now my priority. His conception wasn't ideal, his father sure isn't, and shows how stupid I can be, but I would rather be by myself with him than put him through a traumatic childhood with shitty parents. I had that growing up and it's not ideal."

"I've met your family, Gristle. I have a small understanding of what you went through, what got you in Louis' line of sight." His gaze flicked toward the door, checking we were still alone. "Toby's been through enough too." He reached for my hand that was dry and cracked from so much handwashing, lifting it to his lips he kissed my knuckles, eyes on me, heart stopping with the level of his intensity.

Usually I'm really immature and would have wrangled a way out of this situation, but Jake always pushed me to be something else, to rebel against my own insecurities, so I asked, "Am I just a better option for Toby than his unstable mother?"

He frowned, "I can't decide if that's true, hurtful or mean."

"Jake, there are secrets between us that you told me you could never talk about. I don't want that for myself. I want our only secrets to be the kinky, embarrassing ones that we would never dare tell anyone because they're weird. I hate the idea of secrets that include dog fights and drug lords. I don't think that's unreasonable."

He kissed my hand again, "I like the idea of kinky and

embarrassing secrets with you, Gristle." Then he sighed and dropped my hand to rub his forehead. "Things are different now. I don't have secrets anymore about Louis."

Something about that statement was suspicious, "You're double talking again. I don't care about Louis. What worries me is that I let you in then discover things that might hurt me and Jax or Toby. You want me to be part of his life but I need all the information before I make that decision."

"Alright, I get it." He grumbled. "Fine, tell me what you want to know."

This was easy, there was a topic that my Uncle Rueben had told me about months ago and I had obsessed over it. "Why did you never tell me that you and Michelle lost a baby when she was kidnapped."

Jake gasped in surprise. "Jesus, Sophie. How did you find out about that?"

"Does it matter? Someone could always try to hurt me by knowing things about you. I hate the thought of people knowing more about you than I do when I'm living with you. You know I've always wanted you, Jake and I feel like you use it against me."

"Gristle, it was obvious to everyone that I wanted you from the beginning, you know that. I've never met anyone else like you." He peered over his shoulder, ensuring Toby remained busy. "Why do you think Michelle lost her mind? She knew there was no going back, that I had finally met someone I wanted to be with. But, okay, I get it. You're right, you should know things about me and Toby. I'm sorry, it's just painful to even think about." He bit his lip, peering at the ceiling and my eyes slid down his throat. Why did Jake tie me in knots? It made no logical sense but just looking at him left me wide open for more hurt.

Eventually he nodded, as if to himself and said, "When I was still in the cops, when Toby was about two, I thought I was bulletproof, working too hard, playing way too hard. I had a wife that other men envied, a great career, amazing friends, as much fun on the side as I could endure. Life was good. Then Michelle got pregnant. She said it was the only way to slow me down, instead I had to demand a paternity test when Louis told me she had been playing around. I wasn't even surprised or upset. I wasn't even living the life I wanted, just the one I thought everyone else wanted. Anyway, this guy, it really doesn't matter who and you don't know him, he took Michelle and Toby as retribution for me putting away a couple of his family members. Louis was already undercover but still finding his feet."

"Jesus, how long was he undercover?" My mind was reeling with each statement but I would have to pack them away to ponder when I was alone.

"Way too long, but he always had a good reason to stay in. Michelle and Toby were only gone for four hours, I didn't even know for a couple of those hours. It was Louis who heard about it first and it was Louis who got them back, even though he could never stomach Michelle. He did it for me, and he never let me forget that. A few days after they were back Michelle had a miscarriage. It was early, I didn't even know she was pregnant. She was devastated and lost her shit again. We were not getting on and I knew we would never work, so, being pragmatic, I told her that it wasn't a great time for a new baby. Not saying I didn't want the baby, it's just . . ."

I touched his forearm, "Jake, I get it."

"Yeah. We tried to make it work but just went back to fighting. After a month I knew I couldn't take it anymore and told her I was leaving. She was furious that I would go after she had lost a baby, and she was right, but when was a good time to split? Should I have dragged it out for more years? It was a mess, the whole thing. Mike turned up, I can't even remember why anymore, maybe Michelle called him, when he worked out why we were fighting he was furious that Michelle didn't want me to leave. He never understood it was about control. I doubt she ever loved me, she just liked to have me there. Michelle had told Mike that the baby was his."

My eyes almost fell out of my head. "Holy crap. *Was* it his?"

"Looking back, it was probably his. Michelle and I were rarely intimate."

"How did Michelle explain it?"

"What could she say? If she said it was mine in front of Mike he would know she's a liar, and if she admitted it was Mike's to me she knew there was no going back. So she said nothing. Refused to talk about it again. I ended up leaving the force and going into contracting, I hated leaving Toby but it was nice to get some space and freedom away from Michelle. She made it clear that if I refused to stay with her she would make it difficult for me to see Toby. So I went back and our chaotic relationship rumbled on for a few more years. I knew she wasn't faithful and to counter it I wasn't either. Tit for tat is a vicious, hateful way to live. Like I've told you before, Toby let slip when he was a little older that Mike was always there when I was overseas. Kids shouldn't know that shit when they're five, and so I waved the white flag, called in the therapists and got them to help me leave constructively. Michelle was okay with me moving to the apartment under the house because she still had me on call. I dated pretty, young things to keep her at arm's length and I got to stay close to Toby. We have not had a physical relationship since then."

"Did Michelle want a physical relationship?"

"Only when she was fighting with her newest boyfriend."

"Michelle is beautiful. How did you not cave, just once?" I was trying to give him an out, to admit they had gone back and forth for years.

"Like I said, I always had a girlfriend, an endless string of them. Some vapid, pretty thing that would stir Michelle's endless competitive streak while I said I was a changed man, one that couldn't cheat."

That made sense, I suppose. "I feel bad for you and Mike. It's really unfair to use a pregnancy like that."

He smiled. "I'm sick of me and Toby being dragged along

on Michelle's dramatic neediness. I saved money contracting, and although I hate what you went through because Michelle burned your business down, for once the outcome has worked in my favor. I've been granted full custody of Toby and I'm not giving him up again. He needs me to fight for him this time, to know his adult won't walk away. I want you to be with us."

He knelt in front of me, holding my hands and staring at me hard.

"Sophie, please give me one more chance. I've wanted you from the moment I saw you brawling over a dog. I've never felt like this before. Louis is no longer my problem, I've handed over all responsibility for him and my past is finally done enough that I can move on. I want Toby to know how hard you push for the things you believe in, and to know someone fearless and truthful in their values and beliefs. I want to help you bring up Jax. I don't care who his father is or how we got here so long as we end up together in the end."

"Jake, I . . ." Jax started crying, giving me a good excuse to escape this intense situation.

CHAPTER THREE

I t was five days later that life changed again. Jax had only woken once during the night and I had slept like a dead woman. The antibiotics were doing their job perfectly.

Jake and Toby had taken Sarge out to some hills and were booked in for a trout fishing tour with a nice man they had met in town. I had never tasted trout but was assured, if cooked properly, it was delicious. It was illegal to buy wild trout so the only way to get it was by standing waist deep in a freezing river using a long line and pretending to be a fly. It was an artform. No wonder I had never tasted it. You needed a license and all that equipment. I hoped Jake and Toby liked it and that the taste was worth the effort. If not it was a great adventure for them. Sarge was going too since the old dog's hips were bad and he was happy just being near Jake and Toby, his working days behind him.

I wondered if Jake would like a puppy. He never spoke much about his days as a police dog handler, another thing we needed time to discuss fully. I did love watching him with Sarge. They were so natural in each other's company and would have been formidable in full working mode. This made me think of Captain Pugwash who was with my sister. Just thinking about that little dog that I had taken off a dreadful animal abuser made me smile. He was one of my happy ending stories. I wouldn't think about Pothead, my old clinic cat that was also living with my sister and her family. He was a big asshole and thinking about him made me upset and I had too many hormones for that.

I bundled Jax into his car seat, longing for the days when I just grabbed keys and a phone and was gone. Now I needed a bag to last the Armageddon. I made my way to work, sliding Jax into a front pack that made us both feel warm and content.

Neil and Zoe Hill were the owners of the farm that had almost gone broke years ago and had merged with a scientific company to find a solution to New Zealand's endless possum problem. Possums had been bought to New Zealand from Australia in the 1830's for the fur trade. They are a protected species in Australia, scraggly, mangy looking things, but with the space and lack of predators in their new country the possums had gotten huge and bred like crazy. They were cute, or I thought so. They were not dangerous animals unless cornered. I had a cat once who had tangled with an urban possum and had been virtually scalped. They *were* pests, omnivores that loved eating native bird eggs or chicks. The main solution so far was 1080 poison. I wasn't against ethical trapping and killing but with so much wild, native bush it was impossible for the Department of Conservation to maintain any effective solution and the native bush and wildlife continued to suffer for it. So 1080 poison was dumped by planes and choppers and those poor possums, who were just doing what they always did, who hadn't asked to come from another country, died horribly. I was happy to help find a solution.

Possums were trapped by local farmers instead of being cracked on the head with the nearest chunk of wood, they were then collected in the special cages we provided and were well fed and cared for while the newest contraceptive was tested. Being kind and ethical was important to me and important to my new employers. My role was to ensure the animals were healthy, euthanizing those that weren't and discovering what went wrong.

It was interesting but I had little to do with the actual science behind it. Before having Jax I had contemplated going back to university to study the subject. Then I had him and was just trying to survive.

The farm was stunning, rolling landscape that changed to a whole new level of beautiful with each new season. Neil and his brother had fought bitterly over the family farm, my old vet nurse Primrose, Neil's sister, had told me about it, but Neil and his wife never mentioned what had happened. With my own complicated family history I was not going to bring it up. We all liked Primrose so we were all happy with that.

Neil and Zoe were total opposites. Where Neil was all tall, skinny anxiety and wispy brown hair, Zoe was chubby and laid back, easy to laugh and genuinely a nice person.

Every day I made it to work, they were happy to see me. I could only spare an hour before Jax would need feeding again and I was officially off work for a few more months, but I wanted to come in to check on everything. I had set up my own area and wanted to ensure it was maintained to my standards.

As I returned to my car, laden with an excess of fresh fruit and vegetables from the farm gardens, Neil followed me out.

"Sophie, hold up. Can I talk to you for a minute?" He asked, looking more distracted than usual.

"That sounds ominous." His concerned expression was deeply etched and I worried he was about to tell me my job was not working, that they had changed their minds. What would I do? I could find another job, there was plenty of veterinarian work around, but I had come to Grafton for this job and wasn't sure I wanted to stay if it was gone.

He beckoned me to follow him around the house to a huge bird aviary. I'm not a fan of birdcages, they make me think of prisons, little jails for birds who had done nothing more than be pretty. This one was a little different in my twisty head. It was used for birds found injured or unwell, a holding place until Forest and Bird or the SPCA could collect them. Often birds were returned here to be let loose in the nearby bushland.

There was the usual rabble of birds, not all of them natives. There were kea and morepork, fantail and hawk. The ground dwelling kiwi was rare but had been rehabilitated and released nearby. It was not uncommon to find eggs, the nesting bird then kept until the chicks were old enough to release too. It was a hands-off system, they were wild animals and Neil tried his hardest to maintain that remoteness so they would not come to rely on humans. He caught insects, mice and rats to feed the birds, putting the overflow into a special freezer. It was amazing to work with people who were so dedicated to their local environment.

Neil lifted the lid on an empty nesting box. I gazed at it in confusion.

"What am I looking at?" I asked, noting the cages had been recently raked out.

"There were eggs in here." He said, close to tears, "Four Kea eggs. Now there isn't." He pointed along the other boxes that could be accessed by this small corridor behind the big wooden aviary structure. "It's the same with all the boxes over the past six months. Birds come in and as soon as there are eggs they're gone."

"It must be a rogue rat or stoat. There aren't any possums around, not here. Why don't you just lock this part? Then no one can get in."

"The locks are getting cut, no matter how big I get. You know that no rat or stoat could get into these boxes. I've talked to the cops and they suggested putting in cameras, which I can do, but someone's obviously stealing the eggs. I don't want to pay money for footage of someone in a ski mask, nothing will come of it. I hate that someone is skulking around. We have kids and animals to think about. I understand some people don't like the idea of scientific facilities, even little farms that are trying to fix an awful problem, and I'm worried this is the beginning of some campaign that will escalate or move to the labs."

Jax started grumbling and I knew he would be bellowing for food soon.

"I don't know what to say. I guess someone wants their own kea or something? It's nothing new for people to want something they're told they can't have."

He lifted a pair of thick women's stockings that were knotted every few centimeters and my stomach fluttered in recognition.

"I showed this to the police." Neil said, "They had no idea what it was and I got the feeling they thought it was some kinky rubbish. Why are you looking like that, Sophie?"

Jax started crying and I nodded. "Can I feed him inside before I go? I want to get a single bed on my way home and then I think the both of us will be done in."

"Sure, follow me."

As we walked I said, "I know what that stocking is, Neil." I bit my lip, knowing I was not ready to take on any new wars. I had come here for the quiet, rural community without the bullshit I had endured in the city. Instead I was staring down more hated animal abuse.

"It sounds like I'm not going to like it." Neil sighed, running his hand through his thinning hair and nodding to his lovely wife as we entered the house, saying, "I've shown Sophie the stocking. She thinks she knows what it is?"

Zoe lifted an eyebrow in surprise, hands buried in bread dough. "No one we've asked had a clue and the cops just thought I've been tying Neil to the bedpost with it. Seriously, they tried to make a dirty joke out of people breaking into our property."

Unhooking Jax from the front pack, his mewling was drilling into my head, making me sweat and rush.

"It's no joke." I said, "But it is dirty. It's a type of belt for transporting eggs, usually on planes for the illegal exotic pet market overseas. Some people will pay a fortune to have a thing that someone else can't get, even if it's illegal, immoral and just fucking disgusting." I said a quiet apology to Jax for swearing in front of him, making it my mission to contain my language.

Neil and Zoe stared at me with their mouths dropped open, eyes wide.

Zoe eventually spoke, emotion hitching her voice, "But those eggs, those almost birds, they're to be returned to the wild. We need every single one because of the pests we're trying to get rid of. We've devoted our lives, our farm to ensuring our children have native birds in the future, Neil doesn't talk to his brother, they had a huge fight to ensure this farm stayed in the family, and someone just wanders in and takes whatever they want for some rich guy overseas?"

"Not just rich guys. Some zoos aren't against getting animals via less than legal means, they can always conjure up a lie on how they got it. Either way, the animal, bird, reptile, snake or exotic spider never makes it home."

"But we're out here in the middle of nowhere."

I sat down with Jax on my lap, he was yelling his head off that I wasn't attending him fast enough. I had no qualms breastfeeding here, they were farmers and barely noticed. I was getting quicker and knew Neil and Zoe would let me know if they were offended.

Relaxing into the chair, I stared at the couple in turn, saying, "Then the only question is who is smuggling our native birds out to the world."

◆ ◆ ◆

I t took me longer to get away from the farm than I hoped but it was nice being out and talking to people. Neil and Zoe had a horse and a labradoodle that both needed a little attention and I enjoyed doing it, remembering how much I loved small animal vet care. This made me a tiny bit homesick for Finn, my brother in law, ex business partner and surrogate father. It might have been my fault the clinic burned down, (technically it was Jake's ex-wife Michelle's fault but I had bought her into our lives) it was all Finn's fault that we hadn't resumed working together. By the time he realized he hated working with anyone else I had committed to the South Island. My sister called every few days to complain that Finn was miserable and making everyone around him equally unhappy.

Walking me to my car, Zoe said on a knowing grin, "Rumor around town says some big hunk with a German Sheppard and a cute boy are staying with you. Is this Jax's daddy?"

I smiled, "I wish." It was out before I understood what it meant and I burst into tears. "I'm sorry." I gasped as Zoe apologized and rubbed my shoulder.

"No, it's me. I didn't mean that. I love Jax just the way he is."

Zoe chuckled, "Oh, Sophie. You're allowed to acknowledge life could've been easier if you'd made other choices. Doesn't mean you would give this guy back for anything." She rubbed Jax's head. He was looking around now, frowning like he was unhappy with these new surroundings. It was interesting that I was beginning to see a personality. I hadn't thought about my child having a nature of his own, so far he just felt like an extension of me, an eating, pooping, crying extension of me.

"I know. I'm just tired."

Zoe touched my arm after I deposited my son into his car seat. "It gets better. I promise. Before you know it he'll be a big, smelly teenager, sleeping all day, farting and asking for dinner."

"I can't imagine it." I smiled, "Thank you for being so understanding. I know this hasn't been the ideal situation."

"Are you kidding? It's been perfect. I don't think you realize how good you are at your job, Sophie. You know all sorts of weird shit, like stockings that are used as a transport belt for the illegal egg trade." She blew out a breath and shook her head. "I'm getting lights and cameras installed, not just for the birds. It scares me that someone is wandering around out here and we don't know about it. The kids go out there all the time without us, imagine if they came across the thief? They could get hurt."

"Good idea." I said, ready to leave. "Ask around town. Look for people who pass through, like truck drivers or stock agents, or someone who transports in town. Talk to the science geeks and let them know. Sometimes just getting the word out that you're on to them puts people off."

"Thanks, Sophie. You're a gem."

I stepped into my car and rolled the window down, "And the hunk is just a friend from Auckland. They were having some trouble and Jake decided they needed a road trip to get away from it all."

"His dog is beautiful."

"He's an ex-police dog and he *is* very beautiful."

"The handler's not bad either." She winked. "When are they leaving?"

"That's the problem. He thinks I might want him to stay."

"And what do you think?"

"That he might be right."

Waving, I turned left and headed for town.

◆ ◆ ◆

Pulling up outside the secondhand store, I hoped that like usual it contained what I needed. I had planned to buy all new baby gear but had changed my mind, telling myself that I was helping the environment by not buying new. Secretly, I was not ready to fully commit. The owner was Dahlia Doyle, a chubby, happy woman who had been knocked over in a hit and run years ago and was now wheelchair bound. It didn't slow her down. She always dressed well, usually slacks and pretty shirts in some shade of pink or purple, and her red hair was always curled away from her pretty face. She looked like the aunt you always wanted, the one that would sneak you treats when you were a kid and covered for you when you made stupid teenage mistakes.

Luckily she was there when I entered, Jax again strapped to my chest.

"Sophie!" She called, then made a shushing motion like a librarian and said, "Sorry, and baby Jax. Look how big he's getting already."

"Hi, Dahlia. He eats like a machine. I'm just wondering if you have a single bed for sale. A good clean one. I can even go a new mattress if you have a nice bed frame."

"I've got just the thing." She move the lever on her wheelchair and I followed to the bed section. "I had one come in this morning, still in the plastic. It was going up to the big house on Sansom Street but was the wrong color. Must be nice being rich. I can give it to you for two hundred."

"That's perfect. Could Harley drop it off to the house in the next few days?"

"He's got to take a sofa up to Stretton Road and can swing by and drop this off today, if that suits?"

Harley Punnet was an older man, maybe sixty, with a bald head and a long grey goatee. He had the look of an ex-gang member but I never asked because I knew no one would tell me. He did odd jobs around town, and deliveries for most of the stores. If you wanted something done Harley could probably do it. He barely spoke but I wasn't put off by it, he had the look of someone who just hates people. I appreciated that about him.

"You are a life saver, Dahlia." I told her, holding her hand in a gesture of thanks.

"Is this for the hunk that's been staying at your place?" She asked and I smiled. Small town people really did know everything.

"It's for the hunk's son. They're friends from Auckland and thinking about staying."

"Don't blame them, get out of the rat race. I don't know how anyone can breathe up there in Auckland. I need fresh air to dry my nails." She chuckled. "Now, I've got some brand-new sheets here too, still in the wrappers, they came in a box but they smell good. I'd still give them a run through the machine."

"I've got a few sheets. My sister sent them by mistake with a box of baby clothes."

"I'm guessing your sister had a girl since your baby is always in pink."

"I hope I'm not causing him any damage. I thought I had another week before he came and now I can't find the time to get him anything gender appropriate. He'll end up with issues."

"Don't worry about it." She waved it away, "Just take lots of photos for his twenty first birthday party."

We moved to the register, "Do you have kids, Dahlia?" I had never thought to ask before and wasn't usually so nosy.

"Nope." She smiled, sadly. "I really wanted them but my husband didn't. Had some mental health issues that he didn't want to pass onto his kids. I had agreed when we met, I mean what nineteen-year-old thinks they're ever going to have kids? But then when I hit about thirty-five I wanted them something fierce but he was having none of it." She shrugged. "I could be a grandma by now."

"I've never met your husband." I said, running my card through the machine.

"He died. Left me a freehold home and a pile of money from his parents that he had hidden away. He also had a handsome insurance policy that I didn't know about. That's why I don't have to work full time and can travel a couple of times a year. I love them cruise ships. I know some people say they are floating petri dishes and I've sure been on some that almost put me off, but I like not having to pack and unpack and everyone is always so helpful with this big, old chair. It was nice having the money to buy this place to keep me busy." She gazed around as if at good memories. She was so easy to like and I wondered if I should invite her over for dinner one night. It was time I got back into the real world and made real connections.

"Why did you pick a secondhand store?"

She handed over the receipt. "My husband was bought up in this town. I'm from Christchurch and never felt welcome when I first came here. Once I started working at the SPCA everyone slowly thawed and I was accepted." She looked around lovingly, "This place is like the pulse of the town." I didn't think that was true but it *was* busy. "People pop in just to gossip, who bought sheep, who is sneaking into who else's bed, who's had a baby and moved a hunk into their house." She waggled her eyebrows on a grin. "Everyone tells me everything because they know I don't pass it on."

"Has anyone mentioned stolen native bird eggs at Neil and Zoe Hill's farm."

She blinked a few times, the grin fading away. "I thought they had possums?"

"They have a place for birds that are being rehabilitated back into the wild. The eggs are being stolen. Someone greedy is taking the lot."

Shaking her head on a sigh, Dahlia said, "Those poor birds. Who would do that in our little town? I'll ask around. Don't worry, I'll find something out."

As she led me out, I asked, "How did your husband die? You don't have to tell me." I figured it was cancer or a heart attack, Dahlia had the look of a good cook.

"He committed suicide." I gasped and apologized but she waved it away. "I still have no idea why he did it other than his mental health problems. I've got photos from days before where he looks happy, smug even, but then bang, he's gone. Overdosed." We were out on the road now and people waved at Dahlia who waved back. "I would have been destroyed without the towns support. They saved me and I'll be forever grateful."

I liked this and held a hand to her arm in solidarity. "Yeah, I'm so lucky to be here."

CHAPTER FOUR

Jake and Toby were home when I returned (was I ready to say Jake and I lived together? The thought made me sweaty, perhaps I was getting sick again). Toby was tired from fishing and not interested in talking about his day. Jax wasn't hungry and he wasn't super sleepy either so I put him in the baby bouncer and Toby jiggled him while watching a cartoon on my small laptop. He assured me he was happy enough with it.

From the kitchen, Jake said, "I got food."

"No fish?"

He grinned and my heart did a quick step of excitement. "No fish. Toby and I struggled to stand still for long enough to catch them. We would have been better to give Sarge a pole, he's the only one with the patience for it. We had fun though. It was nice to be out in the fresh air."

"You could have bought fish, I wouldn't have known the difference."

"I'm making butter chicken. Hope that's okay?" I glanced at him again, my eyes unable to stay off him for long. He was wearing an aged, light grey t-shirt that highlighted the muscles beneath. It made my tongue go dry and I glanced at Jax to remind myself why that would never happen.

"That sounds perfect." I said.

I had not been eating much since having Jax, mostly living on tinned beans and tuna. Jake wasn't a fussy cook, mostly one pot wonders, but he was heavy on the vegetables and there was always fruit on the counter.

While he put food away, I noticed Toby was distracted, not really watching the cartoon, absently rocking Jax who gaped in awe. I sat on the floor beside them.

"How are you going, Toby? This must be hard on you, with your mum so far away."

"It's okay. Dad's boring compared to Mum but me and Sarge like it here."

"You know you can talk to me if you need too. I'll always have your back."

He smiled, it was heartbreaking and so like Jake I had the urge to keep Jake purely to keep this kid in my life. He would make an amazing big brother.

"I know, Sophie. You always look after people."

"Don't you mean animals? I'm hopeless with people."

"You look after animals too." He returned to the screen after glancing at Jax who was just staring at Toby in fascination. He was mapping the boy's face, like a baby bird, imprinting on his family, his safe place. It made me want to cry because it could compromise me, make me give Jake whatever he wanted to keep them near.

"Jax loves you." I said and Toby grinned again.

"I love him too. I'll help you look after him."

"I know you will." I hoped Toby believed I would always look out for him too. I suddenly understood my sister and her irrational need to protect her kids. She had even dumped me months before thinking she was protecting them. I had been miffed at the time but now wondered why I had imagined it was all about me. Jesus, this kid thing was really warping my reality and I knew I would never be the same.

◆ ◆ ◆

After the cartoon ended and Jax had been fed and put back to bed, I followed Toby outside to feed Billy the Kid and Kuni the piglet. He did it by himself and I let him. It's good for kids to care for animals, it teaches them empathy and tolerance. It's hard to be self-absorbed while looking after another being (unless you were my sociopathic old clinic cat Pothead. The worst nurse cat ever. Damn, I still miss that furry monster).

Withing minutes, the tabby was back and sitting on the fence, it turned up whenever Toby was out there and I wondered where it came from. There was no collar but that didn't mean it was feral.

"You had any luck with that cat?" I asked Toby who shook his head.

"Nope, he's grumpy. Do you think he's hungry?"

"He doesn't look hungry. Can you let me know if you see him with an owner?"

"He lives a few doors down. He's alright." Toby assured me. "I just want to pat him."

Jake came out then with a beer and sat beside me on the step to watch Toby brushing the baby goat. It didn't need brushing, Toby just wanted to do it and the little goat loved the attention. Kuni the pig danced around them, rolling over Toby's lap like a magic bean. It made me smile and Jake chuckled beside me. Sarge sat outside the fenced off area, panting like he wanted to get in there too. I thought the pig and the goat would annoy Sarge or accidentally hurt him and a warning nip from a dog of his size could do major damage, so the big dog was kept away from the tiny animals.

"I've got a job." Jake said into the silence.

"Really? I didn't think you would want one."

"There's not much point me and you sitting around all

day. I like to be busy and Toby starts school next week. I met a farmer in town with Sarge, we got talking and he wants me to do some work with his young farm dogs."

"I forget you were a trainer."

"Look at Sarge, he's a fucking cool beast."

I chuckled at this unusual boast. "How long do you really think you will stay here?"

"This is a better life for Toby and Sarge. I can't run as far in Auckland as I do here. Jesus, every fucking mini-dog owner thinks Sarge is going to eat them."

"He does look like he would eat them." As if he could understand we were talking about him, Sarge turned to stare at us. "You do realize your dog even looks like a retired police officer. He has the stern, disappointed persona of someone who has seen too much bad stuff and doesn't trust anyone."

"Don't dogs look like their owners?" Jake frowned.

"Exactly."

He grunted and poked me in the ribs, then gently took my hand.

"I've told you, Gristle, I don't want to leave you here alone."

"Please don't call me that."

"It's cute. I can't remember where it came from."

"I do. Right back when we met, you told the police that I was tough like gristle. I've always hated it."

"You're not always tough. I know that much about you."

"Are you here because you feel sorry for me?" I stared at our joined hands, wanting to be swept away by Jake sweet words. But Jax had changed me.

"I want to look after you, but I've always felt that way, ever since I found you brawling with your ex in the street. Jesus, that feels like years ago. I'm sure I've aged a hundred years since I met you."

"That was the same day you picked that name." I grumbled, turning back to Toby and the animals.

"Jake, you used me as bait to get Louis. How could I ever

trust you?"

"I've apologized and I had no option. I knew it was a shitty thing to do but it was my final and only solution. The only way out for me was to bring Louis in. The only way to do that with minimal bloodshed was by using you. It was wrong, we both know it, but it was the best solution I could think of."

"It wasn't just that. What about your doped-up ex-wife burning my clinic down with witchcraft and almost killing Pothead?" At Jake's shrug I added, "You said sleeping with me was work."

"That's bullshit!" He hissed, dropping my hand and checking Toby wasn't listening. "I slept with you because I wanted too. That part of me is not for sale. You made it up in your head, or I said one thing wrong and you obsessed on it."

"But you dumped me. We were together after the pit and then without reason you dumped me. I don't think you know how much that hurt."

"I know exactly how much that hurt and I had no choice. I'm not explaining this again. You either move on or we can't move forward."

"I had a baby to another man. Not just any man but Louis Martinez, the guy you've been protecting."

"None of this is perfect, but we're not kids. And I've got Michelle as an ex-wife. We're both screwed so we might as well do it together."

I felt limp. "But what if I never trust you?"

He ran a hand over my head and kissed my temple. Toby saw it and made a sound like he was being sick which lifted my spirits.

"We haven't seen Louis yet." Jake surprised me by saying.

"What does that mean?"

"That means, you're not the only one with trust issues."

Right at this moment I thought Jake was wrong, mainly because since having Jax I hated Louis. Even though he had no idea he was a father, I hated that he had missed the pregnancy and the birth, I especially hated him for leaving me with a newborn baby, and it was my own fault for not telling him. I hated him the most because if I did see him again he would want Jax and probably me, and I was stupid enough that I might just forgive him.

So instead of telling Jake he didn't know what he was talking about, I said, "Did you know someone in this town is smuggling out native bird eggs?"

Jake stood and threw his hands in the air, saying, "Oh my god! You're postnatal and you still find an animal mission." Then he returned inside, grumbling about starting dinner.

There was nothing else to add, he was right. But what else could I do? Pretend I hadn't found out?

Seeing one of Sarge's brushes (he had more hair care equipment than me) I called him over and gave him a good groom. It's an endless chore with German Shepherd's since they have two coats, the guard coat and the undercoat which is what shed the most. But Sarge loved it which made it enjoyable. I checked for fleas and lumps, giving the scarring on his stomach a gentle once over to ensure nothing had changed. I soon had a huge ball of fur beside me which I thought about clipping to a tree for bird nests but it wasn't the right season and Sarge had been given flea and worm drops a few days ago.

"At least you and Toby are simple." I told Sarge, holding his snout, certain he was smiling at me in thanks, only then realizing that Toby was within earshot. Toby grinned as he put away the milk bottle he had rinsed out.

When he sat beside me, I said, "I know for a fact that goat is over a month old. He's eating and drinking enough. I don't think he's a runt. I think he's a dwarf."

"What does that mean?" He asked, nervous, "Will he die?"

"He looks pretty healthy right now but I'll let the school know in case they change their mind." There could be medical issues but I didn't want to think about it today and I didn't want Toby to worry about it at all.

"What if they don't want him?" Toby said and I could

see the hope in his gaze even as he was trying to appear unconcerned.

"We're going to have a lot of animals coming through this house, Toby. I need you to understand that although I would happily keep every single one, I just can't. If the school doesn't want him there are so many good homes around. What if this goat takes a place that a really unwell animal can't have?"

He took a long breath, "But he's so cute."

"He's utterly adorable and if you really want him and the school don't we might be able to keep him. We'll think about it overnight, deal?" I held my hand out and he shook.

"Maybe I don't want to be a vet." He grumbled, "I don't want to give them up."

"I didn't know you wanted to be a vet."

"It just looks pretty cool."

"It is cool but sometimes it's also sad or really annoying because people can be dumb and mean, which can also make you very, very angry."

"You mean when people abuse their pets."

"Yeah. Toby, sometimes I wonder who the actual animals are, us or them."

I stood and pulled Toby with me, as he said, "It's definitely us."

"You are a wise old man, Toby and I'm so happy you are here to keep me and Jax company."

CHAPTER FIVE

The next few weeks went faster than the weeks before and Jax was suddenly two months old. Having Jake and Toby with me made life busier and more interesting. I had bought home a little dog with caudal duplication, a rare genetic disorder meaning she had been born with two tails and far too many internal parts for such a small dog. She had probably started out as a twin and I had been fascinated to see her, wished I was still doing actual surgery but had to make do with looking after her near the end of her recovery. She was doing well and I prayed we could find a home for her, although her ongoing vet bills were going to be an issue. I also had a small, scruffy, mixed breed dog that had been found on the main road at four in the morning by a farmer. He had been hit by a car and his front leg had been amputated. It was only a week post-surgery and the dog behaved like nothing had happened, dancing around Sarge who would occasionally growl at this new nuisance.

Toby was in love with the new dog and we had to have a talk again about keeping him. Giving the little goat to the school had been hard enough but Toby was beginning to understand that the number of animals in need was endless and was starting to protect himself a little more from the heartbreak. And we hadn't had one die yet. I was dreading it.

My brother in law Finn called to let me know that the insurance money had gone into my bank account. Michelle's father had agreed to compensate us for loss of earnings and emotional distress if we agreed to never speak about it to the media. The amount added to the profit off my Auckland apartment was enough to get me that little farm or a decent house in the suburbs of Auckland.

I'm not sure why that kept running through my mind. I liked it here but I missed my sister and her kids, worried about Jax having no family around him if something happened to me. Finn had also tried to entice me back with mention of our old clinic being rebuilt by the landlord, that it could be purpose built this time to suit two vets perfectly, a guaranteed money maker, so much so that I could probably even work part time, he had reminded me several times in emails and instant messages, bombarding me with GIF's and meme's about random vet things. It was hard to think of Finn as fun when he had spent so much of our working relationship being a grumpy asshole. I reminded him during one phone conversation that the decision to split as business partners had been his not mine, and I had just worked with what little he left me. He had hung up on me then called back to ask if Jax was good and if he could have some new photos. He was an adorable bastard sometimes.

It was a lovely summers day and Jake had gone off to work for a couple of hours while Toby was at his new school. Having the little goat there had been a huge help for Toby on his first few days as the goat danced around with delight and other students wanted to know why Toby was so special. He helped the caretaker feed Billy the Kid, explaining what he liked and disliked. The caretaker soon loved the little monster as much as Toby did and at the end of every day put him on a dog harness and walked him across the rugby field to his house, keeping him in the backyard. It was a great outcome and Billy the Kid was a hit with the school community. His ability, even so small, to eat weeds was unsurpassed.

Toby insisted he didn't need to be collected from school and so walked home with a couple of the neighborhood boys, Jake peering along the road anxiously until Toby was in sight. Toby helped as much as I let him with the animals and he was losing that nervousness to be replaced by a strong, confident boy.

Enjoying the peace while Jax slept, I washed dishes and thought. Jake had made no move on me, and even though I didn't want the attention it was beginning to rankle. Wasn't he supposed to be wooing me? Instead, every night, he helped Toby with his homework, helped me with the animals, took Sarge for a long run, endured my trashy television, kissed the top of my head then went to bed, leaving the bedroom door wide.

He was paying rent, insisting we share the cost three ways because he and Toby were taking two of the three bedrooms. It was already a cheap house and now it felt like I was stealing. The landlord didn't care how many were in the house so long as the rent was paid on time. She even dropped in a few times to see what animals were in the backyard recuperating, letting me know that if we came across more little pigs or goats, she would take them for her lifestyle block.

I was finishing the dishes when Dahlia pulled up in her custom van. I went out to meet her since it took so much effort for her to get out of the vehicle with her wheelchair.

"Hi, honey." She enthused when she saw me, "I just got this in yesterday and you had mentioned you needed one. Go open the back."

I found a white cot, disassembled and wedged next to her chair.

Turning in the driver's seat, Dahlia shouted back at me, "The mattress is new, came from that new place on Matheson Ave. With the delays on the build their little boy was in a bed by the time they got in there."

"How did you get it in here?" I hated the idea of her struggling with all these pieces by herself.

"Harley packed it. Got to get my money's worth out of that old street thug." But she clearly liked Harley, regardless of his scary appearance. "It's been so busy lately he didn't have enough time to deliver for me so I've been driving myself for those I know can get it out of the van themselves. I had a few other things to drop off nearby. I like to get out and about. How's two hundred dollars for the lot?"

"But it's an eight-hundred-dollar cot with the mattress."

"You're doing a lot of good in our little community, Sophie. You sure ingratiated yourself faster than I did. You deserve some help."

"Thank you. Can I put the money into your account?"

She handed me a business card that had her account details on the back, reminding me that retail worked a little different here than in the big cities.

I pulled the cot pieces from the van, grateful that Jake could help me put it together. It was light and easy to move and I thanked Dahlia again as she sparked her van back to life.

"It's my pleasure." She frowned, "I heard that you shut down all the dogfights up there in Auckland." This wasn't a question, she knew.

I chuckled, embarrassed, "How did you find out about that?"

"People talk, talk, talk in little towns. I heard you're a real animal nut, would do anything for them."

I shrugged, "I suppose. It's not noble, it's mostly embarrassing."

Dahlia fiddled with her keys then the buttons on her dashboard. "Any luck finding out about those missing eggs?"

"No, I don't see how I can when no one here talks, or they don't know anything. Whoever it is must be smart and working alone. Otherwise you would have heard." I shrugged, "Neil and Zoe are putting cameras in and I'm hoping that will put the person off."

Nodding, as if in conclusion, she said, "I know about something that might interest you. Could also take your mind off those little eggs."

"I can manage two problems at once." I assured her on a smile.

"Yeah, but this one is about real animals. It's horrible and

I know a few people would sure appreciate some action."

Then she said nothing, just peering up the road as if wishing she were elsewhere.

Eventually I said, "Fill me in."

As if in a dream, Dahlia said, "Did you know the yearly rodeo is coming up?"

And just like that I knew exactly what she was talking about and why she was so cagey about it. "Oh hell no. Give me the details."

◆ ◆ ◆

L ater that day I was in the council offices, waiting to see the Mayor. I had demanded it. Minutes after meeting him I was shaking with rage. He assured me there was nothing illegal about rodeos and that the current Codes of Welfare made the cruel events untouchable. He refused to hear my arguments or engage in any constructive conversation, just delivered his well-rehearsed speech on the benefits to the community then ushered me from his office.

I stood there until a secretary asked if there was anything else I needed.

"I want the name and details of the rodeo organizer." I said, trying to be polite when I wanted to scream.

Like the mayor, the secretary was close to retirement age. She had perfectly puffed white hair that was short at the back and defied gravity at the front. She was short but stern and efficient, daunting, so I couldn't understand why she was debating giving me the rodeo details when it was obvious she wanted too, there was no reason why she couldn't.

Eventually she pulled a plain piece of paper from the

printer, mentioning something about official letterhead, and slowly noted down a name and contact details from her computer, handing it over as if unwilling to leave her fingerprints on it.

Scratching her arm, jittery, she said, "If she asks where you got this, don't say it was me. Promise?"

"Maybe. I won't know until I see what I'm up against."

"You're going up against the devil." She then blanched and covered her lips with perfectly manicured fingers. "You would be better to find her at work." She then printed this out too, so slowly I was suspicious she was using her left hand to hide her handwriting.

"You could have emailed it." I said, confused at the woman's agitation. You would imagine after all the fights and problems I had endured in the past I would be a little wary, but no, I was on one of my missions and took no account of what I was getting myself into. If I had any brains I would have screwed the piece of paper up and tossed it. Instead I left the mayor's office with righteousness pounding at my temples and the name of the woman who ran the local rodeo. I had a distinct feeling we would not be friends.

She was not the rodeo president but managed all official affairs, you know, the actual work, and I found her at her day job at Toby's school where she was the receptionist. As I entered I wondered if this was the right thing to do. I had Jax and Toby to think about now. I didn't want to cause problems for Toby but I needed to see what I was up against.

I had dropped my car home and walked while Jax was sleeping in his stroller, grateful for some exercise. Jake and his daily runs were making me guilty about my lack of fitness.

Darling Roach had about the worst name I had ever heard. She sounded like a bug that wore makeup or was put in a tiny harness and marched around a tiny world. In reality the woman was pretty, stunning in this town of hardworking farmers. She was around fifty-five with ash blonde hair, a tight, trim body fitted into a suit that was way out of whack for this small school office. She radiated hardworking efficiency and I instantly liked her, thought Toby's school was in good hands with this woman at the principals back.

What a pity I would have to hate her.

I introduced myself but she already knew I was a vet who worked at the Hill's farm. She also knew that I lived with a man and his son who wasn't mine. She told me these things, shot them out from her perfect lips at pace, enjoying my uncertainty. Up close it was obvious her clothes were expensive and her makeup immaculate. It was jarring seeing someone so made up in Grafton, she looked expensive and out of place and I could only guess her husband was a rich farmer since reception work would not cover her look.

"Toby Rowland." She said, clicking her manicured fingers. "Lovely boy. Has fit in perfectly."

Oh, man. How was I going to find the necessary rage to shut this woman and her horrible rodeos down?

"I'm not here about Toby. I'm here to talk to you about the upcoming Rodeo."

Her smile brightened. "Oh, well, this isn't really where we discuss that but if you want to offer some sponsorship or help, we always need more hands."

There just wasn't any other way to put it than brutal honesty. Someone had to be the bad guy. "I want it shut down."

Her face fell. "Well, then we are definitely not having this conversation at work. And I'm not even the right person to talk to. Our president is Rick Mussett. Ricky." Her face creased with distaste. "He's the person you should take any complaints too."

"I understand that you mostly run the rodeo."

"Who told you that?" Her eyes flashed and I saw a different woman than the one she had been projecting.

"I'm sorry to do this here but I couldn't find any other contact details for you and no one was answering my calls. I would really like to talk to you and Mr Mussett both about the welfare of the animals. There's a misconception that the animals like it, that their natural instincts are somehow being utilized. Could you set up a meeting with him for me?"

"You might be surprised how many negative comments we get about our event. Not anyone from Grafton, they wouldn't dare, but from the big cities, always poking their noses into other people's business."

"I'm not surprised at all." I assured her, wanting to sing that I wasn't the only one who felt this way. "The public taste for these types of events have changed as people become more informed."

"Information is ruining the world."

"For some." I shrugged, trying to appear friendly.

She grinned in return but it had the warmth of roadkill. "It is a fun community event that is not illegal. I suggest you sign a petition and let the law decide. I know what you did to those dog fighting rings up north and although I agree they are disgusting, what we do here is nothing like that. Unlike you North Islanders, we love our animals and respect them deeply. It is a celebration of the skills of our cowboys and the effort they put in. These animals are respected."

"That was beautifully rehearsed." I grinned too, just as fake, "But we are not in the American wild west and I won't be fobbed off. Set a meeting with your boss."

Her expression hardened, "He's a very busy man. He runs the car yard on Yellow Bypass and his *wife* is very needy."

"Does his wife work for the rodeo also?" I sighed internally, the potential pool of future enemies was expanding. I didn't want enemies here, I wanted a nice quiet existence without animal abuse but I was coming to understand that wasn't going to happen, that abuse was everywhere.

"Are you kidding? The woman wouldn't know a hard day's work if her life depended on it. Sat there with her six kids, proving to the world what a lazy bitch she is, getting pregnant all those times to show the world she likes to screw, now spending all day with her grandkids so her lazy daughters can go back to work instead of looking after their own kids."

That statement didn't even make sense. "So woman

should work or they shouldn't work? You just said both things and I'm confused."

Her eyes became dangerous slits, "I'm warning you, she is unbearable and really boring. I don't understand what Ricky saw in her all these years."

There was obvious historical dislike here that had nothing to do with my mission, so I said, "If she is excluded from the rodeos don't invite the wife. I have no interest in Mr Mussett's marriage or his family life, just the rodeo."

Darling looked at her watch, suspicious, "Who told you where to find me?"

"The Mayor."

She clearly knew the Mayor and knew he didn't do the details, that all those pesky chores were done for him. "But who actually gave you my name, and which one of those town bitches pointed you at my rodeo?"

"That's confidential information and it doesn't matter, I'm here now." I thought of the mayor's anxious secretary and suddenly understood her concern. This woman was formidable, smart and determined, and I wondered what she was doing sitting at a reception desk when she appeared too bright and sparkly for her surroundings.

Darling glanced at Jax who was still sleeping, flat on his back, hands fisted beside his head, all that black hair a constant reminder of his father. I worried that Louis would turn up, out of the blue, like he did, and ruin the little life Jake and I were building, as flat mates.

Behind Darling I noticed a tank with a few little turtles in it.

"Nice basking area." I said, "Is that light bright enough?"

She stared at me then, ready to argue about something before she said, "It's my lunch break, let's go to the staff room, I need coffee."

I followed her behind the desk and into a small room with a tiny kitchen in one corner, brightly colored chairs and old sofa's scattered around the room haphazardly. I wondered if Dahlia had sourced the furniture since it appeared old and needed updating.

Refusing the offer of coffee, I instead filled a glass with tap water and sat with Jax in his buggy beside me. I asked if Darling would be offended if I fed him. She shrugged like she couldn't care less but I noticed a small grimace of distaste.

On a tired sigh, she said, "Alright, I don't know why you're here but whatever. I've worked for the rodeo for the past five years because of our president, Rick Mussett. He led me on the whole time, knew how much I loved him, how far I would go for him while he lies and proclaims loud and proud how happily married he is. I don't believe it, no man is ever truly happy, they can't help their wandering eyes and if you get them at the right time it's simple to get them to admit the truth."

She smiled, all fake friendliness but I had seen this before. Our old vet nurse Keisha had sounded eerily similar and I despaired, all the hard work of my suffragette forebears was blown to smithereens because a woman decides she wants a man and will do anything to have him. I would not rant at her about sisterhood.

"That man you live with. Are you romantic?"

My head was spinning with the change of topic. I didn't come here to talk about my complex relationship with Jake Rowland, I was here for animal welfare.

"No, we're just friends from Auckland. I came for the job with Neil and Zoe and Jake came to give his son a more stable life."

"He's really good looking. I see him running every day with that massive dog. I'm going to ask him out. Just so you know. I'm tired of waiting for Ricky and I'm ready to move on. About the rodeo, you don't need to try and shut it down, every animal sissy in the world has already done your job for you and I'm sick of keeping the thing going so Rick fucking Mussett can prance around like he did one fucking thing." Whoa, she was bitter. "A statement is going out in the next few days, so you can tell whoever blabbed, whoever said that I'm an evil person who perpetrates the abuse of animals, you can tell them that I've seen the light and I've stood down from the association. I've done some dumb shit in the past over men, I'm not doing that anymore and the rodeo can go kiss my ass."

I was stunned silent for a long moment, eventually saying, "Wow, then I guess there isn't anything more to add." I did think about telling her to stay away from Jake but knew Jake would turn her down. Darling was about fifteen years older and Jake was here for me. I felt confident he wouldn't let me down again.

Standing to leave, I was grateful I had come, that this had been fast and that Jax was still asleep. His naps were getting longer, as were the times he was awake.

"How do I know you're not going to continue organizing the rodeo without my knowledge?" I asked her.

"The billboards and signs haven't gone up. The cancelation will be confirmed soon. Then I suggest all you tree huggers hide because there is going to be some upset cowboys."

"You can't really call them cowboys in New Zealand." I said, wanting to go but also wanting to hear some regret. Why did I do that?

"You tell them that and see how far it gets you. Just between the two of us, I'm glad it isn't happening and I'm glad I'm over that Ricky Mussett. He never deserved me."

"Good on you." I said, distracted as the school bell rang and I saw Toby running out to the field with a rugby ball under one arm, a gaggle of kids on his tail. He was laughing and I was glad I didn't have to ruin his fun by fighting with his school receptionist.

There was a fish tank in the corner of the staff room and I mentioned that it needed cleaning. The green tinge was noticeable.

Darling shrugged, giving it no more than a glance. "Harley has been busy lately."

Confused, I said, "What does he have to do with it?"

"He cleans them, also gets in all the stuff, aquariums and

that. It's not like we can get it from the local pet shop. We don't have one." But her gaze was shifty.

"Harley cleans them out?" I'm not sure why I was surprised. I knew he did odd jobs.

On a sneer, Darling said, "He'll do about anything for a few dollars and a meal."

"Harley's a busy guy." I said, wondering if he was too busy to snatch native bird eggs. I might need to talk to him and he looked like the type of man that didn't take false accusations easily. But my own prejudices were fully formed thanks to my family.

"Fair enough." I said and waved goodbye.

On my way I drove to Yellow Bypass, unable to stop myself from dropping in at the big car yard and introducing myself to Rick Mussett.

He was gregarious and welcoming until I said, "I just met Darling Roach and she mentioned the rodeo is being cancelled this year. I just wanted to confirm that is correct." Jax started crying and I was surprised he had lasted so long.

"Yeah, I'm sick of fighting all those caterwauling greenies. Let them plant trees and save those horses from the glue factory instead of watching wholesome entertainment."

"That's a great idea." I was delighted Darling and Rick hadn't lied to me.

He surprised me then by adding, "And I'm sick to fucking death of dealing with Darling Roach. She's psycho, a stalker. I can't count how many times I told that woman I was not going to have an affair with her. For one, my wife would fucking kill me and she's a scary woman, going through the change. For another, I have not one ounce of attraction toward Darling. I mean she's pretty for her age and all that but I've never been into those hard, skinny women, I prefer some meat on my bones, if you get what I'm saying." He boomed laughter, the big personality making me join in.

"She did come across as a little intense." I agreed.

"There's something off with her. She likes to say she's determined and always gets what she wants but if you're the one she wants and don't feel the same way, well, she about makes your life unbearable. Thankfully my wife saw right through her, after she threatened to cut my cock off. I endured Darling for a couple of years but the past few months have been too much and I was quitting that damn rodeo to get away from her."

"I don't think you have to worry. She's moved her sights on to some hunk who just moved into town."

"Then tell him thank you and good luck. He's sure going to need it. I wouldn't say she's crazy but she sure made my life uncomfortable. I should have taken it more seriously and called the cops in, but she always promised she would move on so long as I kept the police out of it. If she didn't resign recently I would have. There was no way I was going through another year of that bullshit."

Something about this unsettled me but Jax was roaring now, I was amazed how his cute little mewls had turned to angry, hungry roars over the past few weeks. My baby was changing fast and I needed to keep up with those changes.

◆ ◆ ◆

J ake was late home that afternoon. He had asked for me to message when Toby was home but didn't mention what he was doing and Darling's offer of a date flicked through my mind. I cast it aside and got on with the rest of my day.

When Jake's car did pull up outside he just sat there, the engine running and I looked out the kitchen window to see that he was yelling into his phone. Soon he cut the engine and slammed the door stalking inside, phone still in his hand but held away from his body like it was poisonous.

He calmly said, "Is Toby in his room?"

I nodded, noting his clenched jaw and flushed cheeks.

"Toby, your mum wants to talk to you."

Sarge was first out of the room, sitting at his master's feet and peering up at him adoringly. Jake rubbed the dogs head and I could see the stress leaching out of him.

Reluctantly, Toby emerged, eyes meeting his fathers for an extended beat, information passing between the two that I didn't like, little boys shouldn't have that look. Toby then took the phone, sitting on the sofa and saying a soft hello.

I turned to Jake, "Why didn't Michelle call Toby on his phone?"

"Toby's not answering it."

"Why? What's going on?"

He ran his hands over his head, still agitated and keeping an eye on Toby.

"Like I told you, she moved Mike in. The culmination of the world's greatest love story. Mike thinks that now me and Toby are fully out of the picture they can get married. Like I ever kept them apart."

"It upsets you?"

He shrugged, "No. Mike won't last long with her fulltime. He'll soon understand I wasn't the jealous monster keeping them apart or whatever other bullshit story Michelle cooked up to make herself look better. She wants Toby back. It's still me versus her and she's threatening to use all her daddy's expensive lawyers to get her way. Like usual."

"Christ, how much money does her father have? They just paid out to the insurance company for the damage to my clinic and even fully paid me and Finn for all the stress and loss of income. Her father must be very forgiving."

"He's one of the country's richest men and does not like to part with money if he can avoid it, but he hates bad publicity more. I'm guessing Michelle is using Toby as the lure. Her father may hate me, and I can only imagine the lies she told him, but Toby is his only grandchild and I'm guessing he's starting to think about where all his precious money will go when he's gone. He had Michelle late in life and is well into his eighty's now. He's a smart man and I doubt he'll leave his fortune to Michelle. He knows she would blow it all. She never thought to work unless you call uploading selfies on Instagram work."

"Some people make lots of money off it."

"But she would never monetize it since she never thinks about money as a thing to get herself."

"But doesn't she want to stand on her own, be her own woman?"

This made Jake laugh, "Nope. She would see that as failure. Anyway, I imagine most of it will be tied up in a trust for Toby. It would never go to charity."

"But Toby wants to be a vet."

"Yeah, he told me." Jake was impressed. "Toby won't be suited to investment banking or whatever shit his grandfather will want him to study. Toby is far too kind, and probably too kind to say no."

My chin wobbled and Jake noticed, sagging he pulled me into a side hug, keeping an eye on his son.

Toby was talking and I couldn't avoid listening as he entreated, "But I really like it at the school. Everyone likes me too and the teachers are nice. We get to go on hikes and things and the school just got a baby goat that might be a dwarf." His mother said something in return and Toby's gaze was guilty as it flicked from me to Jax in his bouncer. "No, it's just me, Dad and Sarge. Sarge loves it, him and Dad are running all the time and his hips are really good." He paused, listening, "No, we haven't found a vet. Dad said Sarge doesn't need a vet all the time anymore. He's better."

I frowned and quietly said to Jake, "I'm guessing Michelle doesn't know you're here with me?" At Jake's tense silence I added, "Please tell me you didn't make Toby promise not to tell? He's a little boy. He doesn't need to keep secrets like that."

"Yeah, he does. She'll tell Louis and he'll turn up and take you and Jax away from me. I'm not going through losing you and finding you all over again."

I gasped on a flurry of uncertainty but Toby started crying and my heart hurt for this boy who was still being the rope in his parent's tug of war.

Jake took the phone off him and resumed hissing at Michelle, stalking to his room and closing the door, leaving poor Toby in the middle of the room crying.

I hugged him hard. "It's okay. I'm sorry you thought you needed to keep me a secret. Your dad has got this one wrong. There is nothing bad about you guys being here and I'll make sure your mum knows. School holidays are coming up. I'll book flights for us up to Auckland for a week. Jax hasn't met his aunt and cousins yet, or his crotchety old Uncle Finn. You need to see your mum. I don't want her to feel pushed out of your life. Can you hold out for a couple of weeks?"

"I don't want to go back at all." He mumbled into my chest, continuing to sniffle. When he pulled away, embarrassed, I found some tissues and mopped his sad little face.

"I'm sorry, Toby. We're making a hash of this. I'll talk to your dad and we'll get this sorted out. I promise."

"What will we do with the animals when we're away." That he thought of the animals next warmed my heart. He was going to make an excellent vet so long as we didn't ruin him before he had the emotional maturity for all that study.

"I'll let them know when we're away. Dog (that was the best name I could come up with for the three-legged dog) is on the SPCA's website and had plenty of interest. He'll be adopted any day."

Toby smiled. "Because he's handsome and people are shallow. They'll take a pretty dog with a missing leg over an ugly dog with nothing wrong with it."

This gave me pause. "Did you hear me say that?" I frowned. At his indifferent shrug, I added, "And Tails can go back to the SPCA for a little longer to heal."

The truth was Tails wasn't healing and I knew within the next week or so she would undoubtably go downhill quickly and be euthanized. But who knew, sometimes animals beat all the odds. Now was not the time to introduce that part of animal care to Toby. Maybe when we were back from Auckland, not with all this drama going on.

When Jake emerged he was much calmer and he hugged Toby tight, Sarge sitting next to them watching. It was an endearing sight, big handsome Jake with his small, skinny son, the big, bushy dog keeping watch.

Instead of swooning I returned to preparing dinner and when Jake was at my side I asked, "Is everything under control?"

"I hope so."

"I've told Toby we're all going to Auckland at the next term break."

Instead of arguing, Jake nodded, "That's what I told Michelle. That I'll see her then."

I sighed, "We have two weeks of peace before we return to crazy land."

"Are you saying my ex is crazy?" But the stress was leaving him and he pushed me aside to take over the cooking. I'd like to say it was because he just loved to cook for me, but truth was, I was terrible, easily sidetracked which was a fire hazard waiting to happen, and he really hated doing dishes and this rental house didn't have a dishwasher. I didn't mind, Toby always dried and we had great conversations about animals, the kid was obsessed and reminded me of myself at the same age. Hopefully his parents wouldn't mess him up as much as mine had done to me.

Two weeks, I thought again as Jake later called goodnight and went to bed, leaving me and Jax on the sofa watching the late news before his final feed. I hoped he slept through the night. It had to happen at some stage, right?

CHAPTER SIX

Several days later Jake had bought a big screen television, unable to endure my little one that was transferred to my bedroom for those long nights when Jax decided three in the morning was an interesting time to stay awake. The new television made me nervous because it indicated that Jake was planning to come back to Grafton and that we were really living together. Before it had felt theoretical, a test, that he would get bored and leave.

Toby was sitting between us on the sofa and Jake was tapping away at his laptop while jiggling Jax in his bouncer with a foot. Jax was staring at Jake hard, he always did and I hoped he wasn't imprinting on a man who would let him down.

It was full summer now and I knew the temperatures would continue to rise, drastically different than what I was used to at the other end of the country.

A car pulled up outside the house but that wasn't unusual.

When I heard the gate open though my heart began to beat erratically.

Toby asked, "Who's that?" But Jake was engrossed in his computer and didn't notice until there was a frantic knock at the door.

Jax had fallen asleep and I gently lifted him as Jake frowned and looked at the clock on the oven. Standing he gave me a nod as I took Jax to my bedroom, gently placing him in his cot, staring at him for an extended beat as Jake opened the door and gruffly said, "What are you doing here this late?"

The angle of the door meant I could hear what was said but not see who it was. I recognized the voice and as I came out of the bedroom, Michelle said, "Where's my son?"

Still hidden from the door, I sat next to Toby who was rigid with fear.

Holding his hand, I said, "There's nothing to worry about."

He gulped and nodded, giving my hand a squeeze and standing while I stayed on the sofa, praying Michelle would not wake Jax. The last thing I wanted was her knowing there was a baby here and telling Louis.

"Honey!" She shrieked and pushed Jake aside to enter, rushing to Toby but not hugging him, like usual, overdramatic.

"Hi, Mum." Toby monotoned. "What are you doing here?"

"You're my son. Of course I would come for you."

Michelle's laser beam gaze turned to me, her lips puckering as she hissed to Jake, "I didn't miss anything. I knew you would run off to your bit on the side." She looked me up and down, adding, "Have you two been sitting around eating? Talk about letting yourself go."

"Hi, Michelle." I said, "Nice to see you too, and calling me a bit on the side is giving me too much credit. We were coming up to see you as soon as the school holidays start."

"Well, I've come to take Toby home. He's not staying at some public school in the sticks. My father pays a lot of money to keep him in the same school he attended. I think after all you've made our family pay through your insurance company, the least you could do is allow my son a decent education."

"I think you'll find that you burning my clinic down was the reason your father had to clean up your mess with wads of his own money. My father wouldn't have paid." I didn't mention that my father probably would have just hunted Michelle down and taken it out of her skinny, greedy ass.

Michelle flicked a gaze to the door. "Is Mike here?" Jake asked at her agitation.

Great, it was going to be hard to get these people out of here without Jax being noticed, and clearly thinking the same thing, Jake said, "Where are you staying. Me and Toby will come hang out for a bit. Sophie isn't interested in this."

"We need privacy as a family." Michelle agreed.

Jake closed his eyes, clearly reigning in his temper. "And I don't want Sophie taking out a restraining order after you torched her clinic. Your father must be getting tired of paying to clean up your mess."

"My father is my hero." Michelle sniffed, eyes still on me, the gleam of competition in her gaze. "The only man that loves me unconditionally."

"That sure is true." Jake conceded, "But Sophie has nothing to do with this and I'm sure she wants to keep it that way."

I nodded, "That's a great idea. I've got work in the morning."

Michelle's cold gaze slid to her son. "You told me you didn't have a vet here."

Trying to take control of the conversation and keep the pressure off Toby, Jake said, "She's not working as a small animal vet. She's doing something else." He smiled a little because we had discussed what I did and he couldn't understand it.

Jake was facing away from the open door, Michelle's attention fully on him, so it was me and Toby that noticed the dark figure appear at Jake's back. Noticing our alarm he turned just as Louis stepped inside and quietly closed the door, the men then coming face to face. Louis was taller than Jake but thinner, both were menacing when they wanted to be and their shoulders widened while Michelle winced just looking at Louis.

Taking a small step backward, Louis said, "I'm sorry for the intrusion." His hands raised in surrender at Jake's clear fury. "But you have not been easy to find, Miss Doctor Doolittle." His gaze didn't leave Jake.

"What are you doing here?" I gabbled, looking to Jake for

what to do but his face was like stone.

"Louis." Jake said, "You're not supposed to be here. Sophie has a protection order against you, and I'm guessing you're on very strict bail conditions."

He smiled, cool and smooth. "I understood she had an order on you too, yet here you are. I won't be long and you will ensure I remain a gentleman."

"I could call you a lot of things, Louis, but a gentleman isn't one of them."

Shrugging like Jake was probably right, Louis said, "I don't think you and I have ever gone head to head, Jake. I wonder who would win."

"Did Michelle tell you how to find us?" I didn't want to sound bitter in front of her son but it snuck into my tone.

Louis looked to Michelle. It was obvious he didn't like her, that he could see past the pretty façade to the woman behind and found her distasteful. He slowly said, "Michelle refused to believe that her precious Jake would run away to find you. The boy wasn't even mentioned once, just Jake, Jake, Jake every fucking moment of the trip." His gazed flicked to Toby but instead of apologizing for such an upsetting statement, he said, "It's always better to acknowledge and accept your parent's weaknesses, Sophie taught me that." His imperious gaze turned to me, "I know Jake better than anyone, and I was right, here you both are. Happy families with someone else's son, Sophie? You know I'm offering you more than that."

Louis looked different, calm and well rested. That jittery anxiety that had haunted his good looks last time I had seen him, when the three of us had been handcuffed on the front lawn of my parent's farmhouse, was gone. He had put on some weight and wore his usual uniform of dress pants and a light blue business shirt that did magical things to his beautiful skin and black hair.

He looked to Jake, "Relax, Jake. I'm serious. I'm not here to cause trouble."

"You've said that before." Jake grumbled. "You step out of

line with my son here and we will have a major problem."

"Understood and agreed." He stepped closer to me and I smiled.

"Always a dramatic entrance." I shook my head, "I knew you'd come."

"Is that why you made it so hard to find you?"

He hugged me then and I held him back, glad he was safe. His memory was always much more rugged than the actual man.

"How did you find me?" My gaze flicked to Michelle who was still to hug her son, standing by herself as if waiting to be rescued. I had never needed anyone to rescue me, I had bumbled through on my own and right now I was glad of that. I had my own son to protect now since I really had no idea how Louis would react to Jax.

Toby was pale and Jake moved to his side, draping a heavy arm across his son's shoulders. Toby slipped his arm around his father's waist looking up as if to confirm this situation was not out of his hero's control. I had no idea if Toby had met Louis before or what he knew of the man. Sarge was outside in the garage, he had free reign of one part of the lawn and I hoped Jake didn't call his big dog in. Sarge might be old but he would still fight to the death if Jake commanded it.

Louis flicked a gaze to Michelle, his lips curling with distaste.

"Michelle called around the local schools, said she needed to talk to Toby, that there was a death in the family. Are any of us surprised that she's a deft liar?" Those black eyes flicked to Toby and he frowned as if annoyed that he would have to censor his thoughts.

Michelle continued, "His school receptionist sounded distracted and ended up emailing me Jake's contact information. She forgot to remove the address, and here we are, in the middle of nowhere. Pack your things Toby. I want to get back to the hotel then book the flight back home."

"You're not taking him, Michelle." Jake was calmer than I

expected, as if he felt sorry for his ex. "I have full custody and he wants to stay here."

"I'm his mother and more important. Come on, Toby."

But Toby didn't move, eyes wide. It was so unfair yet I said, "Maybe you can all go back to the hotel to discuss this? Like I said, I'm tired and I've got work in the morning." Thankfully Jax hadn't made a peep and I was praying this was one of those long sleeps he had, where nothing would wake him.

"I need to talk to you, Miss Doctor Doolittle." Louis purred. "It has been a testing journey to find you, the least you can do is hear what I have to say since I've found no other way to contact you." His gaze flicked to Jake again, "Jake hid you well."

"I didn't ask you to come, Louis, I owe you nothing. Jake didn't hide me. He turned up and wouldn't leave. I don't have any more bedrooms, just in case you thought you'd stay too." I hope Toby didn't think I wanted him to go. I didn't, I loved having him here.

Michelle was indignant, but not that her son was living somewhere strange. "I had to sit on a plane with a criminal and you imagine *you* had a testing journey. You always were a self-obsessed pig, Louis."

Jake and I looked to each other. Michelle calling someone else self-obsessed was outrageous and before I could stop it I laughed. Jake joined in, and Louis, Michelle and even Toby looked at us as if we were insane.

"I just want to talk to Sophie alone for a minute. Just one minute." Louis said when our amusement died down. "Surely you are solid enough in your relationship with her, Jake that you won't mind."

"Jake and I are not in a relationship." I said, "Nothing is going on." It was clear I was annoyed by this and Jake groaned in frustration.

"Say whatever you need to say right here in front of us all." Jake said to Louis, "Unless it's X-rated and Toby can leave the room."

"Fine." Louis said as if it was now out of his hands, that

he had tried to protect everyone. "I'm sorry for everything that happened, Sophie, for everything I put you through. I wasted too many years on revenge and I have you to thank, and you alone," He said pointedly at Jake, "For pulling me back to reality."

I shrugged, surprised I felt nothing for Louis but a sliver of empathy. Like me, he had come from a rough start, how we dealt with our hands was quite different, but Louis had put plenty of bad people behind bars and for that he deserved some respect.

"If you think that, then you're welcome, Louis, but . . ." I was interrupted by the clear cry of a small baby behind a bedroom door.

Everyone froze except Jake who tugged Toby with him a few steps to stand guard in front of the door.

Michelle snarled, "Who's baby is that?"

No one spoke while Louis' gaze dropped to my chest, his forehead creasing.

Michelle repeated, voice stern, "Toby, who's baby is that?"

Tired and rung out, Toby curled toward his father and burst into tears. Jake held him, glaring at Michelle but not saying anything, still daring anyone to go near the bedroom door.

"I'm sorry, Toby." I said, explaining to the adults, "He doesn't want to lie and I shouldn't put him in that position. "It's my baby." I then stepped to Toby and knelt to hug him, sighing as his grasp shifted from Jake to me.

"I'm sorry." I repeated on a whisper, pushing hair from his forehead as he nodded, swiping at his eyes with the sleeve of his pajamas.

Glaring at her ex-husband, Michelle said, "You had another kid and never told me?" She then stepped toward the room and I lifted a hand as Jake puffed up, staring her down, a warning not to come closer.

"I want to see *it*." She growled.

"Stay out of it, Michelle." Jake warned.

"How could you do this to me?" Her voice was confused this time. She covered her immaculately made up face with her perfectly manicured hands and burst into tears. This one thing forcing her to admit that it was over with Jake, there was no going back. He had moved on and had another baby with another woman and Michelle no longer had the only bargaining chip to use against him.

Neither Jake nor I moved to comfort her, both keeping one hand on Toby and remaining before the bedroom door as Jax cried and my boobs began to leak.

I was so focused on Michelle, wanting her to admit defeat and leave, so we could return to our peaceful little bubble, that I forgot about Louis until he said into the silence, "No, it's not Jake's baby." I realized he was holding Jax's hairbrush that had been lying on the kitchen bench. There were several fine but clearly black hairs in it. "It's *my* baby."

Michelle's face cleared and she let out a huge gasp of relief, "Oh, thank god. Toby, go pack your bag, we're leaving."

◆ ◆ ◆

T he standoff collapsed when Louis said, no demanded, "I'm not leaving until I see my baby. I'll stand here all night if I have too."

"Get out." Jake growled but I agreed with Louis, "Jake, he needs to see him."

"We have a son, Miss Doctor Doolittle." Louis said in awe while Michelle beamed in relief, delighted she hadn't lost her control over Jake.

"I knew it wouldn't last, this peace." Jake sighed. "Do what you have to do, Gristle." It would usually annoy me that

Jake was back to that awful nickname but this time it felt comforting, a reminder of past experiences, good and bad. No matter what, Jake and I always found our way back to each other.

"I have a son?" Louis husked, eyes wide in awe, "I have a son with Miss Doctor Doolittle?" His grin was irritating because it was fixed on Jake, the smile of a victor against his foe. This was still a pissing contest.

Sighing, Jake said, "Louis, are they safe with you? You've hurt Sophie before. Can I trust you to behave?"

"I can look after myself, Jake." I assured him.

"Honey, you had a baby a few months ago. You're not back to your fighting best, but I do need to talk to Michelle alone." His worried gaze flicked to Toby who was now sitting on the sofa, shoulders still shaking as he tried to calm down. He was such a brave soul and I adored him. "Me and Toby need to talk to her alone." Toby smiled at his father and moved to find his shoes.

"How long will you be?" I asked, "Toby has school tomorrow."

"Toby is going back to his own school." Michelle sneered, peering around the basic little house as if it offended her, "Not some dump in the sticks."

"It's a beautiful little school, Michelle." I assured her. "They have a goat that Toby helps with." I knew Toby had already told her and I don't know why I thought Michelle would care about Billy the Kid, her shrug of disinterest proved me correct.

For some reason I didn't want to get Jax while Michelle was there but he was giving me no choice, furious now, unaccustomed to his needs not being met instantly.

"You need to let them cry." Michelle said as I turned to the door. "Teach them who the boss is."

"It's a baby." I said, confused. "He doesn't have adult concepts." My gaze slid to Toby and I imagined him as a tiny baby crying his lungs out for comfort, his mother torn between her lover and her husband, his father confirmed by a test. I had an overwhelming urge to claim Toby but he was Michelle's son. Jake's patience and my reluctance meaning we had been found by those with the ability to keep us apart before confirming our relationship.

Louis held his arms out when I returned with Jax, tears springing to those usually empty eyes as I passed Jax over to him. Jake was also emotional but he herded Toby and Michelle from the house.

"How long will you be?" I repeated, scared when Jake held the door and stared at me as if for the final time.

"Call me when you're done. Louis isn't here to mend bridges with *me*."

"Don't be bitter, Jake." Louis chuckled, "Our time will come. There's enough court cases coming up that you and I are going to spend more hours together than you ever hoped for." Louis was looking at his son, smiling big and proud. Jax looked all wrong with Louis, he fit Jake but Jake wasn't his biological father.

"Call me." Jake repeated and turned away. I wanted to chase him, to tell him this was spiraling out of control and not what I wanted. That Jake had made the past few weeks a calm and carefree time that I would look back on with wonder. I had gone from being alone and unwell to being cocooned with Jake and Toby. My memories from the moment they had arrived felt warm and peaceful. Even Jake not trying to seduce me was right. He was giving me time to recover, to return to the Sophie he knew, and I adored him even more for it. Like usual, if I had to choose between Jake and Louis, Jake won.

My history with Louis was so different, unstable and foggy. He was gorgeous and made me want him, but logically, he was not the right man for me. Jax was a wonderful error that I would gladly accept from my moment of weakness.

Watching Jake drive away through the kitchen window, I spotted his mobile phone and ran outside to give it to him. How was I going to call him if he didn't have his phone? What an idiot. I wondered what Michelle would use against Jake this time to get her own way. I might want Jake all for myself but I was not alone in that, Michelle was a master at knowing how to bend Jake to her will, and Jake would do anything for his son.

Back inside, Louis jiggled Jax who continued to rage. "You are amazing, Sophie. Doing this all by yourself. Why didn't you tell me? I would have come. Why do you always run to Jake? You will note that once again he has gone back to his wife."

"It's not like that, Louis." I took Jax off him and sat on the sofa to feed him, Louis sitting beside me and peering at us together on a smug grin.

"Could you get me a glass of water?" I asked, the habit that Jake had instigated now ingrained.

"First, tell me his name."

"His name is Jax Louis Carter."

"You gave him my name?"

"Of course, you're his father."

"That you excluded."

"You threatened to kill me. What did you expect me to do? You made your decision when we were up north and you can't take that back." This was the awful time before I knew I was pregnant, when Louis had discovered I had killed his father. It turned out it was my father who had blamed me to try and get off a prison sentence but Louis hadn't wanted to hear that and had chased me all over the North Island to have his revenge. Jake had used me as the bait to finish it. My trust in both men had been shattered and I had ended up in Grafton all alone with a baby on the way.

Louis needed to know about Jax, the pregnancy, the birth, what kind of baby he was, yet I was surprisingly disinterested in his feelings. Louis had caused the entire mess, starting with our first meeting because of those awful dog fights.

"Being pregnant sucked. I was sick most of the time. I would call his birth traumatic but the midwife assured me it was completely normal. He was almost eight pounds. He eats like a champion and yells like a banshee when he wants something."

"He is perfect. Like you." I rolled my eyes at his cheap words and he laughed. "I want to tell you everything, explain why you don't need to run and hide from me anymore. You can't now. You have my son and you don't want me pulling that link tight."

"Are you threatening me, Louis?" I growled, peering into those fathomless black eyes, warning him with a glare. "I'm not the same person anymore. This baby has changed me. You could push me around, Louis, but you can't push around this boy's mother."

Jake's phone pinged on the kitchen bench with a message and I raged again that he had forgotten it. Jake was not one of those people who were attached to their phone and often forgot to take it with him, right now that was an annoying trait. What if I wanted him to come back? What if I wanted to know what he was doing with his beautiful ex-wife? I had Jake's password and he had mine too. It came about from a weird discussion one night after Toby went to bed. We had been talking about trust, Jake thought I didn't trust anyone and had assured me he had no more secrets, writing the code to unlock his phone on the small whiteboard by the backdoor, welcoming me to go through it anytime, offering to leave a few dick pics to keep me from getting bored. I repeated the gesture but had scrolled my phone and deleted any awful photos.

Louis sat back against the sofa. "You always were the toughest woman I ever met."

"You dated Keisha." I reminded him of my old vet nurse who had been brutal in what she wanted, which was mainly Louis for herself.

"But there was no challenge with Keisha." He peered down at Jax again, his smile proud enough that I felt a little proud too. "Why didn't you tell me?" He asked again.

"Because you tried to kill me." I repeated, exasperated.

"I'm sorry. There are so many reasons why I ended up in that mental space, I've been working on that in prison. I'm better, Sophie. I'm finding the man I used to be, the one that made his mother so proud when I got into the police."

"Where is your mother?" I asked, wondering why she had never tried to pull her lost son into line.

"She died years ago from breast cancer. Her family had it in the genes and she still wouldn't have screenings, thought it was immoral to show herself to anyone."

"I'm sorry, Louis. Do you think the loss made you worse?"

"It sure didn't help." He sighed, lifting his arms high over his head and stretching, reminding me of the long journey to get here. Interestingly I didn't sneak a peek at his stomach like I usually would. Jake really was ruining me.

"I gave everyone up, Miss Doctor Doolittle, even my Australian connections." He smiled then, "That fucker thought he had me under thumb and I fucked him too."

Some part of me wondered at the chances of that connection being to my brother, another undercover cop, but I figured that was impossible. No, not impossible, improbable, but New Zealand was a small country and if an undercover policeman had any links to this it would be my brother. I couldn't hide behind uncertainty anymore. My life was a circle that kept coming back around, a disc that would not stop turning until my story was done.

"I'm free for the first time ever." He said.

"Do you have any family, Louis? Someone who can support you back into the real world." The idea of him having only me made me very uncomfortable.

"I've got a son." He smiled, turning that intense gaze onto me just as Jake's phone pinged again with a new message. I wondered if he had used Michelle's phone to search for his own. My jealousy of Michelle was unfair, she was Toby's mother and I had to trust that Jake wouldn't let me down again. After all, he had moved all the way here to be with me.

"Do you truly understand that I had no choice about what happened with your father? That I was a little kid, sick and traumatized by my useless parents. I never wanted to hurt your dad. Franco was always around, but you must know that he wasn't a very nice man, Louis. Like my father, Franco was a loser."

I saw his jaw twitch, unsure if he should be angry.

"I can't argue with you about it since you probably saw him more than I did."

"No rose-tinted glasses anymore. We all have to admit the truth of our parents, Louis, and ours were hopeless."

"Like Jake and Michelle." His look of satisfaction at this low blow was infuriating.

"I'm not discussing Jake with you. It's none of your business."

He waved his hand like it meant nothing. "It's over. I don't want to think about how close I came to losing you. We have a son and that's all that matters."

"Are you here because you couldn't find Jake?"

His eyes moved around the room as if searching for an explanation.

"Let Michelle have Jake back." He said.

"I thought she was with Mike." God, I hope she was with Mike, I didn't have the energy to fight for Jake.

"Mike was always just a way to keep Jake in line."

"That's disgusting."

"Not everyone is built for monogamy." He smiled, "It can feel like a cage to some, and you are not a fan of cages."

"Not everyone is built for screwing around. Some of us find safety in fidelity."

"I want you, Sophie." He baldly stated into the silent room, Jax now asleep draped over the pillow on my lap. I was thirsty and wanted a drink.

"Your words are good, and you always know exactly what to say to get me to do what you want. But I can't help you this time. Like I said, things are different. *I'm* different." I quickly added before he thought I was talking about Jake.

"It's always been you, Sophie. It doesn't matter that our history almost pulled us apart. We were meant to be together, our son just proves that. It doesn't matter that you sleep with

Jake, it was circumstances, because I didn't know you needed me. Think of the bigger picture of our lives, you know we should be together."

"I don't sleep with Jake." I said, "He has his own bedroom. So does Toby. We're just sharing a house, all trying to feel better after the mess of Auckland."

"It's okay." He assured me, "We've all done things we didn't really want to do."

"What does that mean?" I glanced up, inwardly growling as Jake's phone lit up again with another message. Either someone wanted to talk to him desperately or Jake was trying to contact me. Jax grumbled, his eyes flicking open and his little face scrunching with fury.

Louis watched on with fascination. "It's just feeding a baby, Louis. You don't have to look like a pervert about it. Explain what you just said."

"You use Jake as a crutch and I've slept with awful people to progress my plans."

I felt sick at the thought of it. "You should have told me that before we slept together. I feel like such an idiot. Christ, I thought I was a smart woman and then I end up in another mess. And how did I end up pregnant anyway? Did a condom break?"

"It was a long night." He grinned. I couldn't join in and he mumbled, "I might have forgotten a time or two. It happens."

"I could have ended up with diseases. I trusted you and you turned it into another lesson in control."

"My control didn't work. And I am screened regularly. In my old line of work it was always in my best interest to know everything, even my STI results."

"I'm going to be sick. Thankfully I was screened when I was pregnant."

"I figured you were on the pill, and I don't go bareback with anyone else. Not the women I get tangled with." His lips curled with distaste.

"That's not helping." I groaned. This was so embarrassing, I felt like a fool. "What's the plan? What are you doing with the rest of your life? Can you go back to the police?"

"No chance. They don't want me back and I couldn't do it anymore. What's Jake doing for work?"

"He's training dogs and he helps on farms, shifting hay and digging fence posts."

"I thought he was looking strong. Maybe I'll work on a farm too." His eyebrows waggled and I chuckled at the image of it. Louis working on a farm was as unlikely as him working in customer services.

"Louis, you have so much experience. Can't the police use that?"

"I'm not being used by those fuckers ever again." He growled.

"What about talking to young guys in prison, before they get hardened. Or go into high schools, get them early. Foster troubled kids or write a book about what you went through. You must know everything there is to know. It's a waste to just forget it all."

"Hey, that's not a bad idea. I can just see me as a resident expert for one of them news shows. I'll think about it."

Jax had finished and I sat him up, smiling when he burped and closed his eyes in relief. "Can you hold him while I get a drink." I grumbled, remembering he hadn't bothered to get me one. That phone pinged again and I stood, stretching my back and shaking out my arms that were tight from holding Jax.

Louis took his son, kissing his head gently and pushing black hair from his forehead. I was tired of all this emotional talk. There was no future between Louis and me. I had made my decision and it was Jake. It had always been Jake and I would tell him as soon as he got home. Our home with our children. Michelle and Louis were welcome in but they would not break us apart.

To change the subject and wondering how long Jake would be, I said, "Have you ever heard of an animal smuggling operation around here?"

He stunned me mid-step by saying, "Hell, yeah. There's

someone here who populates every fucking zoo in Australia with native New Zealand birds and reptiles. My Australian contact wanted me to investigate it but my specialty was always drugs. More money." He said proudly like I would understand.

Shaking my head, knowing I shouldn't be surprised, I asked, "Can any of your contacts help me find out who it is?"

His eyes became shifty. "What's in it for me?"

"I won't hate you forever."

"I can't do that from here. I have to go back to Auckland."

"No, you have to go back to Auckland because you are allergic to a quiet life. You would die here."

"You're probably right. Come with me. Just for a few days. Jake won't mind."

"Are you kidding? Jake will flip his lid."

"But you're just flat mates. You told me that."

I guzzled a long glass of water, frowning when Jake's phone went off again. Glancing at the white board I punched in his pin code and opened the text link. One person had messaged him several times in the past half hour and I flicked through the last ten or so, quickly getting the gist of the conversation.

The final text seared my heart right through, *At least tell me where you're taking me. Jean's or a dress? Hard or easy access.* It ended with several saucy winking emojis and the name of the receptionist at Toby's school. So she had followed through with asking Jake out and he had agreed. He was bored of waiting for me, had decided he had needs that I wasn't meeting and he was making his own way while I sat here with another man's son, all fat and disgusting. I swallowed several times to keep the tears at bay.

"If I come with you do you promise to help me find the name of the trafficker?"

"I'll eat the bastards beating heart if you'll come with me right now."

I dropped the phone in the bin and packed some clothes, too angry to talk. As I left my rental I scribbled a note to Toby, leaving it on his pillow.

Just sorting out some trouble in Auckland about the guy that's selling native bird eggs. Have a good week at school and call me if you need me. I love you. Sophie.

I cried as I packed Jax and a few items into Louis car, not talking as we pulled up to a hotel a few hours later, knowing Jake, Toby and Michelle were far behind us. That Jake was now free to enjoy his date fully. As we drove and I cried, Louis' hand remained firmly on my knee while I refused to tell him what was wrong.

I had messaged Zoe at the farm to warn her that I was having a few problems and wouldn't be able to come in this week. Zoe and Neil had already told me to take as much time as I needed, to at least take my maternity leave but I liked to be busy, I liked to learn. I then messaged the SPCA and asked them to collect the animals in my back yard first thing in the morning. I cried again when I remembered I hadn't even said goodbye to Sarge who was alone in a house that was falling apart with dysfunction. It wasn't Louis or Michelle's fault, their presence had just once again highlighted the lies that were the basis of my life.

In the hotel room, Louis took the single bed and I shared a double with Jax, unable to sleep, terrified I would roll onto him. Louis offered for me to share the single with him but I refused, knowing exactly where Louis thought that would take us. I still had no interest in ever having sex again. No wonder Jake had run off so quickly. Men could never keep it in their pants and I was so fat and gross that he had only stayed with me out of sympathy. I stifled my tears, not wanting Louis to know or to wake Jax.

The next morning we were on a flight to Auckland and I looked forward to seeing my sister. I needed Jenny, she would never let me down, would never sneak off like Jake and date some older weirdo who perpetrated the abuse of animals in those disgusting rodeos. I had a sneaking suspicion that Darling fucking Roach would also know who was shifting those eggs. I wanted to lay all my problems on her pretty head.

I couldn't rely on anyone. It was just me and Jax against the world.

CHAPTER SEVEN

B ack in Auckland I refused to stay with Louis, and when Jax bellowed to be fed again Louis accepted it without argument and drove me to my sisters. It was strange being back in Auckland, the air felt cloying with the smells of restaurants and traffic. It was still early but I had sent a quick text to Jenny before boarding the plane letting her know I was on my way, grateful when she said my room was ready. The new baby would be taking that room soon.

When I knocked gently at the door I remembered the last time I had been here. Running away, terrified at being pregnant. Now I was back with a baby.

I felt like a robot as the door opened and my sister lunged, hugging me. Without a word I smiled, knowing I was right to step away from my life with Jake. It was a bubble and I needed to really assess my feelings. I had honestly thought he wanted me, had no idea he would be dating. Maybe I should have made my feelings clear, but seriously, could the man not wait for five minutes?

Jenny looked over my shoulder, eyes almost falling out of her head to see Louis walking in with the car seat in his arms, cooing at Jax.

Jenny had known Louis was the father as soon as I sent her that first photo. She had delighted about how handsome Jax would be. She had also been unsurprised at Jake's easy shift into my life, said it was inevitable and about time.

"Hi, Louis." Jenny said, "I guess I should say congratulations?"

"Thanks, Jenny. It's been a bit of a shock but then that's your sister, isn't it, always doing the unexpected."

"Where's Jake?" Jenny asked, glancing behind Louis who only pursed his lips together. "Jesus, please tell me you two didn't kill him."

This made Louis chuckle and he handed Jax over to my sister, saying to me, "He's left me a few messages so I'm guessing all that time you spent on your phone when we left wasn't to Jake. Are you ready to talk about it yet?"

"He called me too." Jenny said, "He wouldn't tell me what was going on either. Please tell me you and Jake are better at communication. You have kids now."

"No," Louis said, jaw tightening, "My kid, and Sophie needs to come to some conclusions about Jake. I can't keep doing this."

"Then leave me alone, Louis." I snapped, exhausted and worried about Jake. "My life always falls apart when you turn up and I'm left to pick up the pieces. Decide if you're ready to be a dad. I'm not bringing Jax up with a missing weirdo father."

Laughing, Louis draped an arm around my neck and pulled me close for a quick peck. I turned my head at the last moment and he got my cheek.

"I've got to go." He said.

"Where?" I asked before realizing what was happening, "Actually, you know what? I don't care. Keep running out, it makes my decisions easier."

"Cool." Louis said, distracted.

"Go and find me that name."

He winked, kissed Jenny on the cheek, pat Jax on the head and walked away, hopped into his car and left.

"God, I hate him." I said. "Where's Finn?"

"Still asleep. He's taking the day off work. He's always taking the day off work." My sister grumbled then ushered me inside where baby Emma was propped in a bouncer. She was a few months older than Jax and I chatted to her in classic baby talk as Jenny unclipped Jax from his car seat and kissed him silly. Jax just tried to focus on her face, eyes wide.

Jenny poured tea for us both then scurried upstairs to get dressed, returning in leggings and a pretty blouse that was all wrong for the early hour.

"What's going on with Finn?" I asked, "Why isn't he going to work?"

"He hates it. Says everyone there is stupid and won't fight for animal rights or something. Do you remember how much he moaned about the fights you would get into? Now he's acting like no one else but the two of you ever defended an animal. He's such a dick sometimes. His mother was in heaven after the fire and he had a big fight with her when she said he could now be taken seriously since he had gotten rid of you, *that dreadful sister*." Jenny laughed but I couldn't join in.

"Finn defended me against his mother?" I was in awe, he had never defended me against his bullying mother before, just sat there like a whipped dog while she gave me endless jibes and veiled criticism.

"What did I do?" Finn said, grumbling as he entered, flicking on the kettle and scowling at me in a way that had me smiling brightly. If anyone never hid their feelings it was my brother in law.

"What's wrong with your job?" I asked, unsurprised he was acting like my return meant nothing to him. I knew him better than that.

"It sucks. All those pansy ass-faces think they're better than me."

"Are they?" My heart was soaring, not because Finn was miserable but because it meant he would look back at working with me fondly. This made me feel less hopeless.

His gaze shifted to Jax who was now propped in Jenny's arms. His face lit up, "Here's my little man!" He boomed. "Come to Uncle Finn."

As if on cue Pothead sauntered into the room. "I thought

you put that cat out." Jenny said on a frown.

"I did. He gets in somehow." Finn grumbled, glaring at the cat in feigned dislike. He loved Pothead as much as he loved me which was much less than he loved his wife and kids but as much as he could give anyone else. I was up there in his top ten favorite people. He was stupidly in love with his kids, and I was discovering, great with everyone else's too. "There's something wrong with that cat, Sophie." But he was saying this in a baby voice as Jax peered at him then let loose one of his killer grins that Finn melted into.

"Well, you sure are going to be a hunk."

"So long as he doesn't follow his father and become a monster." Jenny chuckled.

"It's not funny, Jenny." I said and hunkered down to pat Pothead who sniffed my hand, flicked his tail and turned away. He was purring though so I took that as a good sign he was happy to see me. "Where's Captain?"

As if on command the little pug Captain Pugwash trotted into the room, his gaze fixated on Pothead, his true master and overlord.

"He's never far behind." Finn then propped Jax over his shoulder, rubbing his back in a way that spoke of experience. Jake held Jax like that too. Jake, I missed him. While my hands were free I gulped my tea and checked my phone. There was only one message, it was from Jake and I wasn't ready to read it yet.

Noticing me on a sharp bark of surprise, Captain tottered closer, his body moving like a baked bean made of jelly as he snuffled at my hand, ruffing as if telling me about his life since I had last seen him.

"You can have them if you want." Finn grumbled, taking Emma, his own baby off Jenny, holding a baby in each arm. "The cat and the dog. They're useless." He then changed direction, "Get a photo of me with these two since I'm the best dad and uncle in the world and if you moved back to Auckland and go back into business with me I'll even babysit while you go and bang criminals and cops."

"You're disgusting, Finn." But I chuckled and took a few photos of Jax with his cousin and uncle, wondering who I could send it to. I wanted to send it to Jake but he was probably lying in bed with Darling with her stupid bug name.

"What's happened?" Jenny took my hand, noting my change of demeanor. "I thought things were going well with Jake."

"So did I but I refused to go to bed with him, not that he asked, and then I found out he's dating other people."

"Yikes." Jenny said, "That's disappointing."

"He's a guy." Finn said, jiggling and bending his knees, in constant motion. When I noticed both babies were asleep I got a few more photos. I would print the best one off and put it in a frame, a constant reminder that my son did have family and people he could depend on that weren't going to be too busy dating.

"Are you saying if I don't put out you'll run off with someone else?" Jenny growled.

"No." Finn husked, "Because I haven't run off yet, have I?"

I never heard my sister and her husband argue, they had four little kids and didn't have time for it. Finn was happy to be the boss at work and the help at home where Jenny ran a tight ship. It was like listening to your parents argue and I stared at my phone, pretending I wasn't listening. I was a little relieved that Jenny wasn't interested in sex either, it meant, like my doctor back in Grafton had assured me, I wasn't abnormal. I wondered if Toby had gotten off to school yet, giving Jake time to lie in with his new girlfriend. How could I ever go back there? But I had a job. I would call Jake today and tell him he had to move out. It was my place. But I hated moving Toby again. This was torture. Why did Jake have to ruin everything by dating stupid Darling? Could I live in the same house with him if he was seeing someone else? Nope, no chance.

Jenny was snappy instead of her usual calm. It was strange and I figured four little kids was their limit. "Don't hang around for me." She said to her husband, "You're not doing me any favors with your shitty moods. You should have thought a little harder before you dumped my sister to mess around with those assholes." She was hissing, not willing to upset the rest of the house.

"She burned our clinic down." Finn whispered in return.

"I did not." I growled, indignant that he still thought that. "It was Michelle."

"Same thing. She was only there because of you."

"She thought I was taking Jake off her. I hadn't even seen him for months."

"Yeah, yeah, ten months, not that you were counting. And now you're living with him, so she was right all along. I bet that sexy bitch is going to get stoned again and blow the world up. I might double the insurance."

"It's not like that. Jake's dating other people. And Michelle isn't sexy, she just has time to look after herself, plenty of her father's money, and she has never had to work with exhausting, self-absorbed assholes like you."

"Oh, she's the self-absorbed one, yet you're living with Jake while you're here with your baby-daddy." He said this like I was being a moron, "Being judgmental doesn't fit this situation, Sophie."

He was right but I was still upset. "Can you take my bag up to my room, Finn?" I said, taking Jax back.

He sagged, "If you come back and work with me."

"Finn," I implored, "Enough. I've got a job."

"I bet the boss sucks as much as those bastards I work with. The work must be boring. Science, yuck."

"No, I love it. It's interesting. I've come back to Auckland because I wanted to see you, and there's someone in Grafton that's smuggling native eggs out of the country and Louis thinks he can get the name."

"Why can't he get the name and just send it to you?" Finn asked, passing Emma back to Jenny who wouldn't even meet his eye.

"I don't know. It doesn't matter." And it hadn't been why I had run. It was the long string of texts from Darling Roach and the image of Jake dating a woman who would wear a sexy, easy access dress.

"Do you need some help down south?" Finn tried not to appear too excited. "I can take a few weeks off work and come home with you, check out this amazing farm. Maybe I could work at a scientific farm."

"Finn, you have a million kids here to look after. I'm fine, I'll get this name off Louis then I'm going home." The thought of seeing Jake again was torture. How was I going to pretend I didn't care when I would probably cry?

"Good to see having a baby hasn't changed your crazy fucking bullshit." Finn grumbled, collecting my bag. He really was moody which made me worry. He had only been this antagonistic after Jenny had the last miscarriage. He didn't often swear unless we were alone together and he never did it in front of Jenny or the kids.

Instead of saying anything Jenny just peered out the window, anxious as if waiting for a visitor. Maybe she had a courier coming. They lived down a long driveway, the gate closed at night or when the kids and Captain were in the yard, so I was uncertain what she thought she could see except trees and the back of other houses.

"If it makes you feel better, Finn." I said, "I do miss working with you. It's cold down there in winter and I don't know if I suit the cold."

"Jesus, Sophie." Jenny said, still peering out the window, "Don't get his hopes up. He'll be even more miserable than he is now."

Finn rolled his eyes and tiptoed up the stairs.

"What are you looking for?" I asked Jenny, wrapping an arm around her waist.

She looked at me in surprise, "Nothing. I don't know what you mean. I'll make us some eggs before the hoard are up. You can tell me all about your job and being a mum and living with Jake." She paused on a sigh, "He's so hot. Louis too, I haven't seen him in ages." She sighed again, "You're so lucky, it must be exciting being chased by two men like that."

"You know neither of them are ideal. Are you sure you're okay? You seem weird."

"Tim starts school next week."

"Of course. I've already sent a present." Tim was Jenny's eldest son and second child. He was a fun, active boy and I figured school was the perfect place to funnel all his energy. Lara, the eldest had started last year and from what I knew was loving school. She was a pretty and kind girl, serious like any oldest sister but without the bullying that I noticed in some families. I hoped Tim could follow her example into his school years.

"I could have just bought it with me." This was the problem, Jenny's second child was off to school, it was a big step and I knew from experience that my sister didn't cope well with change when it came to her children. She was going to be the worst mother in law. I would be the cool aunt they came to for advice.

I couldn't even imagine Jax going to school. I guess I would be scared too.

"Finn's making us all miserable, Sophie." Jenny said, "Not that it's your problem. But I'm just saying, if anything goes wrong, Finn deserves all he gets."

"You adore Finn." I said, dropping my hold from around her, noting her crossed arms and serious expression. I was starting to wonder if staying with Louis was less stressful. "Tell me what's going on? You know you can tell me anything."

"It's just some personal stuff. Don't worry about us, you have enough on your plate." She smiled and opened the door for Pothead and Captain to go outside. Even the animals were on edge. My sister and I needed time alone but first I needed to orient myself.

"Thank you for letting me stay." I said, "I'm glad to be with family."

"It's great having you here. I've been lonely."

"With a house full of monkeys?"

"I'm not used to Finn being around so much. Things change."

I didn't like this. Something was happening and I would find out what.

Taking Jax to my room I smiled at the portable cot set up in the corner and fed Jax, staring at my phone. Was I being unfair to Jake? On a groan I called him. He picked up on the first ring.

"Any explanation why you just leave?" He growled. "How do I explain this to Toby? What am I supposed to tell him?"

"I left him a note that I had to sort some things out in Auckland."

"With Louis? Are you enjoying his hospitality? I imagine he lives well." He was angry.

"I'm not with Louis. I'm staying with Finn and Jenny. I don't even know where Louis lives. He dropped me off and disappeared."

"Could you not have waited until I got back?"

"You didn't take your phone. I didn't know if you would stay with Michelle all night." The hurt in my voice was evident.

"I'm divorced, Sophie. How many ways can I tell you that I'm never getting back with Michelle. This ongoing jealousy is getting really boring."

"Did you find your phone." I asked, jaw tightening.

"In the bin. Yes, thanks for the pettiness. I thought we were beyond all this."

"You're right. I was petty, and I was jealous. I just never knew that if I didn't put out fast enough that you would start dating again."

He paused, "I'm guessing you read the messages from Darling Roach."

"What was the outcome, did you want her to wear jeans or a dress for easy access."

"Why do you always think the worst of me?"

"Because that's the way I work and because there isn't much trust between us. You assume I've run off with Louis, I assume you've run off with Michelle and you're dating again. How much of that is wrong?"

"I didn't run off with Michelle. I thought it best for everyone if she wasn't there. I know her, I know she will do or say anything to make my life harder and Louis hates her. He can be cruel when she's being difficult and I don't want Toby to see his mother being belittled. I might not like Michelle, but she's still the mother of my son. It was clear how desperate he was to see you that he would travel the length of the country with her. Then he finds he has a son with the woman he wants and can't have because I'm already in his place, and he knows I'm not willing to go easily. Louis and I have been through a lot over the years and we know each other well. It's a burden and a blessing."

"You are making this sound really complicated."

"Gristle, you are always fucking complicated." But the anger was out of his voice. "Are you really with your sister?"

"Yes." I said, outraged. "I'm not like that, Jake, and you know it."

"Toby and I were home in less than two hours to find you and Jax gone. Did you read the earlier texts, from Darling?"

"I got through about ten and couldn't stomach anymore. I got the general idea." But I had that sinking feeling that I had messed this up again.

"She came on to me when I picked Toby up from school. She got my number off his file and she isn't taking no for an answer. I'm emailing the principal today."

"She has a history." I cringed. "You might want to talk to the president of the rodeo, Rick Mussett. He owns the car yard on Yellow Bypass. She's been stalking him, trying to ruin his marriage."

"Jesus." He sighed and I knew he was rubbing his forehead, like he did when he was frustrated. I wanted to hug him, and there was something else. Eyes widening I realized what it was, that there might be a little life left below my waist since his voice was doing strange things to me. He always made me feel calm, and sex with Jake had been good.

Biting my lip, wondering if I should tell him. Instead I said, "Do you think the world is conspiring to keep us apart?"

"Usually, and just so we are clear on this topic, I said *no* to Darling every single time. I'm not dating, I'm not going back to Michelle. I want you to come home. I miss Jax and it's upsetting Toby."

"Why haven't you tried anything with me yet?" I quietly asked, feeling homesick.

"Because you just had a baby. I figure you'll let me know when you're ready. I'm not a fucking teenager, Sophie. I can control myself."

"Now I feel like shit."

"Good, you should. Did anything happen between you and Louis?" He said it just like that, blunt, like he didn't care either way.

I had to be equally blunt. "No. Like you said, I'm not ready."

His voice lowered and I could hear the hurt there. "Come home, Gristle. We don't have to keep doing this. I'm not dating, I'm not interested in anyone else. You know that."

"Damn it. Are you going to yell at me?"

"No. We have trust issues but you can't just run off when it gets hard, there are kids involved."

"I did want to see my sister." I grumbled. "Her and Finn hadn't met Jax."

"Are they good?" And we were instantly on much easier ground.

"My sister's losing her mind because another kid is starting school." But I wasn't so sure. Something was off with Jenny, she had been different since meeting our father again. "And Louis *has* promised to find out who's smuggling the eggs out of Grafton."

"Gristle, you need to think. Louis is a liar, he's the best, that's why he's been so good at being undercover. The man could lie to the devil and get away with it. You're an easy target for him."

"Are you saying he doesn't care about me?"

"Not at all, I think he does want you but he still wants his other life too. He sees a normal life with you, and part of him wants that. But he wouldn't be happy indefinitely, eventually he'd want more. He's complicated and more than you can deal with."

"Yeah, I know." I said slowly. He was right, Louis was more than I could deal with. Not the Louis that had looked after me when I was sick, or the Louis that had fought to get me out of that pit, that was the Louis I wanted, but he didn't exist anymore, if he had ever been real in the first place. "I feel bad for Jax. It's not his fault I made a stupid mistake."

"I can bring Toby up next week if you want. I'll home with you and Jax?"

"You're being very mature."

"Because I'm tired. I just put Michelle on a plane and she's exhausting. I'm going to work for a few hours then I need to talk to Toby."

"Someone is collecting the animals. I couldn't leave them. They need special care."

I meant the sheep and full-grown goat that had been found wandering the main road. Rumor had it they had come from a stag party gone too far. The sheep was spray painted pink but was happy enough and the goat had no outward issues. They were yet to be claimed and I was still pondering the blood on the goat's horns, guessing the stag group took the wrong goat.

"No problem." Jake sighed.

"I'm sorry, Jake." I whispered, wishing I was with him so I could tell him face to face. "For believing you were dating."

"There is no way I'm bringing more crazy bitches into Toby's life. My quota is full."

"I'm sorry for that too."

The pause lasted for a beat too long but I was close to tears, ashamed of myself.

Jake said, "It's you or no one, Sophie. I can't make it any clearer than that."

"I'm awful, Jake. A horrible person."

"Not as awful as Darling fucking Roach."

"I'll talk to her when I get back.'"

There was relief in Jake's voice. "I'm not sure she's mentally prepared for that, Gristle. Just come home."

After reluctantly disconnecting, I called Louis. He didn't pick up so I left a careful message. "If you want to see Jax you should come later today or early tomorrow. I'm going home. Just send me that name and next time you want to see Jax let me know you're coming and I'll be ready."

Half an hour later my phone rang and I endured another awkward conversation with Louis where I once again tried to explain how Jax and I didn't fit into his life. He had to work out how to live on his own.

"You're not ready for kids, Louis." I stated the obvious.

"No one's ever ready for kids." He said on a whisper and it finally registered through to my foggy brain how distracted he was.

"Are you busy? Is someone there?"

"I've just got a lot going on." He husked. "I'll be over as soon as I get out of here."

Then he was gone and I looked online for cheap flights, booking one for late the next day, annoyed now at my immaturity. If Jake disappeared with Michelle I would never forgive him. Or would I? Either way, I had one day with my family and then I was going home, the home Jake and I were creating with our children. It was such a weird concept since it hadn't been the plan, Jake had just turned up and refused to leave. He was a stubborn asshole but I was still deeply in love with him, my reason for going to bed with Louis had been to try and get over Jake, and now my immature heart would be broken once more.

CHAPTER EIGHT

I t was later that same morning that I came downstairs to find Finn lounging in front of the big screen. The kids were outside playing and my sister was again at the window, peering up the long driveway. Pothead and Captain were at her feet, all three of them motionless, as if waiting. Jenny had changed her shirt, this one was pretty, pink and floaty, completely wrong for the day, and I knew something was going on.

Suddenly she made a small sound and left the house, the animals on her tail.

"What's going on with your wife?" I asked Finn who slowly dragged his attention from the rugby game on screen.

"She's just hormonal from having a baby."

His tone was bored, lazy, which wasn't Finn at all. He was usually hyper with energy that was exhausting.

The silence stretched out while he refused to look at me. Eventually, I said, "Why are you watching rugby instead of going to work? You hate rugby."

"It's just background noise." He flicked it off and stood, stretching long and wandering to the fridge. He was getting thick around the waist, and for as long as I had known him, since university, Finn had always been fastidious about his weight.

"You need a new job, Finn." I said before quietly leaving the house and wandering up the driveway to see what was going on with my sister.

I couldn't see Jenny and she had closed the gate so

Captain couldn't follow her. He was peering through the fence, clearly dejected. I couldn't see Pothead but he would be wherever he wanted to be. At the top of the driveway I found my sister in deep conversation with the mailman. He was on a pushbike and it took me about half a second to read my sister's body language and know that she was flirting. On a gasp I understood what was going wrong in Jenny's family and I wasn't sure if I should be relieved or furious.

Hearing me my sister turned, her smile dropping, her pretty face going pale while the postman grinned and waved, welcoming me into the group.

"Lovely morning." He called and I understood Jenny's dilemma. This guy was beautiful. He was Polynesian, tall and solid with gorgeous skin barely hidden behind a red and yellow singlet and very short rugby shorts that exposed heavily tattooed and meaty thighs. He was stunning and those big dark eyes and bright, white smile radiated kindness.

I wanted to yell at Jenny and tell her to get back to her kids that were screaming the neighborhood down, instead I smiled, saying, "It is a dazzling day. Don't let us stop you."

Suddenly, from the hedge at Jenny's back, Pothead shot out and launched himself at the postman. I'm not sure if the crazy cat was going for the man or trying to get into his mail bags, either way, the man shrieked and pedaled away, calling, "I'm going to have to get animal control out for that cat. It's insane." Then he was laughing, a big, booming sound that filled my soul with joy.

"What the fuck are you doing? Explain what your mission is here?" I hissed at my sister who shooed Pothead back into the hedge, checking that no one was watching.

"You have to take this cat back. You're the professional." Jenny hissed in return. "He's ruining everything with his fussing and his pissing."

"Are you trying to have an affair with the postman?" It sounded worse when I said it out loud. "That's so cliché."

"Oh, shut up, Sophie. Why are you the only one who gets

to live an exciting life."

"I don't have an exciting life. I've got a boring life that has flashes of stress and upset, and a son with no father." But Jenny's chin was raised in silent protest. "You would ruin your marriage over the mailman?"

"Did you see him? He's gorgeous." Her hands clamped before her heart as if it was too much to endure. "Do you think he looks like The Rock? Maybe a much younger version."

"And probably dating an eighteen-year-old with pelvic floor muscles. I thought you were planning Finn's birthday?"

"What's that got to do with anything?"

Hands on hips, I looked up into the clear blue sky while my sister peered longingly at the mailman's retreating back, sad, wistful, calculated, like a big cat planning her next meal.

A car pulled up then, not even noticing us as it zipped up the driveway, fast enough that Jenny yelped and ran behind it, yelling, "Hey, Lewis Hamilton, there are kids up there."

A tall man with broad shoulders and a shaved head turned, his smile confused then widening as he recognized us.

"Hey girls, your big brother is home."

Once inside we ran through the usual preliminary questions which Tyler sidestepped easily. Finn made him a coffee, poured me and Jenny waters and deposited babies into our laps when they cried to be fed. I thanked him and decided I would not allow his dumb wife to have a midlife, postnatal crisis without him.

Tyler was delighted at all the kids. "Jesus, how many times am I an uncle?" He asked.

"Five." Jenny said, "Why didn't you come home for Mum's funeral?"

"She hated me. It was obvious from a young age that I was gay and she fucking tormented me about it, said it was a choice, that it was against the Lord, that Dad would kill us both, that I thought I was too good for girls. You know what she was like. It took me a long time to be happy in my skin."

Tyler had been ten when he escaped. Had faked a free school trip to Australia to get our mother to agree to a passport. He then hopped a plane after writing to one of our uncles and had remained in Australia ever since. Our mother hadn't gone looking for him for a long time because she didn't want her benefit cut and thought it was a beautiful solution to her son being different. She was still being paid and he wasn't around.

Jenny had been in contact with him but I had not. There was no animosity there and not really any reason. Tyler wasn't very good at keeping in contact and neither was I. It was good to see him, I was happy that he was big, strong and confident. I told him this and he thanked me sincerely.

We talked for long hours as Finn looked after the kids and let us reestablish our relationship. My sister and I were going to have a discussion. If she thought the mailman could do better with her kids, my nieces and nephews, she was wrong. Glancing at Finn I wondered if I could get him into Samson's gym. My sister wanted more excitement, perhaps if Finn got buff, threw her around the bedroom a little she would remember how lucky she was to have a nice husband. Running off with the mailman would be a fast and frantic mistake. I should know, I had a son from my fast and frantic mistake with an exciting and frightening man.

"Why are you here?" I eventually asked when it was clear we were skirting around something. "Have you come to see Dad? He's not in Mt Eden anymore, they moved him out of Auckland."

"No, I'm not here to see *him*." He spat the final word then glanced around as if someone might be listening. "I've come for

Louis Martinez."

Jenny laughed as if it was a joke, "Well, hang around, he should be here any minute."

But this was serious, there was deep strain behind Tyler's eyes. He was trying to cover it but he was on the edge.

He got points for his acting skills, his grin attempted to remain all good guy but I got the sense he wasn't here to see me, Jenny or the kids, he was here for a reason."

"Rueben mentioned you might know where to find him."

"How is Rueben?" Jenny asked, frowning at Finn who put another glass of water down in front of her. She was being so unfair I wanted to slap her. Instead she got a stern glare that she couldn't interpret so ignored.

I might not like Finn right now because he had quit working with me to try some corporate dream but he was still my friend, my brother in law and a decent man. Jenny was being unfair and disloyal to a man that would do anything for her.

Did Finn have a suspicion? Deep down is that why he was staying home? I decided to visit his new clinic in the morning before I headed to the airport. Thinking about the flight home made me homesick again, to take my mind off it I decided to be waiting for the mailman to stamp some reality on the situation. Even Pothead hated him, not that he was a good judge of character. I still missed that furry little batman and his baked bean sidekick.

"I haven't seen much of Rueben." Tyler smiled, "We're busy."

I stood up to take Jax to his cot for a sleep but Finn beat me to him, saying, "I'll do it. Does he need changing?"

"No, thanks, Finn."

Waiting until Finn left the room I then looked down at my brother and said, "Quit the bullshit, Tyler. We know you're undercover and we know you're going off the rails. Rueben was here looking for you months ago. Tell us the truth."

On a long and tired sigh, he stood and stepped to the window, peering down the driveway as Jenny had done earlier.

I knew for certain that he was not looking for the mailman although they would make a stunning couple.

"You better not be luring any bad guys here." Jenny grumbled. "I've got plans and I'm not dealing with anymore of this family's bullshit." I had a good idea that her plans included a buff mailman in a fluorescent vest. I was going to crush her plans.

"Just tell me where Louis Martinez is." He said to the window. Did he expect us to be intimidated? He had so much to learn.

"Why?" I asked, noting Jenny was barely listening, because she had no real sense that we could be in trouble again, her mind cluttered by a pretty face and buff body.

Tyler stretched his neck from side to side and I heard it crack and pop. He said, "That fucker exposed my work and now there's a hit on me. He's ruined all my hard work just because his job is done. He is going to tell everyone that he lied, that I'm not undercover."

Jenny made a distracted snort that could have been amusement, or constipation. "Good luck trying to get that guy to do anything." She flicked hair from her eyes and ran a finger over one eyebrow. "But he'll turn up here soon. He's in love with Sophie."

Tyler's gaze snapped to me. It was full of reproach. "*You're* the Auckland vet?" He growled. "Why did no one think to tell me?" But something was off in that statement. He wasn't as good at lying as Louis but I couldn't interpret how me being a vet in Auckland meant anything to his work.

"Should I email you every time some hot guy falls for me or Sophie?" Jenny said and I knew she was thinking of that mailman again. "Perhaps if you came to see us, just because you want to see your family we might understand things you would like to know."

"Does Rueben know?"

"Yes," Jenny said, "Like we said, he was here trying to help sort Dad out. Like usual Sophie did it for us, hit the idiot in the head with a hammer when he tried to kill Martinez who was cuffed by the police."

"You should have killed the old fucker." Tyler snarled, unresolved childhood despair showing on his face. "After he wiped out Martinez.

Refusing to discuss Louis, I said, "I'm *a* vet, and I don't live in Auckland anymore." I refused to tell him where I lived. I didn't want anyone else turning up on my doorstep and ruining my life with Jake.

"Jax is Louis son." Jenny just said it and my mouth fell open.

"Jenny." I growled in warning, "That's enough."

"He's our brother." Jenny was peering at her phone, distracted. "He's not going to hurt any of us."

"My nephew is Martinez's son?" Tyler was incredulous. "Are you fucking with me? Did anyone think I needed to know this shit?"

"Perhaps you should be a little more involved in your family." Jenny said.

"Louis went crazy then he got pulled in." I ignored Jenny to explain, "I've barely seen him. We are not together and I can't help you find him. It's best for both of you if you leave each other alone and keep me and my son out of your games."

Glaring as if I had betrayed him, Tyler said, "How fucking stupid are you? Don't you know all the things he's done?"

"Yes, thanks, Tyler. I know exactly how stupid I've been. I had a one night-stand and ended up with a son because Louis was too fucking stupid to wear a condom one time, or I was too fucking stupid to check."

He pointed a threatening finger at me and my blood started to pound as he repeated, "That fucker is going to tell everyone he lied or I'm going to kill him."

"You want to kill my son's father." I said, "You would go to jail, live in the cell like your own idiot father. Think about it, Tyler. Don't be a fool. Admit your cover is blown and come in while you still have some morals left. Louis was undercover too long and it's ruined his life."

Staring at me hard, Tyler eventually said, "You realize he has kids everywhere."

It was Jenny who gasped, "What are you talking about?"

But I was frozen, some part of me not shocked at all. His next words penetrated deeper, "You better hope his wife never finds out about your kid. She's some batshit crazy internet influencer. Obsessed with animals."

Finn was back and listening from the kitchen. He whistled and said, "That crafty bastard. He's had another Sophie at home all this time."

CHAPTER NINE

I had sent Louis a text message that my brother was here and wanting to talk to him. Louis had flat refused. He called and said he wanted to see me and Jax, then we had a long discussion that ended in an argument about Louis thinking I would bring Tyler with me or I would let him follow.

Eventually, I reminded him that we were leaving the next day and he agreed to meet in a local mall carpark, I had to go all secretive and not tell anyone where I was going. Deciding this might be the last time I saw Louis I agreed, telling Jenny and Tyler that I needed some products from the pharmacy, taking Jenny's car.

Louis slid into the passenger seat in the mall's parking building then insisted on a long circuitous route before admitting we were not being followed. Only then did he lead me to a carpark beneath a huge apartment block on the waterfront. He didn't get out of the car until the grill rattled shut behind us, then he was out of the car and striding to a bank of lifts, leaving me to unbuckle Jax and follow, not even looking at us.

On the tenth floor, two down from the penthouse, Louis locked us inside the apartment and turned to hug me, frowning that a kid was in the way.

"Finally." He said, in full seductive mode. "I've got you safe, alone and to myself."

"Safe from who?" I asked thinking of his wife, the animal blogging mother of his children. I hugged him back with one arm, truth was, I liked Louis. He was hardworking and determined when he put his mind to something and did whatever it took to accomplish a mission. That his work and mine overlapped in bad ways (like him running dogfights to sell drugs while I was trying to shut the fights down) didn't change the fact that he was easy to enjoy when he tried. It had not been all bad. I had enjoyed going to bed with him and I got Jax out of it, this little human who depended on me to be his family.

"Safe from who?" I repeated and Louis whispered, "Everyone who has tried to keep us apart."

I would never go there again with Louis and as his hand strayed down my back I pulled away, thinking of Jake, about how he deserved better than this.

"You're not going to make this easy on me, are you?" Louis smiled, like he thought he would get his own way eventually.

"My brother wants you dead unless you change your story, tell everyone that he's not undercover."

"No chance." Louis chuckled, "Your brother is a dirty undercover cop."

"So were you." I argued, lying Jax down on a fluffy rug by a huge floor to ceiling window. He blinked up into the sky, birds catching his attention.

Louis continued in that arrogant tone, "But I understood the timing and got out. It's not my fault if your brother can't read the signs."

"Someone has put a hit on him." Why did this not freak me out more? It was obvious I had been on this merry-go-round for too long.

"He's just trying to scare you. No one puts a hit on anyone these days. Why pay someone if you can just do it yourself."

"How? Where can you hide a body."

He raised a hand, lifting one finger, saying, "Nice fishing trip where only one person comes home." He lifted another finger. "A nice walk in the bush where only one person comes home." Another finger popped up, "A nice fall into a construction foundation."

I waved him to stop. "Alright, I get it. But Tyler's your son's uncle. I hardly have any family and you want to ensure one of them is hurt."

Louis' handsome face shut down and he turned to look out the window, past the yachts and motorboats in the marina below, out beyond the harbor toward the open water of the Pacific Ocean.

"There's nothing I can do." He said, "We all have our own exit plan. If he didn't have one or if his contact isn't good enough, he will go down."

"Was your contact good enough?" I couldn't help prodding about Jake.

Louis smiled, "My contact was the best. Even from overseas and with wife and girlfriend troubles he would drop everything for me. What more could I ask for? Except now things have changed."

"Speaking of wives," I said, staring hard into his smug face, "You never mentioned you had one."

Louis returned his gaze beyond the window as if nothing had changed, but I knew him better than that, I could see that he was holding his breath, pressing his lips together.

Gathering his thoughts, he asked, "How did you find out? Was it Jake?"

"Jake knows?" I gasped, only now feeling hurt. Why did Jake have that much more power over me than Louis?

"He has a crafty way of finding things out. I didn't invite him to the wedding."

I didn't think Jake knew. I would trust that he didn't or he would have told me. I was determined to trust that Jake wasn't out to hurt me.

"My brother, Tyler." I said, "He mentioned she's a social media influencer. It's all about animals. Do you have a thing about women who try to save animals?"

This made Louis laugh. "You don't know who it is then."

He didn't care if he hurt me and it fired my blood as I

looked to his son.

"How could you do it? Pull me along while being married to someone else? You knew I would never agree to that sort of relationship with you."

"I wasn't married then." He grumbled. "It's a new thing, sort of."

There was no way I liked that 'sort of'. "How many of us are there?" I was deeply interested. It was impossible for me to understand how you could give yourself to so many people. How could he remember all the details? I pitied his wife, she would never really have him. Just like I would never have had him either. It would start out sweet but quickly become bitter and that was not going to happen to me and Jax.

He didn't answer my question, instead saying, "It was a marriage of convenience. She had connections I needed. I had to prove my sincerity and she wanted to get married." He shrugged like it meant nothing but I had no reference to know if that was true or not.

"That's horrible, Louis. Does she wonder where you go?"

"She understands my work takes me to dark places."

"Does she know about your past, that you were an under-cover cop?" He wouldn't answer so I added, "Was it a big wedding?"

"Why does that matter?" He wouldn't meet my gaze so I remained silent until he said, "I do have an image to maintain, but it was fairly small."

"Show me." I glanced around at the walls as if there would be a huge loving photo there. When he hedged and told me I was being crazy, I growled, "Show me. You've dragged me around all this time, Louis. You won't let me go then I find out I was some affair?"

"You happened before." Then he winced like he had made a mistake.

"Your marriage was *that* recent?"

"A few months ago. It wasn't about love if that's what you're asking."

"I don't know what I'm asking. I don't know why you chased me to my new home with Jake. I don't know why you are so determined to keep me and Jake apart, especially when you have a wife."

"You have my son." He argued.

"You didn't know that when you came to Grafton with Michelle. You were clueless." I hissed in return, mindful of Jax still blissfully unaware. "Why did you come? Was it to find me or Jake?"

"Both." He argued, "I need both of you."

"Bullshit. You don't need anyone. Show me a photo of your wedding, I know you have one on your phone or access to one. You don't go through with a marriage, even one that isn't real, which I doubt your wife feels the same way, without capturing the day."

Grudgingly he scrolled through his phone and found an image, handing the phone to me and peering out that window again. It would be nice if he looked at his son but I had always known that Louis would not make good daddy material. It would be helpful to Jax if Louis and I could be friends, but with each revelation I worried I didn't like him enough to even be his friend.

I took a moment before I studied the photo, knowing the girl would be beautiful and hoping it didn't dent my fragile ego. Louis might sleep with anyone to get what he wanted but I was certain he would not marry someone he found unattractive. He said it was a small wedding so I had imagined a garden event, maybe with casual shirts and pretty sun dresses, instead I looked at the image to find a traditional white wedding with six bridesmaids and groomsmen, all posed either side of the beaming couple outside Parnell Cathedral.

The screen was too small to take in facial details other than big white teeth but I covered my mouth and laughed, taking a few minutes before I could say, "Louis, it's huge."

He was offended at my amusement. "You don't need to laugh. We both had people to impress."

Fiddling with the phone, zooming in on each face in turn, my gaze slid along the line of strangers, wondering at all these people that populated Louis' life. Slowly I focused on the bride and my amusement died on my lips. I knew that arrogant face, that scrawny body jammed into that skintight dress, the perfect hair and make-up.

My stunned gaze found Louis, and as if expecting me to lose it, he took a few steps backward. I had to look at the photo a few times to ensure I wasn't imagining things. But it was obvious who the mystery woman was.

"You married my vet nurse Keisha?" Then unable to stop it, I laughed, bending forward in an unsuccessful attempt to hide my amusement. Jake was going to love this. I wiped my eyes, "How long after the pits?"

"It doesn't matter. She fell in with a crowd that I needed. It was just work."

"Is she pregnant in this photo?" I asked, noting the unusual potbelly.

"Yes."

"I thought you didn't have unprotected sex." Once again he was caught in a lie.

"She told me she was on the pill."

"The pill is still unprotected sex Louis." Jesus, he was dumb sometimes.

"What would she think if I demanded a condom? I married her."

Waving away his pathetic arguments, I said, "I heard you had other children."

"I have two daughters."

My eyes closed trying to work out the number of months since I had seen him. He made it easier by saying, "Two daughters by two different women."

"Here I was thinking I was special."

"You were the only one I wanted to be with. That I had a choice over."

"And beating Jake had nothing to do with it?"

He grinned, relieved I wasn't flipping out. "That was a nice little bonus."

"Just when I think it can't get any worse with you it does. If Keisha knew you were with me she would rip your balls out. She tried to kill me to impress you."

"She didn't have a chance."

"Could you at least be loyal to your wife. Give me some hope for your corrupted soul when you die."

"What do you want me to say?" He complained, seeing I wasn't going to fight for him. "I married Keisha for a purpose."

"But your purpose is over now." I moved to hold his hands, peering into those eyes. "Go home, Louis. Be a decent husband. Christ, be a decent man."

"Like Jake?" He spat, shaking out of my grasp.

"Exactly like Jake. You need to tell Keisha everything. I don't want her turning up enraged because she thinks I'm going to steal you away. I'm not. You're a married man."

"Jake was a married man when you met him."

"Really, Louis? You want to go there? Just leave me and Jake alone. You can have a relationship with Jax but if you can't be a decent role model in his life then leave him alone, let Jake do the job. You know he'll do a good one."

"It's just work with Keisha." He slowly repeated.

"Whatever helps you sleep at night." I gathered Jax, wanting to get out of here. The thought of Keisha coming home and finding me here was unacceptable.

As I backed out of the door with Jax, I said, "Shouldn't you have family pictures on the wall?"

"This is my private apartment. She doesn't know about it."

"I'm not keeping any secrets for you." I quickly said, "If she ever asks me where you are I'll tell her."

"Then I guess I better move."

Glancing around the opulent apartment made me smile. It was a place, I wanted a home and right now that little house in Grafton was calling to me more than any pretty palace could.

"Don't look so sad." I said.

"You're cutting me out. How else should I look?"

Feeling like a mother with a despondent young child, I smiled and said, "Louis, you don't want *me*. I think you might be in love with Jake."

This made him laugh, "He's the closest thing I've ever had to a brother."

"Then stop acting like an asshole. Fix your friendship with him."

"But when he testifies in all the upcoming court cases he'll ruin me." He didn't appear overly concerned. What was the worst that could happen? He'd go to jail. He had worked hard to get into prison before. He was no stranger to the lifestyle.

"You know he's going to tell the truth. It's what he does. And instead of trying to control him by using me, why don't you pull up your big boy pants and talk to him." He thought about this seriously so I added, "You realize I'm only here for that name right? Did you find anything out?"

He was confused which annoyed me but I clarified slowly, "The bird smuggling in Grafton. Please tell me you weren't lying about that too. That would be unforgivable."

His face cleared and he shook his head. "Oh, yeah. I did ask around. The only name I could find was some guy called Baron. Real hard nose. Doesn't care who he hurts, will do anything to move stock."

"Living creatures that have been stolen from the wild. Not stock." I growled. "I'll look around for anyone called Baron but if you find anything else will you let me know?" He nodded and I gave him a finger wave, saying, "Give my regards to Keisha. Please ensure she stays away from me. Your new bride isn't a very nice person. I think you may have married your perfect match, Louis. She'll do anything to get what she wants too."

He rubbed his face as I winked and closed the door. I was relieved, feeling lighter than I had in a long time. I was rid of Louis, over him, there was nothing there. I knew he was married and had other children and it didn't upset me at all. I passed the burden of the man over to Keisha. She could have him.

CHAPTER TEN

Tyler was still at Jenny and Finn's house when I returned. "Did you get what you need?" He asked and my heart did a double beat. Did he know I had been with Louis? His gaze remained on his phone, he wanted to leave.

"Fine." I said, nervous. "All good."

His hooded gaze lifted to me and he asked, "Where are the things from the pharmacy?" There was a mean glint in his eye that I didn't like.

"None of your business, Tyler." I snapped, refusing to be intimidated by my own brother. He knew nothing about what me and Jenny had gone through with our father, and worse, he didn't even care.

"Maybe." He smiled and I got a hint of the man who worked undercover, all fake smiles with hidden thoughts and agendas.

"Where's Jenny and Finn?" I asked for something to say, mostly wanting to have some time to myself to work out my feelings about Louis and how I was going to explain myself to Jake.

"They had a fight, one's outside and the other's gone off somewhere in a huff."

"Who went in the huff?"

"Jenny." He slowly replied, disinterested, still focused on his phone. "They hissed at each other like two old men. They need to scream it out."

"Damn." I knew she was out searching for that postman. This needed to be sorted out and I was going to do it. "They have kids, Tyler. They can't have screaming fights without upsetting them. It's part of being a responsible adult."

"I'm out of here too." He said, ignoring me, smiling at his phone. "Work to do."

"What kind of work?"

"Just the usual kind."

"You're an undercover cop, Tyler. You don't understand usual kind of work."

"Sure I do. It involves taking down scumbags and making sure no one rats me out."

"What are you going to do about Louis?"

"What I have to do. He knew what he was doing when he named me, what the ramifications of that would be for me. He wants me dead."

"Why would he want you dead?"

"Because I know plenty about him too."

It was on my lips to ask what he knew, instead I raised a hand to still the words. "You know what? Louis is not my problem."

Tyler gave me a hard glare of disgusted disbelief. "You have his kid."

"I'm not the only one with his kid. He'll move on. People like you always do."

Tyler chuckled then, "You're right, and we like to win."

"You'll reach a time, Tyler when you'll be too old for this sort of life. What will you be left with?"

He stood then, towering over me. He was a big, handsome man, his shaved head giving him a hard look that I didn't think was an honest representation of his soul. He had been a sensitive boy and I wondered what his life choices would eventually cost him. Taking a long breath he let it out slowly before saying, "Because of Louis, I have nothing and if he was in my position he would do the same."

"He has been in your position, he's done this for a long

time, he's crafty and brutal and you might not survive taking him on." Seeing Tyler wouldn't be swayed, I said, "Which way did Jenny go?"

It was clear that he was debating telling me something and eventually he said, "I want his contact details."

There was no point asking if he meant Louis, he wasn't interested in anyone else, not his dead mother, his sisters or his nieces and nephews. Tyler was a selfish asshole, but he was also my brother and I had empathy for the childhood that had bought him to this point.

"Why?" I asked, "So you can kill him first? Or beat the shit out of him? He's not easy to take down, Tyler. I've seen him in action and he's terrifying."

"So am I." My brother smiled, cold and hard.

"It's not a competition, you'll both just lose."

"It's always a competition. If I talk to him, make him understand why he needs to change his story we can all avoid a whole heap of violence."

I studied my brother. How hard had he become because of our parent's rejection at such a young age?

"Remember Nana?" I asked, "Mum's mother?"

"Nana Te Wiata." Tyler shrugged, "Sure. She was great. It was after she gave Mum the farmhouse, when Dad moved back in, that things really went to shit."

"Do you think she would have understood you?"

"That I'm gay you mean?"

"No, she wouldn't have cared about that. I mean, would she have understood that you were so sensitive and crazy clever?" He said nothing, so I added, "I only remember a few things about her, like how much she hated swearing and how she would say words I never understood. She was smart too, and fierce, a fighter. I think that's where we get it from." Tyler was staring at me, fully focused now. I continued, "She told me a story once, about how her family tried to hold her down and tattoo a moko on her chin. She went wild since she didn't want it. Instead they put something on her arm. Even when she was so sick, just before she died, she still raged about it. I remember thinking I wanted to be just like her. Be the type of woman that if you were going to mark her, you would have to bring a whole gang and be prepared to fight, and if I survived I would never forgive. All mum said about her was that she liked the white boys too much."

"Only our mother could turn someone's life into something dirty." Tyler scowled. "Nana planned to take us off Mum, did you know that?"

"No."

"I overheard her talking to one of her sisters, said Dad was going to kill us all eventually and she wanted to get us kids out, she even made a deal with mum, she would sign the house over if Mum left Dad for good. Mum agreed, got the house signed over then just moved him back in. I knew as soon as Nana died that I had no hope staying at home. Rueben had written to dad, wanting him to get help for his addictions and mental health problems, I got the letter out of the trash and wrote him back, told him if I didn't come live with him I would kill myself."

"You were ten." I sighed, horrified all over again at our parents. "It's a miracle any of us survived. You don't have to be alone, Tyler. We're not those sad little kids anymore. Jenny and I have worked hard to be a better family for our kids. We want you back."

As if a man-eating monster had just left the room, Tyler sagged, "I would love to be the big brother you need, the person you and Jenny deserve, but I'm just not that guy. I'm sorry. What happened to me made me different and I'm making the best with what our childhood left me with. I get shit done, Sophie. I get it done and I take bad guys out."

Taking a long breath, I studied my brother again. "I can give you his number. That's all I'm willing to do."

"That's all I need." He smiled, standing and hugging me. "And congratulations on the baby, sis. Being a mother suits you."

He left then and I took Jax with me to my room. Outside

the kids were screaming, and when Jax was asleep I would go out and spend time with them. First, I wanted to rest and decide what to do about Jake. I couldn't do this back and forth, the jealousy and confusion. It had to change. Either we were together or Jake had to go, and I knew that saying goodbye to Jake was going to be a whole lot harder than getting over Louis.

◆ ◆ ◆

L ater that night I made dinner since Finn and Jenny were still uncomfortable with each other. I had hissed at Jenny about the mailman but she just turned her nose up and told me to butt out.

Louis arrived when the kids were all in bed. My first instinct was to be annoyed at him. Like why couldn't he turn up at a decent hour to see his son? Why was it always a performance or a drama?

My annoyance was quashed at the state of him. He was sweating and shaking, trying hard to contain his emotions.

Jenny and Finn unthinkingly huddled together.

"Which one of you told your brother where to find me?" Was the first thing he said.

We were all silent as he paced and ran shaking hands through his hair.

"I gave him your number." I said, gulping when his dark gaze turned to me. "I didn't tell him about your secret lair, remember the place where you hide from your wife."

He rubbed his eyes, "He's a fucking cop. He traced my phone. Fuck." He murmured, waving away my apology. "I'm leaving. I don't know for how long. I just wanted to come and say goodbye and see my son."

"Where are you going?" I asked, already knowing he wouldn't tell me.

"I can't trust your brother won't find me through you."

"I'm sorry. I didn't want you to get into trouble."

"I know." He hugged me then I followed him up the stairs so he could lean down and kiss his son.

"Should I be scared of Tyler?" I asked.

"He's *your* brother. You tell me."

"I barely know him. But I imagine he can be as ruthless as you to get what he wants."

"That's what I'm afraid of, and since I've come in I don't have any of my supporters."

"You mean those big thugs you were always hanging around with?"

"Amongst others." He smiled and strode down the stairs and for the door. "I'll be in contact but it might be some time. I'm trusting you with my son."

And just like that my worry bled away. He always said the thing that would annoy me the most, and it concerned me that he had no idea. "Oh, shut up, Louis." I growled, "I'm not one of your idiot lackeys."

He stopped then. "Did you tell your brother where to find me? Do you want him to hurt me, as revenge? Tell me the truth."

"No, why would I do that?"

"Because I married someone else." I realized then that behind his stern façade he was hopeful that I would fight for him.

There was nothing for it but to be honest. "I'm sorry, Louis. I don't want you."

He looked up at the ceiling, jaw tight. "It's always been Jake, hasn't it?"

"Yes."

"Even with my son?"

"Even with your son." I agreed.

He nodded and I followed him as he said a quick and terse goodbye to Jenny and Finn. He stared at me for a long moment after that then turned away just as a figure emerged from the gloom. An outside security light flicked on to reveal Keisha who took one look between me and Louis and burst into furious tears, racing for me. Louis grabbed her around the waist while she shrieked and swore.

Finn emerged then, "Shut that bitch up. My kids are asleep."

"Fuck you, Finn." She cried and after a moment of confusion Finn gasped, "Jesus, Keisha? I didn't even recognize you. What happened to you?"

She did look terrible. Emaciated and exhausted. "My husband keeps disappearing and leaving me alone with his kid."

"I told you what you were signing up for." Was her sweet husband's great reply.

My sister pushed past Finn to ask Keisha. "Where's the baby?"

Keisha must have walked up the long driveway since her car wasn't parked behind Louis'. Keisha's huge sad eyes remained on her husband, rubbing at her nose with one wrist.

"She's in the car. She won't stop crying."

Jenny took Keisha by an elbow and turned her back toward the driveway while Louis peered around as if for another exit.

"You really are a bastard." I told him. "You can't just leave her here. She's your wife, she has your baby."

"What am I going to do for them? I never asked her to get pregnant. She just did it."

"You had a little input." Finn grumbled, peering up the driveway as if anxious to get the baby. Jesus, sometimes I remembered why I liked Finn. He was an eternal caregiver. A great dad, a brilliant vet and a loving husband. My sister would regret what she was trying to do with the mailman and I loved her too much for that to happen without a fight.

God, I just wanted to get home to Jake and Toby. I was missing the quiet life.

Louis stepped toward the backyard and Finn growled, "No, you stay here and face what you've done. I'm sick of you leaving the mess to me and Jake."

"What mess?" I asked, thinking Finn was involving himself more than he had any right too.

"Sophie, every time this guy comes into your life it's a disaster. Would you and Jake be in constant chaos if Louis just stayed away from you both?"

I looked at Louis then, hands on his hips, arrogant and gorgeous.

"I know that, Finn. I've told Louis that too."

Keisha returned then, Jenny holding a baby that Finn took inside.

Louis said, "I'm going. I don't know when Tyler could come back."

"What do you mean, you're going?" Keisha asked.

"Their brother's out to get me. I don't have any supporters right now. So, I'm going." He turned to me, "You tell her."

Then Louis Martinez once again left me with his mess, or according to Finn, left *him* to clean it up.

Keisha crumbled and Jenny walked her to the dining table, sitting her in a chair while Finn jiggled the unsettled baby.

When the room was silent, Finn said, "You have to sort your shit out, Keisha. This baby is feeding off your emotions, the more upset you are the more unsettle she is."

"Who are you, Doctor fucking Phil." She hiccoughed, taking the tissue Jenny pressed into her hand.

"Finn has about a million kids." I said, "I'd listen to him if I were you."

Continuing in his smooth, calming tone, Finn said, "This baby is highly stressed and needs to calm down. Are you feeding her?"

"God, no." Keisha gasped. "I'm not a fucking cow." She looked at the two bouncers beside the sofa and asked, "Finn, did you have twins?"

"No, there are two babies here." He said, eyes widening at me. "My youngest baby and Sophie's baby."

Confused, Keisha asked me, "You had a baby? Was that to

that cop, Jake?"

"No, Keisha. He isn't Jake's baby."

Her gaze snapped to me then filled with more tears. "You got pregnant to Louis? Some lame way to try and keep him. How could you? With a married man."

"Get a grip." Jenny snapped, "She only found out today that he had married you. They had a one-night stand and that self-centered asshole never bothered with her. She's living with Jake yet Louis dragged her back here with the promise of names to shut down a bird smuggling ring down south." Jenny was outraged, she had never liked Keisha who had been totally useless when working with me and Finn. Then there was that little issue with Keisha masterminding a plan to take over the dog fights, kidnapping me to keep Louis in line, then trying to get me to fight her in the pit. Who wouldn't dislike her? To be honest, Keisha is a generally unlikeable person.

"Did he want to stay with you?" Keisha asked.

"It doesn't matter." I said, "The same still applies, I don't want him."

"But saying that makes him want you more."

"Jesus, I can't win. Look, I don't want Louis. I told him that. More importantly, our kids are siblings, that's all that matters to me. I went over to look at the little girl who was now peering quietly at Finn. She was small and skinny but then so was Keisha so she might have taken after her mother. I didn't want to imagine Keisha wasn't feeding her enough.

"She's really cute." I told Keisha who looked confused as she replied, "Well, yeah. Of course she's cute. Look at her parents."

On a sigh, I added, "I don't even know her name."

"Savvy." She said, sitting up straighter, wiping more mascara onto tissues.

"Savvy?" I asked, "Is that short for anything?"

"Sauvignon." She smiled now. "It's that wine we export overseas so it sounds exotic. Don't you think?"

She looked between me and Finn expectantly, while we

were both frozen.

Eventually, I said, "Lovely." I smiled while Finn turned away. I could see his shoulders shaking with amusement and wished I could join in.

"My son's name is Jax." I said.

"What is that short for?" She asked and I bit my lip. No one had queried his name so far and I had hoped to avoid explaining.

"It's not short for anything." I said, "Just Jax."

My sister added her unwanted opinion, "I thought you wanted to call him Jake but freaked out at the last moment and changed it to something similar."

Damn her, that is exactly what had happened. I had no idea Jake would turn up on my doorstep, faint then move in. Jax could have been called anything.

"Do you want our kids to know each other or not?" I snapped.

"Like you look after my daughter or something?"

"I live in the South Island. I can't offer babysitting but when I'm here we can meet up, let them get to know each other."

Finn had the baby in the crook of his elbow and she had stopped crying, continuing to stare at him. "I can help you, Keisha." He said.

"Really?" Keisha asked, "I'd love another person I trust to look out for her if I'm out with Louis. We have a very active social life." It was like she was ignoring the fact that her husband had a kid with someone else. She clearly wasn't surprised and I understood that.

More concerning was the glint in Finn's eye. I knew that look and had a hint of what he was up to when he asked Keisha, "Are you working?"

"No. I was helping some guys with . . ." Her eyes flicked to me before she added, "But Louis fucked them over and so I'm out too."

"If I find out you've been doing anything illegal with animals I'll take you down."

"Yes, Sophie. I know you well enough to know that you would. I've been blogging about animals actually and I've got almost ten thousand followers on Insta with my posts."

"What kind of posts?" I imagined she was replaying some of my greatest moments, putting herself into my place and saving animals one embarrassing street brawl at a time.

Instead she said, "I find cute pics online and post them. Especially cats and little dogs, the world is full of pet weirdos."

Finn spoke then, his eyes widening along with his smile, about the first real one I had seen since I'd been here. "We have a vacancy at my new clinic. I'd love you to work there. It's exactly what those guys deserve, I mean need, a hard-working vet nurse."

Jenny and I looked to each other. Finn was angry, taking Keisha to the new clinic was like slipping a stoat into a chicken house. It would be the eventual downfall of them all, and as complicated as my brother in law could be, he wasn't mean or vindictive like this. I knew his new colleagues from university, we had hated them then and them us, but that was years ago, we had all grown up. I needed to go meet them again to get a handle on what was going on with Finn. I had a good idea I would really hate them too.

"Part time?" She asked, taking Savvy off Finn and opening a bag of bottles.

"Whatever you need." Finn said, holding fingertips to his lips as if unable to believe what he was doing.

Jenny helped her with the microwave and Keisha sat on the sofa to feed her baby. I sat next to her and smiled at the little girl.

"She really is pretty, Keisha. You're doing a great job."

Scowling, she said, "Not as good as you, I bet."

"It's not a competition, and I found having a newborn pretty tough."

Her frown cleared and she grudgingly said, "Thank you. I'm trying really hard."

Pothead slunk in then and Finn said, "I know that fat bastard was locked out."

"He's coming down the old chimney." Jenny said, "I caught him in the act this afternoon. It's impressive, he's almost silent but I thought a bird had been caught in the chimney so I put a torch up there and found him perched on a little ledge about halfway. He fell down after that, or he was trying to attack me since I'd found his secret passage."

Shaking his head, Finn said, "See, this is what I mean. What kind of cat can run up and down a brick chimney? He's not normal in the head."

Keisha was delighted to see him, "Pothead! I thought he got cooked in the fire."

"No chance." Finn grumbled. "But he did start it." At Keisha's blank expression he clarified, "Sophie's boyfriend Jake, you remember him?" Keisha nodded, "Remember his wife who came in that time with the big dog and the kid?" Keisha nodded again. "She broke in using the code the beefcake left on his phone from when Sophie neutered your brother's dogs. The wife was stoned and used hemp candles and Pothead thought she was like those teenagers Sophie saved him from and had some relapse. Apparently he was running around with a rat in his mouth and knocked over a candle that hit something flammable and the place went up like a rocket."

"Why are you smiling?" I asked Finn, "I thought that ruined your life."

"It did but I'm sure it's going to be one of those stories I tell my kids about when they ask what it was like working with their aunt."

"Don't forget all the street fights." Keisha chuckled.

"And that time she did Periodic Detention." My sister joined in, looking less stressed than usual.

"I'm here to entertain." I grumbled.

"I always knew that cat would ruin you guys." Keisha said, "It's got something wrong with it. Like he thinks he's a person and we are all just his minion."

"He's gorgeous." Jenny enthused, picking him up and

cradling him like a baby. If anyone else did that, even Jake, Pothead would jab their eyes out. Instead he flicked his tail in delight and closed his eyes gently, telling my sister how much he loved her in return. It was galling since I had saved that cat and he treated me like everyone else, a burden he had to endure. Well, he had hated Keisha, like most animals. For a vet nurse she was not exactly an animal person. She wasn't a people person either.

"He's trying to get me out of my own bed." Finn growled.

"He won't have to try very hard." Jenny muttered and Finn glared at her, reminding me of the mailman.

Keisha stood on a gasp of delight when Captain Pugwash rolled into the room in search of his overlord.

"You kept him?" She picked him up and Captain Pugwash turned into a trembling baked bean, huffing in pleasure at the attention. "Can I have him?" She asked Finn who instantly said, "Yes!"

My sister put Pothead on the floor to take the little dog who morphed into a magic bean, moving in a way that should be impossible with that little body.

"No chance." Jenny said, "The kids love him and he keeps Pothead honest."

Finn clarified, "The dog warns me when Pothead's near. I'm swear he's trying to kill me, sleeping on my face like a big furry cushion."

"Better than a pillow." Jenny joked in a way that wasn't very jokey.

Turning the conversation away from my messed-up family and back to Keisha, I asked, "Have you had much help with Savvy?"

"My mum's been better than I expected. She hates Louis and likes to say it's all my own fault that he runs off, that I knew what I was buying when I got him to marry me. Nathan hasn't been around. He hates me after what went down at the pits. Says his dogs wouldn't have been ruined if I had of just left you and Louis alone. That's probably true." She sighed, staring at Savvy sadly.

"We're all doing the best we can." I told her, once again astonished that Keisha and I failed to hate each other every time. "And you should have known better than trying to change Louis. Although who am I to say anything. I messed up even worse, and I had no interest in marrying him. I was just lonely after Jake dumped me." I thought of Jake and Toby at home and wanted to hit something for what an idiot I was. "I'm such a loser."

She thought about this, peering around the room as if searching for something. I hope she wasn't casing the joint for any of her less than savory connections. "You're right." She said, "Fuck Louis. I thought once we were married he would settle down, that a baby would force him too. Instead he just carries on like we don't exist. My father did that. I don't want to go through it again."

I pat Keisha's shoulder, remembering that when she dropped the hard façade, she was a decent human being. Not that I would ever forgive her for using her idiot brother to kidnap me and haul me to a dogfight. My worst nightmare.

I said, "Find a nice guy, or even better, be her hero on your own."

After feeding her baby, Keisha stood and said to Finn, "Are you on the same mobile number?" He nodded and she said, "I'll call tomorrow about the job."

"Great, I'll let them know you're the best." He laughed like a lunatic and it made me happy. Before Finn had been my business partner or clapped eyes on my sister, he had been my best guy friend from university and we had pushed each other to be the best vets.

Keisha turned back to me and said, "Just so we're clear, Louis is mine."

"All yours." I agreed, grinning at her confusion.

When she was gone, Jenny snapped at Finn, "You're getting bitter to want her at the clinic."

Finn glared at Jenny in return and even I wanted to weep

at the hostility in his normally amiable face. "Fuck them." He said then turned toward the stairs. I heard him say under his breath, "Fuck you too." I was unsure if he meant me or Jenny. I hoped it was me.

CHAPTER ELEVEN

J ax only woke once during the night and although the sleep was welcomed after the frantic and emotional day, I woke anxious about going home. I wanted to be there but I didn't want to face Jake at all.

Downstairs, I found Finn pottering in the kitchen and asked after Jenny.

On a sigh, he said, "She's taken Tim to school."

"Oh, god. Is it his first day?"

Finn nodded, "Jenny didn't want me to go. Said I would only upset him and that I needed to get to work."

"Then why aren't you at work?"

"I'm going." He grumbled. "If I'm not gone before Jenny gets home she'll probably divorce me." He sighed and I felt bad for him.

"Can I have a quick look at the clinic?" I asked, stealing Finn's toast.

"Would you?" He asked as if unable to believe his luck. "Then you can tell Jenny that I'm not just a miserable asshole, that these guys are shit."

"They can't be the same as Uni. Why do you hate them so much?"

"They think they know everything. Seriously, you would think I've just graduated. One of them comes in to watch over me every session."

"Maybe they want to learn off you."

"I'm not that dumb." He lifted a finger when I thought to disagree. "Get Jax in his car seat. Let's go."

We took only one car, Finn telling me to drive his car home and he would walk.

"That's like an hour." I argued.

"Yeah." Finn sighed as if in pleasure.

The clinic was a lovely, modern space, big and busy with three receptionists. It was on the main street in Remuera with lots of parking so easy to access for older people or those with kids. What was not to like?

Inside, I didn't recognize anyone, not that I was looking hard, too busy gaping around at the purpose-built surrounds, seeing exactly what had drawn Finn to the place. Our old clinic, the one Jake's wife had burned down, was an aged house that had been forced into a life as a clinic against its will. How much did this place cost to run?

Finn introduced me as an old colleague who was interested in buying into the clinic. I just smiled. In Finn's room a man followed us in, shaking my hand and smiling brightly.

"I remember you from university." The man grinned like a crocodile. "I asked you out once and you turned me down."

Looking at him hard, I clicked my fingers, "Chester Canasta. I didn't turn you down, you puked on my new shoes then passed out." God, he had been the reason I had lost my slot as top of the year. Damn, I had hated him back then and by the smug smile on his face I wouldn't like him now either. Finn was an idiot to try working with this guy.

He boomed with amusement. "I was hoping you would forget that. Good times."

I didn't agree. I would have received a scholarship without that incident and it wouldn't have taken me so long to pay off my student debt. I shot Finn an annoyed look that he had kept Chester's identity a secret when he knew how much I had loathed him.

"You want to buy into the clinic?" He asked.

"It doesn't look like you need any more vets. This place is

huge."

"The more vets means the less I have to do since I take a percentage. It's a genius set up that keeps me in the life I've become accustomed too."

"But I have to buy in? Then you take a cut of what I earn?" Seriously, what? Had Finn agreed to these terms? Had he been that desperate to be rid of me. My blood was firing.

"Think of it like a finder's fee." Chester chuckled.

"But Finn found me." I wanted this clear in my head so I could yell at Finn about it later. "So does that mean I give my fee to him?"

"We're not in university now, dummy. No professors to impress. I make the rules."

Now it was crystal clear and I understood what was going on with Finn. He might be a smart man, but he was also dumb. "Wow." I said, "Awesome. I'll think about it."

Chester nodded as if he thought I would seriously consider buying into a clinic that I would then have to pay for. What was wrong with the world?

He held the door wide as if ushering me out. "Now if you don't mind, Finn has a full load today since he's taking some of my clients. I've got to go out."

"What?" Finn then sagged. "Sorry, Soph." He was defeated. "I'll talk to you later."

"I think I've seen enough." This was gross and I wanted out of here, no wonder Finn was such a mess.

On the way out I noticed another vet walking behind the pretty receptionists, asking what they were doing, barking orders and instructions like a drill sergeant. I imagined Keisha here and smiled brightly as I said goodbye to disgusting Chester Canasta.

"You never paid me back for those shoes." I said.

He snorted like I had made a joke, "I should have charged you for stealing my drinks straight from my stomach." He boomed, embarrassing and obnoxious.

I added, "If you remember anything about me from university, you'll know that I always work hard and I hate to lose."

His ruddy, chubby face flushed right into his thinning hair, "What does that mean?"

"It means, Chester, that one way or another, I'll get what you owe me."

He looked me up and down, attempting to belittle me. As if I cared what he thought.

"You always were fucking nuts." He said before checking who might be listening. He added, "I'll send you through the information about buying in."

Something was off here and I wondered if this seemingly busy clinic was not doing as well as it appeared. I would ensure Finn had his own accountant look over the books. There were other vets from university that might want to work here. If Finn could bring in Keisha, and I now fully understood why he would want too, I might know just the lady to blow this place to shit and back. I could think of no finer gift to my brother in law. Not that he deserved anything after dumping me but I think he had learned his lesson.

I turned back to look at the clinic and noticed Finn staring longingly out the window. It took him a moment to realize I was watching him and he pressed his face and palms to the window, mouthing *help me.* I smiled and shook my head at the sad state of Finn's life. This could be fixed, I just didn't know how yet. One thing was for sure. Finn had got me through some hard times at university and I was not going to let him down by allowing Chester to beat him. We both deserved better than that.

On my way back to Finn and Jenny's house I thought about getting to the airport on time. I wanted to get on the plane and get home, to be near Jake and Toby, but I had a job to do before then. I was waiting at the end of the driveway when I thought the mailman might come by. It was heartening that my sister wasn't there. That she hadn't been peering out the window like a milk-mad puppy.

Pothead escorted me to the mailbox which was nice. Instead of hiding in the bush he sat on a fencepost and peered around like a snooty king on his throne, occasionally tossing me a disdainful look.

Half an hour later Jenny wandered up the driveway with Jax.

"What are you doing?" She asked, "Jax is hungry."

Honesty was all that would work here. We needed a confrontation before I left. "I'm waiting for the mailman."

"You're not having him." She snapped, furious. "Are two hunks not enough for you?"

"Don't be an asshole." I growled, reaching out to pat Pothead who rubbed against me, a sign that he was on my team about this. "I'm going to tell him to back off, that you're married to a very nice ... sometimes nice man, who adores you and your four kids."

"You wouldn't dare." She snarled, passing my son and lifting Pothead as if I wasn't allowed to touch him.

"I would." I assured her, "You are going to ruin your life over a pretty face. Do you want your kids to be bought up poor like us?"

"This isn't about money, Sophie. I can get a job."

"And leave your kids in daycare? It'll cost more than you'll earn, and you would hate someone else teaching your kids anything."

"This is about me. I want to fall in love. I want excitement again."

"Then get Finn to slap your ass a few times. I don't care, just sort it out. Go and get counselling. Your kids deserve better than this."

Jax was crying now and I peered along the road. "Where is he? I've got to get to the airport soon."

"You don't have to go until after lunch." Jenny argued, tears pooling in her eyes.

"I'll have lunch there. I want to go home." It was clear I was exasperated with her.

"Are you going to pick Finn's side?" She lifted her chin, pretending she was tough when we both knew, when it came to family, she was hopeless, we both were.

I jiggled Jax, exasperated, "There are no sides. You're both being gross, that's why you suit each other, you've even synchronized your breakdowns."

"I'm not awful." She was genuinely offended.

"You're trying to run off with the mailman. You don't even know him. It's so shallow. The poor man's just trying to do his job every day. You're deplorable."

"The mail hasn't come every day for about a million years, Sophie. See, you don't fucking know everything." She dropped Pothead back to the ground and he hissed. I liked to think it was in solidarity to my position on this situation. "Finn can take you to the airport."

"Finn's at work." I said, annoyed all over again at the memory of that clinic. "Have you even been there? It's horrendous, yet he does it for you and your kids while you stay at home and dress up for the postman."

"If you can't support me then I won't tell you anything in the future."

"Oh, what's that, Mum? Emotional blackmail looks ugly on you." We hadn't argued like this in years but I was furious at her.

Wordlessly she stormed up the driveway before spinning

back to say, "You just don't get it. You don't understand what I go through every day."

"You're right. I don't get it at all."

She stormed back toward me. Thankfully Jax had calmed down and was now staring at Pothead who was trying to climb a spindly tree.

"You got the education, not me." She cried, "I've got all these kids, what will I have when they leave?"

"Is this about Tim starting school? You still have two at home. Jesus, Jen. You're smarter than this. You love Finn."

She turned away again. "Do I?" Then she was gone, Pothead thinking it was a game and chasing her, causing her to scream and run. I figured she deserved it.

Finn arrived soon after, I didn't ask if he was supposed to be home yet. He looked close to tears as he said, "I'll take you to the airport."

"I can call an cab." I wanted to brighten him up.

"You've been to my work. I don't need much of an excuse not to be there."

Jenny gave me a terse goodbye as I packed Jax into the car, and on the way to the airport I asked Finn, "What's going on with you and Jen? I've never seen you guys like this."

"It's me." He said, gloomy. "I hate my job so much that I'm making us all miserable. I don't know what to do without quitting. How will I feed them all and pay the mortgage?"

"What are your options, Finn? If she leaves you, you'll be paying for two homes."

He was silent for a long time, checking the road compulsively in case of runaway cattle in the middle of the city, knuckles white on the wheel, as always, the best grandad driver around.

At the next lights he relaxed his grip and said, "You're right. I'm miserable. I'm going to pull out of the clinic. I'd rather work on my own and be poor. I'll get another mortgage if I can't get the money out but I don't care. Are you joining me?" He glanced at me then which was surprising for Finn who would never normally take his eyes off the road.

"Even if I came back to Auckland to work with you again, I can't go back to how it was. I've got a baby."

"Just work part time. Whatever you need. I want to get the band back together." His face cleared and he looked genuinely happy. It was hard not to get sucked into his enthusiasm. "What if I get another mum to take half a share with you? I know a couple of vets who might like to do that."

I was about to say no, but that wasn't what he wanted to hear and he was so hopeful that I just said, "I'll think about it." But I had a new life down south. It was what I wanted. A life of my own with Jake.

Then Finn helped me get Jax to the departure gate, kissed my cheek, smooched Jax and was gone, looking happier than I'd seen him since I'd been back. His last words were, "I'll email you some properties. If we go back to Parnell we'll even get out old clients back. I wonder if Primrose is enjoying her new job. I might call her. It'll be amazing."

CHAPTER TWELVE

It was late afternoon when we made it back to Grafton. I thought to let Jake know we were on our way, to ask for a ride, but I couldn't keep telling him we were flat mates then ask him to help all the time. Instead I found a cab, nervous to be back.

My return was stealthy because something unwholesome was stewing in the back of my mind, it stuck with me on the plane then grew in the cab. It started with me worrying that I was putting too much expectation on Jake. Would he let me down? What had he been doing while I was away? Was Darling Roach still messaging him? Had he decided to meet her? Maybe just to shut her up, but things could have progressed naturally. Was I about to be devastated all over again? I would be justified in all my concern about Jake but that felt like a shallow victory right now.

Jax slept for most of the cab ride, the car rocking him gently, and the driver wasn't the talkative type so I just peered out the window and worried, talking myself into a frothy mess. The closer we got to home, the more I was certain Jake was right now in bed with Darling Roach, trying to coax her from the house before I returned, both laughing at what an idiot I was. It was my own fault, I wouldn't put out so what did I expect would happen?

What would I say? Would I scream and be dramatic, tell him to leave and take his lovely son? Or would I be stoic and agree to talk about it? I hoped Toby hadn't heard them going at it like wild cats. Toby's reaction was going to either make or break me.

I was so absorbed in my daydream that it was a shock to pass Jake and Sarge on a run. They were moving fast but I knew Jake liked to warm down with a walk then take his time to stretch and water Sarge before coming inside. I would have time to slink in and find Darling draped over his bed, her lingerie tossed about the room from the spent passion, the scent of her expensive perfume and their lovemaking heavy in the air.

When we pulled up I left Jax while I grabbed my bag from the trunk of the white Prius. The driver suddenly decided to give me a business card and tell me all about a new driving service that was cheaper. I was anxious, words stuck in my mouth until Jake and Sarge turned the corner and spotted me. Jake sped up and I was mesmerized by it. He had no shirt on and I wondered how many neighbors were watching him running around half naked. I wouldn't blame them, he was worth the shame of being caught.

At the car he dropped Sarge's leash and the big dog sat, huge tongue lolling from the side of his mouth. Without looking at me Jake opened the door and unclipped Jax's capsule from the backseat.

Jax opened his eyes, face scrunching to cry. Jake stopped him by cooing, "Hi, buddy. Why didn't you guys call? I would have come and got you." Jax grinned and my heart wanted to burst out of my chest.

Unable to speak, not sure what I would say, I carried my bag into the house, Jake following, chatting to the baby who was being more mature about his feelings than I was. Inside Jake quickly changed Jax and asked if he needed feeding.

I shook my head, "He slept in the car and most of the plane ride."

Jake nodded then slipped him into his bouncer.

"I better take a shower." He sighed, noting I couldn't look at him. Jesus, how could I? The guy had been keeping fit and it was showing while I was a mess.

When he emerged I took my turn in the shower to get away from him, still unable to meet his gaze. By then Toby was home and I yelped with delight, hugging him tightly.

He pulled away to open his school bag, producing a strange bald creature. "I found this on the road. I don't know what it is but I didn't want it to get run over."

I smiled and took it off him, finding a box and placing it inside.

"What the heck is it?" Jake asked while Toby followed, watching what I did closely.

"It's a hedgehog." I said, "It might have mange or mites or maybe an infection. We'll give him food and water, he'll be okay till the morning." To Toby I said, "Good job, you saved his life." Glancing at the clock, I added, "You're so late."

"Yeah, I was trialing for the rugby team." He peered at the floor and I thought he might cry.

"You must have gotten in, the school's tiny, lucky if it can put a team together." I dropped a hand to his shoulder, confused by his concern.

His bottom lip wobbled. "I wanted to play winger but the coach says I'm too big and not fast enough."

I frowned, "So maybe play another position."

"I probably won't make the team, or I'll do the water, even if there aren't enough players. I don't want to play anyway." It was obvious he did.

"Do you want me to come and talk to him?" I asked, "Just to ask what's going on."

"Her. It's Miss Roach, our receptionist."

I glanced at Jake who rolled his eyes. "She called again today." He said, ruffling Toby's hair. "The principal wants to see *both* of us tomorrow."

"Is something going on at school?" I asked Toby, worried now and holding his hand.

He smiled, it was lopsided and confused. "I don't think so. I'm not sure what it's about. I've been doing really good at math, maybe I'm getting an award."

To Jake I said, "The principal wants me there?"

"Requested by name." He stared at me then, blowing out a breath when I stared back for the first time, my heart slowly thudding.

"Sounds exciting." I told Toby who shrugged out of our anxious hold to play with Jax, bouncing him then reading him a book.

"He missed you, Toby." I added when Jax broke into a beatific grin.

"I missed him too." Toby said, "What's for dinner?"

Jake was in the kitchen and called out that it was butter chicken and Toby made a fist pump of delight.

"You have time for a shower." Jake said pointedly and Toby sniffed his armpit, laughed and stood, eyes still on Jax.

"Are you guys fighting?" Toby said before leaving the room.

My heart went out to him. He was a bright kid who had watched his parents behaving like spoiled children, and here I was doing it all over again. I decided to just be honest, he deserved the truth.

"Me and your dad have both had complicated people in our lives in the past."

"You mean Mum?"

"Yeah, amid other people. Me and your dad are figuring things out and we won't always get it right but don't ever think we don't adore you. You're a wonderful guy, Toby. Me and Jax are so lucky to have you and your dad in our lives."

He hugged me then, a fast, hard squeeze before shuffling to the bathroom.

Jake had his back to me, working over the stovetop. I wasn't sure how he felt about what I had just said, after all, I had explained it better to a ten-year-old than I had to him. Jax had nodded off, like an old man in his favorite chair, meaning Jake and I had a few moments alone. I touched his back and he glanced down at me, his smile sad.

He started to speak a few times before saying, "You almost picked Louis, didn't you? Be honest."

"No, I . . . I don't think so." I really wasn't sure. My feelings for Louis were now tied up with Jax. It was always going to be complicated. I took a long breath, staring into that handsome face, remembering what we had been through to get to this point, that we were still fighting to be together was the whole point. "I thought you were dating." I said, "Darling Roach is more like Michelle than I am and I panicked. I was terrified that you've made my son fall in love with you and then he wouldn't have you or Toby in his life."

"We knew this wasn't going to be easy." He said, cupping my cheek.

I shook my head. "In the name of honesty, I'll admit that my first instinct was to find that name, to know who is smuggling those eggs. Louis said he knew or that he could find out, that if I went with him he would get the name for me, so I took the opportunity."

Jake turned the stove off and carefully placed the wooden spatula down.

"Are you for real?" He was trying hard to contain his anger. "You carted your new baby to Auckland for a name that Louis could have messaged you." I tried to defend my position but he held a hand up, saying, "He calls and you jump, every fucking time and I can't deal with that. He knows exactly what to say to get you where he wants. He's a manipulative mother fucker. Believe me, I know better than anyone what he'll do to control a situation. How many ways do you need to know that?"

"I'm sorry."

"Did you get the name?" He peered out the window over the sink, hands propped on the bench highlighting mouthwatering arm muscles. It was dark outside but the heat wasn't letting up and I could feel sweat forming. I should have taken a cold shower. I glanced at Jake again and wanted to fan my face. Maybe it wasn't the heat. Was it getting hotter?

"Yes, Baron."

"Do you know who that is?" He was cringing, not wanting me to know.

"Not a clue."

"Thank fuck." He blew out a breath of relief.

"Did you know that Louis got married?"

The shock on Jake's face was obvious. "No, who the hell did he marry?"

"Keisha."

His jaw dropped, "Your old clinic nurse? The one that kidnapped you?"

"One and the same."

"Why? That makes no sense. I know it isn't love because he isn't capable."

"He said she had new connections he needed. She turned up at Finn and Jenny's to stake her claim. Louis did his usual disappearing act and left us to pick up Keisha's disintegrating pieces. She's got a baby to him too, a little girl called Savvy, short for Sauvignon."

Jake rubbed his face, "Are you fucking joking?"

"Keisha thought naming her daughter after wine was classy. Savvy's not much younger than Jax and she's really cute. I don't blame you for questioning my feelings about Louis, Keisha thought I wanted him too."

His anxiety froze as he asked, "Does she still think you want Louis?"

"No. I set her straight." Jake nodded, lifting his eyebrows, knowing that Keisha wouldn't have walked away if there was any uncertainty.

"Louis has another daughter somewhere to someone else too." I said, testing what Jake knew.

Propping his hands on his hips, looking out the window again, Jake said, "I'm surprised. He doesn't like anyone having a hold on him. Perhaps he's growing up."

"He has nothing to do with any of his kids. Spreading them all over the countryside isn't growing up. It's just being an immature idiot. And I'm an even bigger one for ever believing any of his lies."

"Don't beat yourself up." Jake rubbed my arm, "You will never meet a better liar."

I sighed, "My brother's in the country too. He wants to talk to Louis before all the court cases start. He thinks Louis ratted him out as undercover."

"Would that really surprise anyone. Louis would rat me out if he had anything on me. He's just that type of guy."

There was nothing to argue about there. Louis *was* that guy, always looking out for number one. "You never mentioned there would be so much legal stuff after Louis."

"I was his contact for a long time." He was watching me carefully, interested in what I knew, what Louis had admitted to.

"He says he only survived because you were the best at what you did."

"I knew him well."

Unable to stand there any longer without touching him, I wrapped my arms around his waist, grateful when he accepted my hold without question.

"I'm sorry I took off like that." I said, finding it easier to speak without his heavy gaze on me. "I don't want Louis."

"Because he's married with kids?"

"You were married with a kid when we met."

"No, I was virtually divorced."

"Another complicated situation." I rubbed my cheek on his shoulder, the scent of him like coming home. "I did miss you, Jake. I like our life, but I'm worried we're avoiding the world by staying here."

"What are you saying?" But his arms wrapped tighter around me and he kissed the side of my head.

"My sister's losing her mind, trying to rape the mailman, Finn is depressed and wants me to work with him again, Michelle wants to see her son, and you need to be in Auckland for the court cases with Louis. I think we need to go back."

He held me away by my shoulders, staring at me before

pressing me to his chest again on a groan. "But Toby's settled in school. I don't think I want to go back. I'm tired."

"You can take over the rent here." I said, pressing my forehead into his shoulder, his presence, like always, a problem for my celibacy vow.

He pulled my head from his chest with his hands covering my ears.

"Let me think about it." He said as we stared at each other. Eventually Jake was the braver one who leaned down and pressed our lips together, slow and gentle as if unsure of my reaction. Hello, this was Jake Rowland and I still had blood in my veins so I melted into him, relieved, in awe, as always, in love with him.

The kiss deepened, Jake's hands shifted to hold me carefully while mine roamed the wide expanse of his back. I could think of nothing else but Jake, his touch, his taste.

Then suddenly Jax made a noise in his sleep at the same time Toby unlocked the bathroom door and Jake and I leapt apart, both laughing as we turned pretending to be busy with the meal. I pat Jake's butt when he returned to cooking and his next gaze at me was different, less stressed, layered with promises.

After eating Toby and I did the dishes while Jake rocked Jax and watched the news.

After the kids were in bed we were perched on the sofa, nervous, both unsure.

Jake had always been braver than me and soon said, "Should we talk about what's going on between us, Gristle? What we both want out of the rest of our lives?"

"Can we talk tomorrow?" I said, "I'm too tired and I'll just cry."

He stared at me for a long moment before saying, "Alright, tomorrow."

Then he said nothing more and I cursed men and their ability to compartmentalize emotion, wishing I had that skill. By ten I was still obsessing over every single word he had said, terrified I would say too much and my immature heart would be crushed all over again. What if I had a bad night with Jax, how would I explain to Jake all my complicated emotions about him without sounding like a complete idiot.

But Jake being Jake he just went right back to our usual routine patting my shoulder to say goodnight before remembering, "That woman from the secondhand store came by to see you. You might want to stop in and see what she wants."

"Oh, she lets me know if something comes in that I might need."

"You know you can buy new stuff, I know you've got plenty of money from the insurance. Michelle mentions it every chance she gets."

"Is that why you're here." I joked, "The insurance money from a fire that ruined my life." This wasn't a very funny joke so I changed the subject, "It's a waste to buy new baby stuff when the things she has is just as good. It's not like I'm having more kids." Once again my lame joke fell flat on the floor.

Jake glared at me for a long beat before saying, "This might surprise you, but I'm not a money guy." He gazed around the small rental on a smile. "Michelle had to have everything new. When I couldn't afford the ridiculous things she wanted for Toby she got her father to pay. Her father already openly disliked me because I wasn't providing. I'm guessing she told him some line about how I blew money or something, which isn't true. She just never wanted me and her father to get along. She had to have control over him too."

"And he's still paying for her." I said. "You're taste in women is appalling." I hoped to take away some of his stern sadness.

Instead of going to bed like he usually did, he stared at his mobile phone. I figured he had finally lost his mind until he handed it to me, saying, "Read that."

Confused, I looked to the screen, finding a text message from Louis, *Congrats. Like usual she picked you. I'll give you this one but next time I won't be so forgiving*

"When did you get that?" I asked, feeling sick that Louis would make our relationship sound so emotionless.

"Yesterday." Jake said, assessing my reaction.

"Next time? What does that mean?"

As if deciphering a code, Jake said, "In Louis language that means that if we both fall for the same women again he won't give up. He thinks of you as a prize that I won over him. Everything with Louis is a competition."

"Will there be another woman?" I quietly asked, looking down at Jax who was dramatically draped over my arms, I played with his tiny fingers, wondering if Jake would be part of his life. Would Jax be one of those cliché kids screaming that their stepparent wasn't there real parent, even though their real parent was a waste of space?

"Not if you let me in, Sophie." It always scared me when he said my real name.

"I never locked you out, Jake. Remember, you were the one that left me." I raised a hand before we could have this argument again. "I made it clear to Louis that I'm not interested. That if he wants to be part of his son's life he needs to get his shit together, otherwise he has to leave Jax to you."

Jake scratched his chin and nodded, emotional. "Thank you, Gristle." He then smiled down at Jax who resembled a drunk old man. "Come on, it's time to get this baby into bed."

We took turns brushing our teeth then I put the sleepy baby in his cot, crossing my fingers that he would go through the night. It had to happen at some stage, didn't it?

Jake surprised me then by silently entering my room, taking my hand, gently towing me to his bedroom. I let myself be led.

Standing beside his bed I worried about my body. What it would feel like to him?

He gave me no time to obsess over it, undressing me quickly, down to my bra and underwear, he then pulled the covers back and pushed me into his bed. I got comfortable while he left to check the doors. When he returned Jake flicked on a small lamp, letting me watch on in awe as he undressed, down to his boxer shorts. I was anxious, shaking, not sure if I was ready for sex but also knowing I didn't want to be anywhere else. The door remained open while I watched Jake's muscles shift and move, deeply attracted to his body, almost as much as I was attracted to him.

In bed he relaxed on his side, head propped on an elbow as he looked down at me and smiled. Then he wordlessly flicked the light off, pushing me to my side and wrapping me up tight, my back to his front, skin to skin, the heat of the night nothing in comparison to our own warmth.

He whispered, "Thank you for picking me."

"How could I not pick you, Jake. Thank you for being patient while I worked my feelings for Louis out on my own."

"I know you're not ready to be physical, but I want you close. Just for tonight."

I relaxed into him, feeling the hard contours of his body at my back, wanting him but too tired and wrung out to push it.

"Soon, Jake. I'll be ready soon." I assured him.

"It doesn't matter." He husked and I was asleep faster than I had been in months, knowing that if Jax woke Jake was there. I felt safe, no, I felt at home.

CHAPTER THIRTEEN

It was dark when I came awake on a jolt. Sarge was going crazy and Jake disappeared from my back. I wasn't sure what had changed. Sitting up I dragged on my t-shirt that was draped over the end of the bed.

Jake's voice cut through my foggy thoughts, I hadn't slept that deeply for months. "Sophie, someone's trying to get into the house. Get Jax and go to Toby's room. Close the door and don't come out until I tell you to." Jake was in full police mode while Sarge sounded like he was eating his way inside from the backyard, the fence to get around the front far too high for him to jump with those bad hips.

"No, Jake. We're in this together." I argued.

"Then look after the kids." He was moving, pulling on his trackpants and I followed him into the living room, my hand at his back.

I stepped toward my own bedroom, guilty that I had left Jax alone. Lifting him from the cot I scurried to Toby's room. The boy didn't even move, deeply asleep as I slid Jax into one of the clothes drawers, ready and able to help Jake if necessary.

A lock clicked then the backdoor creaked open and I wondered what Jake was waiting for. Suddenly the door slammed and the lights flicked on, Jake had doubled around behind the intruder to trap him inside. Was it my brother or Keisha expecting to find Louis here? Maybe it was one of my idiot uncles, sent on a mission from my idiot jailbird father. Perhaps it was just a run of the mill junkie looking for a PlayStation to pawn at the local bar.

My gaze bugged finding who was standing in the middle of our living room and without a word I stepped from the bedroom, closing the door firmly behind me.

Like a possum caught in headlights stood Toby's receptionist, Darling Roach. She was dressed in only a bra and underwear with suspenders and stockings, she had her phone in one hand and seeing Jake she relaxed, grinning and saying, "I wanted to meet you in bed."

"What the fuck are you doing?" Jake growled, "Get the fuck out of our house. We've got kids here."

"And I was in his bed, Darling." I said, making her jolt in surprise.

"You told me you weren't sleeping with him." She snapped, turning to Jake to hiss, "Pissing dirty cheater. You've been leading us both on."

"This is breaking and entering." I said, "What is wrong with you? Do you want us to let the dog loose then call the cops?"

"You better leave *him* alone." She jabbed a finger toward Jake, "He's mine."

Behind me, Toby called out for his father and Jax began wailing. Checking the clock, I realized it was not even midnight. Instantly furious, irrational, I took two long steps and snatched Darling by the hair, pulling her face to mine to say, "Get the fuck out of my house, and stay the fuck away from Jake, or you and I will have a very big fucking problem. Do you like spiders? I'll leave them wherever you fucking walk and fucking sleep and fucking fuck!"

"Woah, Sophie, calm down." Jake said, hands raised.

"I'm sick of people trying to pull us apart."

With that I grabbed Darling by the upper arm and towed her to the front door that led straight out to the footpath. Flinging it wide I pushed her out.

"There will be a protection order tomorrow," I told her,

and Sarge will be sleeping inside from now on. Come in again and he'll fucking eat you." Then I closed the door.

Jake let Sarge in and he raced through the house, nose to the ground, looking to Jake for direction. Collapsing to the sofa, Jake commanded Sarge to sit by his knee dropping a hand to the big animal's head to let him know all was well. Both man and dog turned to me, Sarge with a big lolling tongue, Jake with a finger over his lips, listening for the boys.

"I think they're asleep." He finally said after a long minute, then he started to giggle. It took me a little longer but soon we were both gasping for breath, trying not to wake the kids while laughing hard at the image of Darling Roach in her underwear.

"How did she get here?" I wondered aloud, "She hadn't been carrying any keys. She either walked here half naked or left her keys in her car."

"In Auckland that car would have been gone in a minute." Jake said.

"That is going to haunt me forever." My amusement was gone.

Eventually, Jake said, "There's nothing we can do tonight. Let's go back to bed."

I collected Jax from Toby's room and Jake knew I was going back to my own bed.

"Auckland might be easier." He said as we stood at our respective doors to say goodnight. "I don't think even Louis is that batshit."

CHAPTER FOURTEEN

After a few hours at work I met Jake at Toby's school during the lunch break. We entered together, still unsure what was going on.

Thankfully Darling wasn't at her post, the principal meeting us instead and ushering us into his room. I felt myself relaxing. He had heard about Darling and had us here to apologize.

Instead he confused me all over again by saying, "I understand you wanted to see me?" He crossed his arms and leaned back in his big chair, not even bothering to introduce himself, already bored. He appeared far too old to still be working full time but then maybe working in schools had worn him down.

"We were told *you* wanted to see *us*." Jake's eyes flicked to me, worried for his son. "Is there a problem with Toby?"

"Toby?" The principal flicked through a pile of paperwork on his desk then clicked into his computer before conceding, "I'm not sure which one is Toby."

Just then Darling entered, smiling and closing the door behind her. "I called the meeting. I was sidetracked by those moaning teachers in the staffroom. Seriously, if you don't like kids, don't become a teacher."

She then perched herself on the edge of the principal's desk, blocking out her boss from Jake's view while blatantly letting her short skirt rise to inappropriate heights. My blood pressure began pounding again and I glanced at Jake, seeing his bunching jaw.

Without a word to her boss, Darling said, "Toby is a difficult child who is causing disruptions in class, the rugby team as well. I suggest that *you*," She pointed at me, "Leave Jake alone and I will guarantee that Toby will be named as the school's top scholar and athlete for his final year in primary. It's proven that top students go onto better careers. Do you really want to ruin his life because you won't leave his father alone?" She said this as if it were a no-brainer, that I was going to ruin Toby.

"Are you fucking kidding me?" Jake growled, standing and saying to the principal. "Your receptionist broke into our home last night dressed in her underwear. I'm an ex police officer and I'm getting a protection order against her. She's stalking me and I want you to do something about it."

The principal gaped from me to Jake with watery eyes. "There's nothing I can do. She seduced me when she started and got photos. She'll go to the Board and I'll lose my job."

"How can you trust her with children?" I asked.

Leaning back in that big expensive chair that was paid for with our tax dollars, he steepled his fingers in a superior way, chuckled and said, "She's not interested in children, just their father's."

"That's it." Jake said, "Get Toby. I'm pulling him out of this school, and I'm writing to the Board to let them know exactly what's going on."

"You can't leave." Darling said with uncertainty.

"You're a fucking nutjob." Jake pointed right at her nose, "Even if I was single, which I'm not, it would not be you." This made my heart flutter with surprise and joy. I guess Jake and I were officially a couple now. Wow. Thanks Darling.

With that he held his hand out to me and I grasped it, following him out. Should I have made a scene to show this woman I was not to be trifled with? I didn't because Jake had said all that needed saying.

Striding to Toby's room, Jake entered while I waited outside. Soon, Toby emerged, and if I didn't know better, I would say he was happy to leave. I put my arm around him and he leaned into me.

"Are you okay?" I asked him.

"What's going on? Am I in trouble?" He asked. "Dad's losing it in there."

"The receptionist just threatened your father and he's not impressed."

Toby made a fake puking gesture, his new favorite thing, and said, "She told me this morning that she was going to be my new stepmother."

Now I was offended. "She's disgusting and a liar. No one's taking my spot without a fight. Come on, you don't go to this school anymore. Your dad is going to talk to the Board but we're not happy for you to stay here. Are you okay with that?"

"Yeah, I don't mind. I don't really like it here, everyone's related."

"Why didn't you tell us you didn't like it?"

He shrugged, embarrassed but determined to tell the truth. Sometimes he was exactly like his father. "I didn't want to be a bother, and besides, I don't like my old school either because school sucks. At least Billy the Kid was here. Can I go say goodbye to him?"

"Maybe another time." I said, holding him close, walking quickly to my car, leaving Jake behind still talking to Toby's teacher who left the class crying.

Darling followed me and I ushered Toby into the car, asking him to clip Jax in before closing the door, ready for battle if I had to.

Darling said, "You think you've won?" She growled, "I don't lose."

"What does that mean?" I asked.

"Do what I want or everyone in the district will know it was you that got the Rodeo shut down. You will be dirt in this town. This is your last chance. Dump Jake, let me have him and I'll ensure you are a beloved part of this community."

She smiled like this made complete sense and there was

no way I could refuse her kind offer. She didn't know the first thing about me or what Jake and I had been through to be together. She didn't know about Jax's father or Toby and his mother.

"I don't think you understand who you're messing with or why we came here, what I was running away from. And you definitely don't know anything about Jake. He's going to spend years in court, trying to explain his part of a massive under-cover police case."

Instead of the distaste I expected, Darling's eyes became dreamy and she sighed. "He's a hero."

I didn't realize Toby had lowered the passenger window until he said, "Just hit her, Sophie. She's dumb."

"You brat." Darling spat. "You'll be shipped back to your mother, I assume you have one, or you can live with *this* one." She flicked a perfectly manicured finger at me. "I spend all day with children, I'm not having them ruining my time with Jake."

"You really are dumb." I said, knowing there was no way of getting through to this woman. She had a fantasy life with Jake all mapped out and it did not include kids. "If you think Jake would leave his kids behind you're dumber than dumb." She wasn't even listening, so I added, "You know what? You do you. I'll talk to Jake about you." I knew threats against Darling were pointless and I was not going to jolt her into reality. She would move onto the next poor sap when the focus of her ardor was not available. Jesus, living in a small town was not as simple as I had hoped.

Her threat about the rodeo was forgotten by the time I got the boys home, and hello, I didn't care if I was blamed for helping animals.

Jake pulled up behind me, perplexed at what had happened.

"I'm not sure if I'm flattered or terrified." He said.

"Then you're as dumb as she is." Toby shocked us both by saying before busying himself with the bald hedgehog's cage.

CHAPTER FIFTEEN

O ver the next few days it was obvious that my life in Grafton was over, that Darling had made good on her threat and told the world that I had singlehandedly ruined the rodeo. Anytime Jake or I left the house we were barraged with car honks or nasty comments. A few people whispered their support but mostly it was gross. I tried to defend myself, claiming the rodeo had been cancelled before I had anything to do with it, that it was Darling trying to steal Jake. Only one woman believed me and she had then burst into tears, saying Darling Roach had ruined her life before she ran off as if being chased by a wild boar.

Jake had thought about taking Toby to another school but it was almost the end of term and so decided Toby could stay home to let things settle down.

The grand finale of our life in Grafton came swiftly less than a week after the confrontation with Darling and I marveled at the stronghold she had.

I went to work for a few hours, however when I got there, Neil and Zoe pulled me into the office and without looking me in the eye fired me, pleading that I went without a fuss since they couldn't afford an employment grievance.

"What does Darling Roach have on you?" I asked Neil but he shook his head. His eyes ran around the room, searching for an exit, his wife suspicious.

Zoe eventually said, "I'm not sure about Darling but I was

threatened for supporting the outsider who was trying to destroy the rodeo and our farms. What did you do, Sophie to upset everyone so much?"

"Darling wants Jake and tried to shoehorn me out, regardless of what Jake thought."

Zoe frowned, "No, it's more serious than that. Everyone hates you, just like that." She clicked her fingers and her husband jumped in fright as if he had been miles away.

Keeping my gaze on Neil, I said, "She gets local men in precarious situations then blackmails them into submission. She hasn't had a chance with Jake yet because she hasn't caught him vulnerable or without me. She broke into the house the other night in lingerie, not even embarrassed, just furious that she failed to sneak into Jake's bed."

Zoe's pretty, round face curled with distaste. "She's always been such a nice person. Does so much for the community." But her eyes returned to her husband who was still not talking. "Anyway, we're sorry, Sophie but this could ruin our farm and you know how close to the breadline we are. If there's any hint of scandal the big company could dump us and move elsewhere."

Raising my hands, Jax strapped to my front, looking around, I said, "I understand. There's plenty of work around town anyway. I'll be fine."

As I walked away, Neil called, "Someone stole more eggs. I had two kea and even a Kaka that had dropped an unexpected one. There was also some pukeko, three blue duck, a tui and a few fantails. Oh, and a hawk and two owls, any of them could have dropped eggs that I hadn't spotted yet. It's giving me anxiety, thinking they all had eggs that have gone even though that's impossible."

I blew out a long breath, not wanting to be involved but knowing I was all the same. "Who knew about the eggs?"

He shrugged, "Just the usual, Department of Conservation, wildlife rescue, SPCA, since a couple came from them. It's part of the deal, we all keep each other informed."

"One of your informants is using the information for their own purposes or telling the person who is." I assured him, adjusting Jax who was getting heavier every day.

"No one would do that to us." Neil assured me in return.

"You'd be amazed what people will do when they want something." I was thinking of Darling and her determination to have Jake. She looked young for her age, well-groomed with expensive clothes and accessories. This reminded me, where was a primary school receptionist getting money enough to dress so well? Could Baron be a woman?

Once again I was so flustered by a man that I didn't read the signs around me.

"Have you ever heard the name Baron?" I asked, watching them closely. These people were not liars.

"There used to be a man in town called Baron." This was Zoe and she was not happy. "I think he ran off with his mistress or something."

So it *was* a man, and he still had links to this community. I would bet that the link was Darling. She knew how to work this town like a vulture at a carcass. She was the only person I had met who was mad enough and egotistical enough to do it.

"Does Darling have a history with the police?"

The couple shrugged, Zoe saying, "Not that I've heard. Look, she's been a good friend over the years. She's done so much for us all, fundraising for whatever is needed."

"Yeah, and that little fox has had a field day in the henhouse. Where does she live?" But the couple were nervous and mumbled something about a new subdivision on the other side of town, right on the border of the national park. I had to ask someone else and thought Dahlia Doyle at the secondhand store might be a good source of information, after all, she claimed people told her everything. She might know how much information Darling had on the men in town too. Perhaps it was time to push that little flightless Darling bird off the perch and see if she could fly.

◆ ◆ ◆

I returned home to find Jake and Toby scrubbing the side of the house. I left Jax sleeping in his car capsule with the door wide open.

"What are you doing? What's that on the house?"

"Graffiti." Jake said.

Toby's eyes danced with delight. "It said you're ruining the town." He chuckled.

Jake added, "With more colorful language."

"Dad thinks it was blood, and he just got fired."

"Me too." I said, hands on hips, staring at Jake who had snapped the hose off to stare at me in return.

"You might be right about going home." He said.

"Does that mean I can go back to my old school in Auckland?" Toby grinned.

"I thought you hated that school." Jake said as a car roared past, tooting its horn, an elderly man giving us the bird which Toby returned and got scolded for.

"I hate school because school sucks but the office lady never tried to rape my dad."

I pressed my lips together and Jake gave me a stern glare but I couldn't help laughing. When I finished, I said, "I'll get on-line and find a rental in Auckland. It's time to go home. I just need to find out who Baron is."

Jake complained, "No one's going to tell you anything, Gristle. Not in this town and not now. You have to let this one go."

I wanted to deny it but he was right, there was nothing I could do. That didn't mean it would stop me from trying.

It took the rest of the day but I managed to find a three-bedroom apartment in Auckland city for a short-term lease. It wasn't ideal and it was closer to Louis than I wanted but it was cheaper than a house and more flexible with the termination date. Jake and I needed a home and we both had money to buy so it was pointless wasting money and energy on a rental. An apartment was the fastest and cheapest solution to our immediate problem. Did this mean Jake and I were in this for the long haul? I was anxious at talking to him about a house together. What if he hated the idea?

It was close to five and Jax was grumpy when I decided to go for a drive to settle him down. The witching hour is real, people.

The apartment we were moving to was fully furnished so I unthinkingly made my way to Dahlia at the secondhand store. I figured it was closed but I was just driving, wondering if she would take back all the stuff she had sold me. It was also a chance to talk to her about Baron and Darling Roach. If Dahlia was right and everyone told her everything there must be gossip about what was really going on with that primary school receptionist and community fundraiser.

My mind was wandering when a van going the other way caught my attention. I glanced over in time to see Harley Punnet. He was driving while talking on his mobile phone. It wasn't that he was breaking the law that I turned around, he was yelling, furious and I was suspicious I knew why. He had more eggs and was trying to move them on. But I would follow him and find out where he lived or who he was taking the eggs too. I would find Baron on my own then call the police.

Harley turned onto Yellow Bypass and I got a suspicion of where he was going. The car yard owned and operated by Darling's paramour, Rick Mussett. I just knew he was a dodgy guy, that he had something to do with this. Scenarios and outcomes flicked through my mind and I pulled across the road to watch as Harley slid into the yard, staying in his van. Ricky came out of the office but just waited, and unable to endure the suspense any longer I pulled in, right up to Harley's bumper, the big van even uglier and dirtier this close.

Leaving the safety of my car, I was grateful that Ricky was watching as I stormed to the side of Harley's van and knocked on the window. The man was frightening up close, tattoos snaking from the side of his bald head down his neck and into the torn black t-shirt. His gaze when it cut to me was unsettling and he held a finger up to make me wait while he finished his phone call. I wanted to be annoyed but he was too scary so I just stood there and Ricky was soon at my side.

"Did Harley not drop something to you?"

"I want to see what he's delivering." Was all I said, Ricky's anxiety feeding into my own. He was guilty and wanted me gone so I wouldn't find him taking delivery of the eggs. "I'm not going anywhere until I see them."

Harley flung his door wide then and clambered from the van, yelling, "Fuck you!" I think it was the first time I had ever heard him speak.

"Everything okay?" Ricky asked and the older man nodded, eyes flicking to me.

"Just the ex-wife. She wants more money. Always more and more. What do you want?" He glared at me and I wilted a little.

"She wants to see what you're giving to me. I think I've got a good idea."

"Me too." I growled but needed to see it with my own eyes.

Harley and Ricky were staring as if I were insane but I was onto them and we knew it.

"Move the car or I can't get in the back."

So I backed my car up, moving fast as Harley swung his big double doors wide and leaned into the van. I scurried back just as he turned with a huge bouquet of flowers.

Ricky sagged and growled, "I told you not to bring that shit here anymore."

Harley placed them on the ground when Ricky refused to take them. "I'm just paid to drop them off. Sort the rest of your own shit out yourself."

Turning to me, Ricky said, "You take them. My wife will rip my balls out."

I wasn't completely convinced, Harley could have pulled the flowers out to put me off his real delivery, so I plucked the card from the front of the flowers, deciding they were an expensive purchase. The card was drivel from Darling Roach about how she would take him back, how she would do anything for him, how she loved him.

"She told me she had given up on you," I couldn't take my eyes off the handwriting, it was annoyingly perfect. "That's why she had moved on to Jake."

"She always says she's given up then this shit turns up." Ricky shook the bouquet that Harley had picked off the ground to thrust into his arms. "You take them, Harley. Send them to your ex-wife, might soften her up."

"Are you kidding me? She would complain about me wasting money." He gave the flowers a glare, "And there is no way I want that crazy Roach bitch after me for not delivering them."

Staring between the men I decided just to say it. "What have you two got to do with bird smuggling?"

"Are you on drugs?" Harley said after a long and confused pause.

"Come on, I bet you know where to get them too." I countered.

Harley's eyelids drooped further. "You one of them that judge a man by his looks?"

"No, but ..."

"You think because I've got a goatee and I wear black shirts and jeans that I'm a bad person?" He didn't give me a chance to answer, on a rant now, "I've been dealing with this shit my whole adult life. Alright, I went to prison but that was a long time ago and I just want to work and be left in peace. That includes from my ex-wife."

I rubbed my eyes, tired and unsure what else I could do.

"Someone in town or someone who regularly visits is smuggling native bird eggs out of the country."

"I heard Neil and Zoe been having problems." Harley shrugged, at a loss.

"Are you saying you don't know anything about smuggling?"

"I only go out to the Hill farm when Zoe needs something taken back to the courier center. That's it. I don't know nothing about smuggling, I don't have the first idea how people would smuggle but I'm guessing you need a passport to get them to the other end, and I haven't had a passport ever in my life. Have never once left New Zealand."

I turned to Ricky, about to question him but he wasn't interested in the conversation, peering at the flowers, pale and anxious. A man worried about being caught out as an international smuggler would not be more concerned with flowers from a stalker.

Sagging, I said, "I'm sorry. I just don't have any leads and it's driving me crazy. I want to find this Baron and shut him down but I can't even find a link."

The two men nodded, Harley saying, "It's alright. I know I look rough but it keeps people away from me and that's all I want for the rest of my life."

I wondered at Harley's life story but he was already slamming the doors on his van, mentally moving on to his next delivery.

Stumbling back to my car I called out another apology but Harley was already behind the wheel, impatiently waiting for me to back out so he could get going, while Ricky was walking toward a dumpster, surreptitiously glancing around at who might see him discard the unwanted flowers.

As I resumed my trip I wondered at small towns. Were they more dramatic than the city or were the dramas magnified with less people? Either way, it was clear if we stayed in Grafton, Darling Roach was going to cause more problems than Jake and I could endure. We had a shaky start to begin with and were not mature enough to deal with a cataclysmic psychopath. Jake's ex Michelle already had that role.

CHAPTER SIXTEEN

As expected the store was closed when I pulled up but seeing Dahlia's van gave me hope that she was still inside. I could imagine her doing paperwork when the store was quiet and peaceful.

I unclipped Jax's carseat and knocked on the big glass doors. When no one answered I wandered around to the back, surprised to find it unlocked. It ran through my mind that something might have happened to Dahlia, perhaps she had fallen out of her chair and needed help. With pounding heart and worry for a friend I entered the brightly lit storage area behind the shop.

Expecting blood and doom, it was a shock to find Dahlia standing unassisted, strapping a thick stocking belt of bulging egg pouches around her waist. I was disoriented by her wheelchair that was parked by a door meaning she had walked across the room.

We were both frozen, Dahlia's eyes big with surprise while my gaze was trapped by the eggs, snug and warm in the thick stocking.

My anger quickly caught up with reality. "Going on holiday?" I growled.

Dahlia smiled, it was smug (I still hate smug) mixed with a little annoyance. "A cruise." She sung, resuming her careful belt placement. "I won't tell you where because I can't have you ruining my plans."

"Do you work for Baron?"

She laughed, "He wishes." Then she carried on as if I wasn't even there.

"Put the eggs down." I said, pulling my phone out and waggling it at her. She rolled her eyes like I was an annoyance she didn't need right now. The handle to Jax's little car seat was looped over my left forearm, the plastic digging into my skin so I placed him carefully at my feet, worried this could get physical. I wanted to message Jake but couldn't take my eyes off Dahlia for a second, expecting her to make a run for it through the store to freedom.

Seeing I wasn't about to leave, Dahlia sighed, "Look, princess, you've already made enough enemies in town by getting the rodeo shut down. No one here will help you, believe me, I know them all."

"To clarify, I didn't get the rodeo shut down, and you are going to jail."

"I know all the cops. I've known them all for years. If I tell them you're lying, who are they going to believe? Me or some uppity bitch from Auckland?"

"You're right." I said, quickly snapping a few photos of her.

Instead of demanding my phone like I expected she slid a shirt over the belt and said, "Look, I'm a businesswoman, you're a single mother. Have I ever judged you for being a tramp? And this is the way you thank me." I said nothing so she grumbled, "You must appreciate how us single girls have to survive."

"Not by destroying ecosystems and animals."

"It's not animals, just some dumb birds and lizards. What do they care?"

"They are natives to this country and some of them are critically endangered."

She groaned like I was pathetic then yanked a spongy vest over her thin shirt, finishing with a baggy blouse over the top. She was not as big as she appeared, most of it a suit that could hide all sorts of horrors.

"I don't know why you tree huggers are so dumb." She grumbled, eyes flicking to Jax before she returned to her desk, throwing things into her handbag. "If creatures are endangered, just make more. You should be thanking me for helping."

"It's about protecting their ecosystems for our future generations."

She turned to me on a triumphant smile, "Why would I care about future generations? I don't have any. All I've got is this lifetime and I've made sure it's exciting, interesting and I'm rich, honey, rich!"

At her yell Jax started crying and she boomed with laughter then tossed her handbag onto her wheelchair and raced with it toward the store front. I ran too, figuring Jax was safe by the closed backdoor, safer than if it got physical with Dahlia.

At the glass front door she spun and pushed her wheelchair right at me. It hit me in the knees and I fell awkwardly. Dahlia darted to my left up a narrow aisle of beds and dresser drawers. She must have put the brake on the chair since I couldn't budge it.

It wasn't until the door to the storeroom behind me slammed that I realized my error. She had doubled around to another door and was now in the room with my baby. Running on instant fear I ran, stunned the door wasn't locked and I burst through to find Dahlia panting and holding Jax in his car seat in the crook of her meaty arm.

"You're not going to stop me." She said, still smiling like a deranged grandmother. "I have a timetable to keep and some interloper from *Auckland* isn't going to ruin that."

"Why did you say Auckland like it was another country, a bad one that you hated."

She was confused, "Because everyone hates Aucklanders."

"Why?" I didn't even know what I was saying, just talking, trying to keep her attention off my baby.

"I don't care why. We just do. You don't live here so you're all assholes."

"But when we move here we're still assholes." I was babbling, my focus only on Jax who was howling in outrage now. I was scared the noise would annoy Dahlia so much she would drop him and I didn't want to test the efficacy of my car seat choice.

"I'm walking away, Sophie. Let me get into my van and I'll put your little baby down." She glanced down at him, "Jesus he's noisy."

"Okay." I said instantly.

We then did a weird walk where she backed toward the door and I followed, my blood pounding, the yearning to get my baby back leaving me shaky and sick to my stomach. I meant it, I would do anything to get him back. She could get in her van and leave so long as she left Jax unharmed. When we were back at the wheelchair she unlocked the door to the store, put Jax into the chair and pulled it outside.

I glanced around, hopeful a local would see what was happening, that they would notice the kindly, disabled second-hand store dealer was suddenly walking and they would intervene, or just take her attention off me for long enough that I could grab my son. But the streets were empty, everyone had gone home to kids and evening meal preparation. It was like a ghost town.

Opening her van, Dahlia pushed a button and lifted her chair, Jax and all inside. She was much stronger and fitter than she appeared. As I stepped forward she snatched the handle on his car seat again and held it before her like a shield. Sidestepping around the driver's door, she took two small paces toward me then placed Jax carefully on the ground.

"He's all yours. See you around."

I raced for Jax, snatching up the car seat as the van roared to life and Dahlia tore out of town, no doubt heading for the tiny district airport in Charlton which could link to Christchurch or Auckland airports for an international connection, unless her cruise was to the islands or Australia. All these thoughts ran through my head as I stood in the middle of the road with Jax, both of us crying hard.

◆ ◆ ◆

Thankfully Jake and Toby were together so I wasn't worried about Toby being alone with this crazy woman around. I drove straight to the police station, a two storied squat building on a roundabout. It was soon obvious that no one was going to help me in time. Dahlia would be out of the country with a pile of native eggs before anything was done. Even the police had a stake in the rodeo and I was ruining their fun too.

Instead of causing a scene, I called Mike in Auckland, not sure who else could help. He was the only working police officer I knew, I could only hope he thought my problems were worth police time.

He answered on the third ring, "Sophie Carter." He sung, "Long time no hear. If this is about me and Michelle, forget it. I don't care if Jake's angry . . ."

There wasn't time for this, I could almost sense Dahlia's delight at getting away. The story came out in a long breath that left me winded by the time I was done. Thankfully Mike didn't interrupt. "This has nothing to do with Michelle, and Jake's not angry. You two are free and clear. Good luck to you both. This is about Baron, a native bird smuggler that I've been looking for while I've been down south. I thought Baron was a man then I thought it was Toby's receptionist, a woman who is stalking Jake and breaking into the house almost naked. That's another problem. I was almost certain it was a man called Harley but that was just me being judgmental. Anyway, turns out Baron is a woman called Dahlia Doyle. She snatched Jax. I got him back but she got away and now she's heading somewhere, probably Christchurch airport to meet up for a cruise to smuggle a pile of eggs out of the country. Those eggs are vital to repopulating the native stocks down here, Mike." I knew I was talking too fast but there wasn't time for his usual bullshit. "She is in a wheelchair and she looks overweight but it's a body suit. The eggs are under the suit in a special harness made of thick stockings. It keeps the eggs warm near the body and safe if she isn't thrown around. Whoever finds her will have to be careful. I'm texting you a photo of her right now."

After a stunned pause, Mike said, "You vets are a pain in my fucking ass."

"You don't know any other vets."

"You're right. *You* are a pain in my fucking ass."

"But you'll help."

"Naturally. Give me a minute."

I heard him tapping away then I was put on hold for what felt like a long time. Jax was wide eyed as if sensing my agitation which reminded me to contact Keisha, to ensure she was getting her life together. Savvy was Jax's half-sister and if Keisha found mothering too much I would take her baby, even if the thought of two babies boggled my mind. How the heck did anyone cope with twins or more?

Eventually he came back on the line. "Sophie, this is going to take some time. I've got the photo but give me her name again, the full spelling."

Diligently he noted it all down and said he would call me back as soon as he could. Before he disconnected he added, "Relax, Sophie. We've got this one."

"I've heard that before." I grumbled.

"I mean it this time. Let us sort this. Michelle told me you just had a baby. This is not the time for vigilante adventures."

"Will you let me know if you get her."

"You don't think we will?" He was amused.

"You don't even know where she is."

"Trust me." He chuckled, smug prick.

"Can you talk to your brother for us?"

The change of topic made my head spin. "My brother? About what?"

"There's word around that this big Australian is here to wipe Louis out." Mike was trying to sound cool but I didn't think he felt cool at all.

"How do you know that it's Tyler?"

"Because it's a big Australian called Tyler and I know you have a big Australian brother with that name. I have had reason to investigate your history a time or two. How the scum, no offence, got into the country is irritating but he's after Louis and if he wipes him out a big shit-pile of shitheads will get off their charges." The only thing that makes the past few years with Jake and Louis feel bearable is the hope that all our sacrifice would get criminals off the street." This was off since Mike hadn't even known that Louis was undercover. He had been furious at being the only one left out.

"Jesus, I'll talk to my sister, see what I can do."

"You rub my back and I'll rub yours."

The way he said that curled my stomach. "Did you just hit on me, Mike?" My voice was stone cold.

Mike spluttered, "Don't be crazy."

"Then don't talk to me like that again."

He laughed but it was uncertain. "You're just wishful thinking."

Biting my tongue, noting he didn't ask after Toby or Jake, I said goodbye and drove home to find Jake busy with Sarge in the back yard. They were working through his obedience. Jake was methodical and consistent. When Sarge was in working mode he was stern and professional, just like Jake and I loved watching them together. The dog trusted Jake and I knew this was why Sarge had been so badly injured when things went wrong.

Seeing my unease, even as I tried to hide it, Jake took me inside and I ran through what had happened at the secondhand store and afterward at the police station. Jake was furious and was soon on the phone, talking with the local police, yelling enough that Toby came inside to ask what was going on.

I wrapped an arm around his shoulders, grateful when he held me back. I needed the human contact. "I found the person who has been stealing all the native bird eggs."

Toby was round eyed with interest, "I knew you would. Is he arrested?"

"It's a her, and they are trying to find her now."

"Wow. That is so cool." Then his attention shifted to Jax and he lifted him from the car seat and into the bouncer. It surprised me that Jax was now strong enough to look around, his interest in the world growing daily. Toby was great with the baby and as my gaze flicked back to Jake, again dressed in his fat pants and a black t-shirt, I found him mouthwatering and wondered if we could manage more kids together. It was nice to feel part of a real family, I understood Jenny's need for more kids, although why she was now screwing it up so cataclysmically made no sense at all. Damn that hot mailman.

Jake got off the phone, his humor instantly returning. "That got the lazy bastards moving. They'll head over to the store now. If not I said I'd bring in the police from Auckland, that motivated them."

"Everyone hates Auckland." I said, "Have you noticed that?"

Jake shrugged, "Smaller places always hate the bigger places. It's nothing new." He hugged me then, "Are you sure you're okay?"

"Yeah, I just want to hear that she's caught and those eggs are returned."

He rubbed my head as I buried my face in his neck. "I know, but there's nothing we can do for now. Why don't you go have a bath while I sort these handsome guys out?"

Toby was making Jax laugh at something weird and Sarge was standing guard at the backdoor, surveying the road like a bouncer expecting trouble.

"A bath." I said like it was a mystical place but Jake wasn't listening, he had hunkered down beside Toby and they were talking to Jax like he was about twenty.

CHAPTER SEVENTEEN

J ake's phone shrilled a couple of times while I was in the bath and unable to stand the suspense I was ready to get out when Jake entered.

The water was up to my neck in the old tub but there were no bubbles and I tried to cover myself. My body had changed since Jake had last seen it. Instead of perving at me he dropped the toilet lid and sat down, propping elbows on his knees and rubbing his eyes.

"Jax is asleep," He said, "He won't be long. Toby's talking to his mother. I came in here to give him some privacy."

"You're a good dad, Jake." He shrugged and covered his eyes.

Sitting up, I wrapped my arms around my knees. "Mike hit on me when I talked to him on the phone."

Jake wasn't surprised and didn't ask what he had said. "It's what he does."

"I don't want any secrets between us. He said something saucy and I told him to shut his mouth."

"Mike might complain about how no one can see past his looks but if he doesn't get the attention he believes his looks deserve he doesn't like that either."

"Why is he obsessed with who you are with?"

Jake chuckled, tired and humorless, "It's not just me. I was the only one with a wife. A dumb wife who was flattered by Mike's pretty face."

"So he cheats on her."

"I imagine so. Didn't you see how stressed she was when she was here? I bet she thought you were here with Mike."

"What about you and Toby?"

"We're just an afterthought. Mike is currently putting up the biggest challenge so that is who she will focus on."

"You know I'm not like that. I won't ever be interested in Mike."

"I do know that." He paused, pressing his lips together as his eyes skimmed my naked back, making my skin tingle. "Gristle, I hope you're getting closer to being ready." His voice was deeper.

I knew exactly what he meant and it was flattering. "Are you getting desperate?" I asked on a smile.

"Yeah." He sighed, then looked away.

"I'm worried I won't feel the same for you. I don't feel the same to me."

"Honey, it's not what's between your legs that ruins me, it's what's between your ears."

His words made my breath catch since Jake didn't say things like that. I tried to fob it off with humor. "I wouldn't blame you for any horror or disinterest, it's probably a mess. I'm pretending it doesn't exist although the nurse assures me it's all still in working order. She even suggested I give it a workout."

Jake peered at the ceiling on a smile while I studied his thick neck. He said, "Let me know as soon as you're ready. I can give you critical feedback."

"Okay." I said and Jake took a long breath before saying, "Looks good to me."

"That's because you've been stuck here for too long. Maybe when you get back to the city you'll find plenty of women that aren't ruined."

"Gristle, that you think I'm young enough, or have enough energy to bother is nice, but get your shit together." This was more like it.

"Sorry. Old habits." Being brave, I stood from the bath

and Jake handed me a towel.

"Don't get out because of me. I'm enjoying the view."

"My ego's still a little battered." I reminded him.

"I don't know why, Gristle. You look good to me."

"You are crazy fit right now, Jake and I'm not."

"You had a baby a few months ago, Soph. Give yourself a break."

I wrapped the towel around myself as Jake stood and I hugged him hard.

"Sometimes you say the best things. Thank you."

"For what?"

"For coming, and for looking after me and Jax. For being a good dad and letting me share Toby. For cooking and calling the cops when someone other than me needs to yell at people. It's exhausting being alone."

"I've been alone for a long time too." He rubbed our noses together and I wanted to kiss him but didn't.

"Are we living together in Auckland?"

His gaze hardened. "Do you want to live separately?'

"No. But it doesn't seem right. You turn up at my door, faint like a princess and then move in. Life is more complicated than that. *Our* lives are more complicated than that."

"Thanks for reminding me about that faint. I was tired from a long trip." He kissed my cheek, moving his lips down my neck, giving me undeniable proof that there was life below my waist.

"You thought you had another kid. Is the fear of having more kids that scary?"

"Not at all. I just want a better experience than what Toby and I endured."

"Jax is having a wonderful time." I rubbed my jaw against his bristles, digging my fingertips into the hard muscles of his back.

"That's true." He husked, hands straying to my butt. I pressed my lips to his shoulder and Jake added, "I don't want to give him up. I never imagined I would raise Louis fucking Martinez's son but I can't see my life without him. And Toby's in love with you both."

"What if things change when we get back?"

"Honey, we are the most boring people."

"But everyone around us is crazy."

"That's true, especially Finn. Please tell me you aren't going back into business with him?"

"Not sure yet." But I grinned. Finn *was* nuts, but he was family nuts. "My sister's in love with the mailman," I mumbled as Jake pressed closer, "I need to fix that too."

Jake went rigid, giving me one of his patented glares, "No, Gristle, you don't have to fix that. Stay out of your sister's marriage."

He kissed me, slow and easy. Then Toby burst into the room, backing out when he found us in his way, telling us we were disgusting then pretending to puke.

Jake ushered him out, laughing at the dramatics.

After dressing, my mind returned to reality and I asked Jake, "Should something have happened with Dahlia by now? Should the police have caught her at the airport? What if she got away with all those eggs? She'll have to come home at some stage." I collected my phone, "I'll let Neil and Zoe know who's been taking the eggs. Do you think they secretly had something to do with it? I know they're pretty desperate for money."

There was a message on my phone from Mike. It said, *DELETE THIS MESSAGE*. Then there were three photos. One was Dahlia standing from her wheelchair while two uniformed police officers stood beside her. Another showed her running for it, the officers chasing her. The third showed her being handcuffed, a female officer lifting the fat suit to expose the eggs beneath.

The photos had been taken surreptitiously, were on a weird angle as if snapped by someone's side.

I showed them to Jake who laughed, wrapped an arm around me and kissed my temple. "You did it again, Gristle. Congratulations. We need to celebrate."

Toby was at our side, "Did you get her?" He was jumpy

with excitement.

"Yep. No more birds will be smuggled out of here for a while."

Wordlessly, Toby hugged me. I held him back, thanking him for being so understanding. He just shrugged and went outside with Sarge, a tennis ball in his hand that would never make it back alive.

Jake said, "You keep charming my kid like that I might have to marry you." He had Jax propped up in the crook of his elbow, the baby looking around with interest. They were so adorable together a lump caught in my throat that I swallowed down.

"Ditto." I said just as Mike called.

"Did you delete those photos?" He barked but I could hear the excitement in his voice. Was it the thrill of the chase for Mike or did he enjoy following the law? I had known Mike for a couple of years now and still didn't understand what motivated him. He was a good cop but no one took him into their confidence when Louis went undercover. That must have really stung.

"How did you get them?" I asked, thinking about Dahlia with those eggs strapped to her white skin.

He chuckled, slow. "I know the arresting officer."

"Let me guess. A woman?"

That easy humor disappeared. "What's that got to do with it?"

"Nothing, Mike. Thank you for believing me." I meant it, he could have easily fobbed me off and Dahlia would have been out of the country by the time I got any action from the local cops, they had made it clear they hated me.

"Don't thank me yet." He said, returning to his big boy, serious voice, "You'll have to give a statement first thing tomorrow at the local station. They know you're coming in."

"I'm getting good at those statements." I sighed.

"And maybe lay low for a while. She'll get out on bond since it's only animal related. Looks like you've picked up another enemy."

"Yeah, I know all that too." It would be nice to think Dahlia would be locked up for years but she would be back home in the next day or so with a fine and a note on her police record. "What about the eggs?" I asked, hopeful that some good would come from this. "What happened to them? When can I collect them and bring them back?"

"You'll have to talk to the zoo. They already picked them up."

"New *assets*." I hissed, "We'll never see those eggs again."

"They won't be leaving the country." Mike couldn't see the problem.

"They won't be restocking the places they're needed, the places they belong." I had accomplished nothing. The eggs were still gone.

He was silent for a moment while I seethed and wondered if I should go to the media. Perhaps the zoo would happily return those eggs.

Into my anger, Mike said, "Another thing, what you thought I said, don't say anything to Jake."

I groaned loudly, "Don't make me complicit in your games, Mike. Jake's sitting right beside me and I already told him. Your crazy behavior has nothing to do with Jake and nothing to do with me. You ever try anything like that again and I'll tell Michelle, let her deal with you. Jake and Sarge will bury your dismembered remains."

I disconnected before he could say anything more. Like I had just sorted out something annoying, I nodded at Jake who was staring at me hard before sidling close, turning me to face him with a finger under my chin.

Unfortunately Toby reentered the room and yelled, "Gross! Don't you two ever stop." But he was smiling and I said, "That's not fair."

It wasn't fair. I still hadn't gotten far with Jake. But the way we were circling each other showed I might not have long to wait. He had made it clear the first move was on me and each day that passed made the inevitability less terrifying. Next time I saw the doctor I might even discuss birth control. Just to be on the safe side.

CHAPTER EIGHTEEN

Dahlia was back in town within two days. I saw her ugly big van outside the store. By then Jake and I had sold most of the furniture to another secondhand store and had packed what we wanted into our two cars. Jake and I had not had a moment alone together since Toby was unsettled at moving again and was sneaking into Jake's bed every night.

The landlord was delighted we were going, saying she was about to terminate the tenancy agreement anyway since I had ruined the rodeo, destroyed Neil and Zoe's farm, and she hated Aucklanders.

The morning we left Grafton was raining, we had slept in a local motel since the house was now empty and clean. We left Sarge at the house for the few hours we slept and collected him the next morning, grateful there was no more graffiti. I didn't want to start the day with more cleaning. As I drove out of town I looked in my rearview mirror, remembering coming here, scared, pregnant and alone. I felt stronger for the experience, knew I could depend on myself, but I didn't want to live that life again. A future with Jake was unsettling but I had to try, I couldn't let fear drive me. Besides, Jake gave me no choice, he had turned up, fainted and refused to leave. He understood my fears, no doubt had a pile of his own, but if he was going to be brave and trust me, if he would understand my weird relationship with Louis and believe that I would never go back there, then I would do the same with him and his ex-wife Michelle.

Hopefully, eventually, I would remember Grafton fondly, not the end bit, but my son was born here and I had learned a lot about pest control in the wild. There were successes too, the rodeo was not going ahead and although I was getting blamed for shutting it down, I would happily live with that. I had also uncovered a smuggling ring and people would watch Dahlia closely now. That had to be enough.

My life was back in Auckland.

Remembering that final confrontation with Dahlia gave me shivers up my spine. She had snatched my son to escape. I tried not to think about it since it made me cry. I would have nightmares about Dahlia holding Jax for years to come.

Darling Roach was another burden I didn't have to deal with. She gave me the creeps and I wondered who her next target would be with Jake gone. She didn't take rejection easily and I wondered how Rick Mussett had endured her for so long.

Driving behind Jake, we stopped every few hours to feed Jax or Toby who swapped from car to car.

Toby was beside himself with excitement on the ferry but within an hour, when we were out in the straight, he found his iPad and became immersed in a movie, headphones covering his ears. We were at a small booth, Jake holding a coffee since the boat was swaying. The boys were on the window side, Jake and I facing each other. Jax was in his car seat or bouncing on our laps, snoozing and waking, Jake and I taking turns to hold him.

We had debated putting Sarge into the onboard kennel but Jake went and checked it out, concluding that the big dog would be better left in his car. We had taken him for a decent walk before boarding so he would snooze for most of the three-hour trip. I knew Jake would still go and sit with his dog if he could sneak down. I also knew Sarge would enjoy the peace.

My sister called and I smiled, excited to let her know I was on my way home. It had been such a frantic time that I had yet to tell her.

Before I could speak, Jenny said, "I've left Finn."

"No you haven't." I assured her, "Look, I'm on my way

home, for good."

"This isn't about you, Sophie. I know what I'm doing."

"What about Finn?"

"He's not talking to me. He doesn't understand what I'm going through."

"What *are* you going through?" I growled, crossing my eyes at Jake who sipped his coffee, holding Jax on his lap, looking delicious. When Jenny said nothing, I sighed, "Have you told Finn about the mailman?"

"No, it's none of his business. If he wasn't so moody I wouldn't have looked at another man. He's got no one to blame but himself. It was his decision not to work with you and he's been an asshole ever since."

"You agreed to that, Jenny." She wasn't snaking her way out of any blame.

"He didn't have to listen to me. It's his career, not mine. I don't have a career. I don't have anything."

"Do you think you're postnatal?" This was a serious question, Jenny was far from her usual calm, logical self.

"Don't be stupid. I'm alive for the first time in years. I thought I was creating this lovely family but I was just doing what Mum did, attaching myself to a man and expecting him to make me feel whole. I don't need Finn to be whole."

"You need the mailman?" I said flatly. "You need another man to make you feel whole? Look, leave Finn if you really believe you have too, what do I care? But don't say you don't need a man then jump straight into a relationship with another one. Be alone for a while, learn what you really need on your own, and look after your kids first. Then you would be doing something different from our mother."

There was a long silence then my sister hung up.

I looked at Jake who was cringing as I said, "I don't care what she says, I'm taking her to the doctor when I get home. She's losing her mind again."

"Leave me out of it." His coffee was done and he pushed the empty cup across the table for me to toss in the bin. He lifted

Jax who was awake and taking in his surroundings, grinning as Jake made a face at him.

It was impossible to imagine Jake as a helpless baby or a clingy toddler. I could imagine him as a surly teenager. He knew most of my dysfunctional upbringing but I knew little about his past.

These were things I suddenly wanted to know. "I meant to ask, you said you were adopted, did you have any siblings?"

"Nope. Only child to older parents who both died, my mother the last one about six years ago. They were lovely people and I miss them."

My heart went out to him for his raw honesty. "Did you ever find your real parents?"

"My birth mother contacted me a few years ago. I met her and found her lifestyle distasteful. She had a pile of kids to a pile of men and no one was happy with my existence so I decided to leave that relationship in the past. I don't need a mother, I had a great one."

What adopted kid didn't want to believe they had come from decent parents who had made a mistake? Discovering they were weak could be traumatic. Jake Rowland was the only person who had been stable since the mess in the pits. To imagine he had been saved from an awful life by a lovely couple who couldn't have kids of their own was strange. It made Jake feel different. What man would he be now if he had been left in an unstable environment. Would he have become like Louis? Lost, alone and full of rage at the world?

"Was she a criminal?" I asked.

"Worse, a swinger. Had been since she was in her early twenties. She had no idea who my father was because it could have been half her shitty little town."

Pressing my lips together, I stared at Jake. His head tilted to the side, "You can laugh if you want but you better not ever tell anyone."

I held up three fingers, "Scout's honor. This will be one of our kinky and embarrassing secrets."

He glanced at Toby, ensuring his headphones were firmly in place and he wasn't listening. He leaned over the table to take one of my hands, the other holding Jax to his chest. "We are going to make lots of our own kinky and embarrassing secrets that will be kept just between us."

I giggled then, "You're good pedigree, sexually."

"Yeah, the best." He said on an annoyed eyeroll.

Squeezing his hand I was lost in those eyes, the clean scent of him drifting toward me, my gaze sliding down the neck of his shirt.

"I'm sick of denying what I want, Jake."

"Explain what you want, Gristle." He said, that handsome head tilting again, just like Sarge when he was trying to hear something. It made my stomach jump with excitement and gave me confidence. Jake was my kind of man and I wanted him to be all mine.

"I pick you, Jake. I always picked you. Going off with Louis, part of me was relieved to run away. I'm terrified of you, that I'm copying Jenny, repeating my mother's mistakes by depending on a man. I'm scared you're still using me, that you'll get what you want and dump me again. But I'm equally certain that has nothing to do with you, that I'm projecting my insecurities. I know enough to know you wouldn't include Toby unless you were in this for real. I want this to be for real. I'm sorry for everything with Louis."

He lifted my knuckles to his lips. "There is no professional connection anymore between me and Louis. He was part of my job, a part that got me out of a whole heap of trouble and I promised him right at the beginning that I would have his back till the end. I kept my part of the deal. I almost lost you to keep my word. I won't hurt you again, Sophie." He glanced at Toby again, whispering, "Well, not in a way you won't like. I adore our fucked up little family. I want this. I want these boys and I want you. Marry me."

I stared at him, my eyes bigger than bug eyed Captain Pugwash's when his dark overlord Pothead sauntered into a room.

He smiled and it blew away all my concerns. "Too much too soon?"

I shook my head, unable to unlock my frozen jaw.

He continued, "We'll find a home first. Something big enough for all the animals you'll undoubtably bring home, and for a garden wedding. I like living with you and Jax, Sophie, and I want to make it official."

Thankfully Toby glanced between us then and pulled his headphones away, saying, "Are you two fighting?" It made me sad that every time Jake and I looked serious he thought we were arguing. His past was still holding tight and only time would change that.

His father smiled and said, "No, I'm trying to convince Sophie to marry us."

"Gross." Toby said and returned to his movie but I could see the smile on his lips. Jax took that moment to giggle, it was beautiful and simple and Jake laughed along with him as I fumbled with my phone to capture the image unable to process what Jake had just asked.

CHAPTER NINETEEN

A few days later we were settled in our Auckland apartment. It was nothing like Louis' and was far back from the waterfront but it was clean and comfortable while we looked for a house to buy, bank and lawyer visit's breaking up the day. No lawyer thought it was a good idea to blend our finances but since Jake and I had about the same amount of money, and it was no one else's business we carried on with our own plans.

My sister called a few times, pretending nothing was wrong until I asked her pointblank, "Are you still leaving Finn?"

"Yes, I'm in the spare room." She wouldn't say anything else and I was terrified she had already started something with the mailman.

I called Finn. "Jenny says she's left you."

He was distracted. "She's just hormonal. Look, I'm standing on Parnell Rise with our old landlord. He's rebuilding, it's almost complete and he's willing to have it used as a clinic again, a new and more purpose built one if we want it. What do you think?"

"We got his old building burned down." Was all I could think to say, not ready to discuss my work options with anyone yet.

"He's a businessman. It was fully insured and it saved him spending money on the old place. If I didn't know it was that sexy Michelle that set it on fire I would think it was him or his mistress." He laughed, loud and carefree and I got a better idea of how disengaged he was from his wife.

"Finn, I told you, I'm not sure."

"Rubbish, you know you miss it."

He was right, I did miss our old clinic but that isn't what I was calling about. "Can you sort out your wife before you get obsessed with a new job. You haven't even finished working at the other place."

"Yeah, I did. Remember Olive Fletcher from university?"

"How could I forget. She hated us."

"She hated everyone and was an amazing bully, so I got in contact with her, asked her where she was working, said I could probably get her into my clinic if she had some capital to invest."

"You didn't. Finn, that's so cruel."

"Those fuckers deserve it." Remember how I said that Finn rarely swore. His anger stilled my tongue. "She started last week."

"How's it going?"

"Great. They are all terrified of her and she hates them. They wouldn't dare peer over her shoulder like she doesn't know what she's doing. Olive would eat their spleens."

"I did a one-day handover, that was all I could endure. She's paid me out and now I'm in the clear. I only ended up losing a few thousand dollars. It's worth every cent. Oh, and Keisha started too."

"Oh sweet Jesus."

"Yeah, she was late to work one day and when they threatened to fire her she threatened them right back. God, I wish I had seen it. Anyway, I'm out, the money cleared on Friday. I got shitfaced and didn't go home." He was proud of this but it indicated the deep trench between him and my sister.

"No wonder Jenny wants to leave you."

This time it got through to him. "She wants to leave me. Why?"

"Because you're an idiot. Look, you need to talk to your

wife. Tell her that you've been an asshole but life will get back to normal now."

"When are you moving back?"

"I'm here now. Did Jenny not tell you? I'm looking for a home to buy."

"Then I'm going to sign the lease. Come see me tomorrow and I'll have paperwork for the lawyers."

"I'm thinking about it, Finn. Talk to your wife first and sort out your home issues. If your wife really is dumping you it's not wise for me to go into business with you again. And I can't forget what you did to me last time."

"I've apologized." He grumbled.

"No you didn't." I assured him.

"Do you want me to beg?"

"Yes please." I said and I want it in writing that you won't behave like an asshole when I'm at work."

"I'm never an asshole."

"What about when I got into trouble trying to help animals. Remember that stoat?"

"You tried to take it off the crazy owner."

"It looked like a wild one." Our voices were both scaling up octaves and there was something soothing in it so I disconnected, looking at Jake who drawled, "Sounds like you're going back to work."

"I'll have to look into childcare." My breath caught at the thought of leaving Jax with a stranger. "Maybe Jenny could take him for a few hours."

"I can do most of it. I'm going to be security consulting, mostly from home."

"You never mentioned work." I said, or had he? We had been busy since returning, shifting and settling in. We had been taking long walks with Toby, Sarge and Jax, talking, eating and learning about each other.

"Word got around that I'm back," He shrugged, "I've had a few emails just today. I'm not hiding anything if that's what you mean."

"I'm sorry. Just tell me things, Jake. It's important for us to keep talking."

"I agree." He dropped a hand to my shoulder and looked at me in that way that spoke of yearning and frustration, I thought most of it was about sex. "We can juggle it, Gristle. Go back to work. You're the best at your job. Sarge wants to come see you for free."

"You only ever wanted free services."

He smiled, slow and hot, "Yeah, but not vet services."

We still had to decide about moving into a room together. Jax had started on formula which meant Jake and Toby could feed him and which also made him sleep more. It wouldn't be long until he didn't need me at all for feeding and instead of being sad about it I felt liberated. I had tried my hardest and my son was moving on, growing up, thriving and becoming his own person and I couldn't be happier.

I hadn't heard from Louis and didn't mind. I had never asked for a cent, had not received any government money either. I was independent and didn't need Louis. I had contacted Keisha, asking after Savvy and she assured me that she was fine, that she had baby duties under control. She had been snooty about it, like I was checking up on her. We didn't mention Louis although Keisha did ask if I was still with Jake, delighted when I said he had asked me to marry him, even inviting herself to the wedding. No chance.

CHAPTER TWENTY

Jake had gotten into a routine of dropping Toby at his old private school then taking Sarge and Jax for a run, Jax strapped into his three-wheeler buggy. But after talking to Finn I decided this morning was the time to intercede in my sister's life. I kept it to myself in case it was a disaster, telling Jake I was going to see Finn, annoyed that I told Jake not to keep secrets then doing it myself. But this didn't feel like my secret, this was fixing my family and Jenny would not thank me later if Jake knew all the details of her relationship.

Jake being Jake he knew something was up and confronted me as I packed the buggy into the car.

"Is this secret mission anything to do with me and Toby?"

"What do you mean?" But I was unable to hide the guilt. "I'm going to sort out the mailman."

"How? And do you think it's wise to get Jax in the middle of it?"

"This isn't some criminal monster." I assured him, "It's a beautiful mailman and my idiot sister. If she can't sort it out with Finn I can't work with him again. I'm not getting in the middle of another divorce."

Giving me a long look, Jake then surprised me by nodding and kissing me goodbye, saying, "Call if you need me."

Taking him seriously and keeping my phone in my jeans pocket (oh, I forgot to mention that I was back in my jeans, not quite where they used to be but close enough to make me happy) and parked not far from Finn and Jenny's home. Waiting like a super spy while Jax chewed on a rusk and a big squishy foot shaped thing that I kept in the fridge, his teeth were coming in and making us all grumpy. (There is nothing natural about teething.)

Eventually the mailman turned the corner on his bike and I quickly packed Jax into his seat and set off.

It was a long road and it took the mailman some time to make it to where I was ambling along, Jax cooing. It was fascinating to watch the hunk as he made his way up the middle-class suburban road, and I took photo's as women stopped him to talk or he paused to pat dogs and cats.

Glancing back toward my sister's driveway showed her loitering. Certain she didn't recognize me in my disguise of baseball cap (I never wore hats), I noticed a rustle in the hedge and knew that asshole Pothead was in wait. Jenny wasn't focused on me, not with the mailman around and I intercepted him as he bent to pat a huge tabby that curled around his legs in delight.

"Good morning." I said, smiling. "Lovely day."

He grinned in reply and my toes curled. He was outrageously handsome and the twitching curtains proved I wasn't blind.

"Sure is. I'm going to get in trouble if I keep stopping to talk to all these animals."

"Do you like animals." He was getting more handsome by the second.

"Sure." He shrugged. "Although my husband thinks I'll get ringworm."

My grin widened, "Your husband sounds like a very wise man." For the first time I didn't feel the need to clarify that animals were not the only way to contract ringworm, that you could get it from humans, infected objects and even sitting on the ground.

Feeling the need to ask, I said, "I've seen you around. How

do you cope with all the woman that want to talk to you?"

"People are just being kind." But I could see the strain at the corner of his eyes. "It would sure be nice to finish work a little earlier but a postie is part of the community, right?'

"Not if the community is looking at you like a side of meat."

He nodded and it was sad. "Yeah, maybe I need to talk to my boss. He's getting annoyed that my routes taking so long. Maybe I'll go back to the warehouse."

"Have you thought about modelling?" I couldn't help it, he was that good looking.

"Me? Are you crazy?"

"You should. Anyway, I've got to go. Nice to talk to you."

"You too. Cute baby."

He peddled a few feet down the road and stopped as a dog whined through a fence and the lovely mailman stopped to pet it.

I continued on my way then doubled back slowly since Jax had fallen asleep. It was nice to walk in the sun and think. What was I going to do about Jake's marriage proposal? I had wanted to fob it off as a spur of the moment thing but he had bought it up several times and each time I said nothing. Scared out of my head. I had picked Jake, we both knew that, but it was a big step to marry him. I could imagine Keisha's delight but what would Louis think, and Michelle, she would make my life miserable.

My sister had disappeared from the top of her long driveway, I was still mad that she was ruining her good life, but she was my sister and whatever was going on was out of character. Even if Jake had told me to butt out I wouldn't, so instead of going home I knocked on my sister's door, confused that the kids were screaming the house down.

Jenny looked harried when the door opened.

"Why aren't the kids at school?"

"One of them is." She said, defensive and I could tell she had been crying.

"Jen, what's wrong?"

She stepped from the house, closing the door on her screaming kids. Captain Pugwash was dutifully at her side until spotting Pothead who was sitting in a tree that looked way to skinny to hold his bulk, he was surveying his territory slowly before deigning the small dog with a glance and lifting a back leg to lick his own butt. Working hard not to fall off his precarious perch.

Jenny glared at him, "You have to take that cat. He's ruining my life. He attacks people for no reason."

"You mean the mailman?" At Jenny's silence I added, "You know what that cat is like. He's territorial and a bully. Pothead can smell all the other animals on that man and thinks he's getting all those other animals in line in one brawl."

"Was that you talking to him?" I didn't have to ask to know she meant the mailman.

"Yes, I wanted to see what he's like. If he's going to be my future brother in law. Where's Finn?"

"He's looking at new clinics. Do you know he quit his job?"

"He sold his share, big difference."

Jenny was linking her fingers together, agitated and on edge. "Are you going to work with him again?"

"Probably. It was the best job I ever had, owning it was awesome."

"Even though I'm leaving him?" She couldn't meet my eye. After all the times Jenny had dragged me out of some emotional disaster it was unsettling to see her in such a state.

"I've thought about this, Jen. He was my friend before you met him."

"That's not very loyal."

"I need a job and Finn's promised to be flexible. I like Finn, I enjoy working with him. I've got kids to pay for now. You know that mailman won't ever want to be part of our wacky family, especially with all your kids. They're insane, it's genetic. Finn is the only one who could endure our mongrel blood. I can't believe you're ruining it."

"They're high energy." She said but there was no menace behind it. "If I was single I could at least try."

"You realize half the neighborhood waits for him. Everyone wants him. He's just a kind man who wants to pat the cats and dogs."

"Finn called. He didn't even notice that I had moved out of our bedroom. He said you had told him I was leaving him."

"I thought he knew." Had I put my foot in my mouth again? The last thing I wanted was to make matters worse.

"He was crying."

"Yuck." Was all I could think to say. Jenny and I were not good with our emotions.

She looked at me then. "I haven't even been to see you. Where's your new place?"

"Don't worry about it. You've had a lot on your mind." I had yet to mention that Jake and Toby were living with us, and I was holding his proposal to me closely. It felt like something I wanted to keep all to myself for a little bit longer.

She sighed, "Come inside. Finn will be home soon and I guess I need to tell him what's going on."

"Don't tell him about the postman." I warned, knowing Finn would forgive most things but not another man, even one she had only looked at.

"But I have to. It's not fair. I've been blaming Finn for my stupid insecurities." Just like that I knew the storm was passing. That Jenny was looking at the situation from another point of view, one I would find easier to stomach.

"That mailman is crazy good looking." I conceded. "I understand your interest." But that was all I was going to give her.

"I know, right?" She sighed longingly.

"Imagine poor Finn if he thinks he needs to compete." I didn't mention that the mailman was gay. It made no difference. My sister might have tried to take it further but I was certain she would have reached a point and backed out.

Smiling at her sad face, I unthinkingly said, "I can take the kids for a night if you need some time alone with Finn, although if you end up pregnant again I'll disown you."

"I can't be pregnant again. Finn got a vasectomy." She cried then, deep sobs of misery. "He never even told me, well, he says we talked about it and I told him he had to have it but I must have been sleep deprived and can't remember. I'm not having any more kids." She was tripping over her words in her haste to get them out.

This time I frowned, "Has this all been about having more kids?"

"He doesn't want more." She sniffled.

"And you do?"

"Heck no."

"Alright, you are officially insane. I'm taking you to the doctor. Are you still seeing your therapist?"

"Yeah, she says I'm pushing all my anger and dissatisfaction on to Finn. She thought I could probably put all that energy into studying."

This was news to me, Jenny had never mentioned studying before. "What do you want to study?"

"Teaching. I always wanted to be a teacher, helping everyone in the community."

I smiled, bright with relief. "Jenny, you will be an amazing teacher."

"But I'm too old."

"Nope, you're the perfect age."

"But I'm not smart enough." She was just trying to argue now.

"You're way smarter than me and if I could make it through university, so can you. You'll have Finn to support you and think how proud your kids will be when they're older."

She lifted Captain Pugwash into her arms and hid her face in his stocky little back, sniffling. "I've been the worst wife. Finn must hate me."

"Finn's an idiot, but he loves you. I'll take the kids tonight and you can roll around the house naked and remember why you had a million kids together."

She put the dog on the ground and hugged me tightly. "I'm going to be the best teacher ever."

"No doubt." I said.

"And the best wife and mother."

"Jesus, don't go overboard. Just do the best you can, and if I see you near that poor mailman again I'll post you a snake."

I felt her shiver. "I'm such a fuck up."

"You're in fine company." I chuckled, holding her at arm's length, "Your cat and your dog a fucked up too." My mind turned to Jake. Was he going to kill me for bringing a pile of kids into our lovely apartment? I had to remember that Jake was an adopted orphan who was getting all my family. Poor guy.

CHAPTER TWENTY-ONE

Jenny's kids were in love with Toby who was overwhelmed when he arrived home from school to find three kids under six in his bedroom (Jenny had kept Emma, the baby since she was still feeding). Like Jake, he just dealt with it. We fed them a mountain of lasagna for dinner and the apartment was silent by eight that night, Jake and I side by side on the sofa. We didn't speak but when I snuggled into him Jake pushed me to my back and kissed me deeply and completely. After long minutes he stood and wordlessly went to bed where Toby was already asleep beside him, his bedroom given over to the hoard of kids.

If Jake was trying to push me toward sex he was doing a fantastic job. I was feeling completely recovered from having a baby.

During the night I had a text message from Dahlia asking me to call her. That she needed to explain something. Yeah, no chance.

The next morning we fed all the kids then Jake took Toby to school. The poor boy was swamped before he went and I would talk to him later to ensure he was comfortable with so much attention. Toby was an only child and if I couldn't stop him being mauled I could at least give him some strategies to escape.

When Jake returned we took the gaggle of kids home, intending to visit a few houses on the way. We had to take two cars since there were too many bodies, Jake decided to take Sarge and Jax with him.

Jenny was clearly expecting us, the gate wide open and the kids raced inside. Jenny was excited to see them and listened carefully as they retold tales of their adventures. Who knew lasagna, a movie, and a ten-year-old boy were so exciting?

I warned Jenny that Sarge was coming over with Jake and Jax and she shrugged. Everyone knew Jake had complete control of the dog who might look at little Captain Pugwash with slobbering delight but would never do anything unless Jake told him to.

"Are you back in your own bedroom?" I asked and my sister grinned.

"Yes, thank you for your help."

I nodded as a strange car pulled up behind mine and I frowned, knowing Jake was now going to have to park on the road with Jax and Sarge.

Jenny shepherded the kids outside to play as Louis entered, kissing my cheek and glancing around.

"Where's my son?"

"Jake has him." At Louis' frown, I added, "They'll be here any minute. Any chance you can park on the road so Jake doesn't have to bring a baby and Sarge up the driveway?"

Louis waved me away so I flicked the kettle to life, deciding to let the little things go.

"How's it all going, Louis?" I asked for something to say.

"My life would be infinitely easier if your brother wasn't trying to find me. That's why I'm here. I assume he's following and he won't try anything violent in front of his sisters. I need to work out a deal with him," He shrugged, "Or I can beat the fuck out of him to prove that he needs to back off and change his plan."

As if he had been conjured, Tyler walked in then, just as Finn wandered down the stairs, looking flustered and ready to leave.

Finn eyed the two men and growled, "Take your pissing match somewhere else. There are kids here and a cat that's on the edge." To me he said, "Pothead is a fucking pest."

"There are plenty of pests around here." Louis drawled, looking at Tyler. "I don't have a taste for violence right now, Tyler. I suggest you don't push me today. Who knows what might happen?"

"You want to talk to me about pests?" Tyler hissed at Louis, "You are a fucking pestilence in my life."

Lips pursing, containing his anger, Louis told my brother, "You need to back off. My job is done and your work is none of my business. You are collateral, so suck it up, princess. It's been done to me a hundred times before. Forget about me, move on or there will be bigger problems for you than you can comprehend."

What did that mean? Was Louis still working? I thought he was uncovering his true self, finding out what he wanted to do with the rest of his life.

Concerned only with his own problems, Tyler said, "I have people who need to know that I'm not undercover. You are going to tell them that you lied."

Like usual, Louis didn't care that he could ruin someone else's life. "Nope. I've got court cases coming up. I'm not perjuring myself to save your ass. Find your own way out."

"You fucking prick." Tyler's fist clenched at his sides but he took a deep breath, closing his eyes to calm himself. "You have taken me out with you. Do you know how close I was to ending it?"

This amused Louis, "You wouldn't have ended it. Like me you would have found a way to keep going. Like me you like the lifestyle, the power, the luxury, the sex. Don't forget I've been there. I know exactly why you won't finish, why you want me to keep the ride going, and I'll say what I've said to a hundred guys before you. Fuck you. Fix your own mess like I had to fix mine."

Tyler propped his hands on his hips and peered at the

ceiling as Jenny returned, finding this standoff. "You better not be causing trouble in my home." She growled, "Either of you. There are children here."

It was obvious that Louis was sick of my brother. He appeared calm, arms hanging limply at his sides, but I knew better, Louis was ready to fight. He was always ready to fight.

Instead of punching and threatening, Tyler leaned over his knees, crying so the rest of us became uncomfortable. When the children became interested, Finn herded them upstairs and we could soon hear a movie booming from the big screen.

He returned, saying, "You have exactly forty-five minutes before my kids are bored. You sort this shit out then get out of my house."

Jenny sucked her lips between her teeth and stared at her husband in a way that felt inappropriate right now.

Wiping his eyes on his shirt, Tyler said, "My husband dumped me. He's taken the kids because I've been so selfish. I've tried to do the right thing and it's all collapsing. I don't know how to get out of it but if Louis doesn't tell the Toa's that I'm not undercover it's going to get messier than I can deal with. If I go to prison I'll never see my family again."

"You never told us you had kids, Tyler." I said.

Pothead sauntered in then and, like an idiot, Tyler picked him up. Pothead rolled over until Tyler was holding him like a baby. It was a cute image until Pothead hissed, long and loud, like it had taken him a moment to vocalize his outrage, then he tried to claw Tyler's face. Tossing the cat away, Pothead bounced off the sofa, executed a perfect midair spin, landed on his feet, shook himself off then sauntered to his cat bowl.

"That cat is fucking badass." Tyler said, "If I'm forced to stay in New Zealand he's mine."

Jake entered with Jax, not seeing what was happening since he was commanding Sarge to wait by the door. He turned to find Tyler and Louis facing off, with me, Finn and Jenny at different levels of annoyance.

"Is this a family reunion?" Jake asked as Louis took the

car seat and smiled at Jax, going so close that Jax couldn't focus.

"How's my big man?" He said.

"Is that your kid?" Tyler said, looking to me instead of Louis.

In reply, I said, "One-night stand."

"How dumb are you?"

Ignoring his barb, I asked, "How many children do you have?"

"Twin girls. They're four." He didn't produce a photo or any proud parental thing which I found suspicious. Is it normal to be distrustful of your own brother? My family had proven to be unworthy of trust and I was wise to be wary.

"I would love to meet them." I said but Tyler's focus had returned to Louis.

"You took my kids." He reached out and snatched Jax. "So I'll take yours. "Louis was so surprised, or so fucking stupid that he just stood there. Did he think a smoldering look was going to stop this?

"Put him down!" Jake unexpectedly roared and Sarge was instantly at his side, barking hard at Tyler as Jax jolted at the noise, his face scrunching up as he began wailing.

"He took my children, I'll take his." Tyler repeated, stunned at Jake's menace.

"Give him to me." Jake ordered, "Right now or I let Sarge go."

Jake and Sarge were covering the nearest exit so Tyler looked to me and Jenny as if we would offer him an escape.

"Put my baby down." I said, trying to control my emotions as Jax continued to wail, scared by the unusual noise coming from Sarge. "What is wrong with you?" I turned to Louis, "And you. This isn't some pawn in your game, this is a little person who depends on us, and what are you doing? Using him."

"He's not yours, Louis." Jake growled, oblivious to the noise. "He's mine."

Louis smiled, mean, ugly, smug. "No, he's mine. My blood."

Without thinking I lifted the first thing at hand and threw it. It was a plate and it smashed on Louis' forehead, causing a gash. He leaned forward, yelling in surprise. I expected him to rush me, but he just stood there until Finn told him to get outside so he didn't ruin the floorboards. Finn really had the constitution of an ox, nothing fazed him.

Tyler was still holding Jax but I was following as he side-stepped to the door. Jake rushed him, surprising my brother enough that he let Jax go.

We were all panting when my Uncle Rueben, Tyler's contact entered. Seeing Jake turning away with Jax, he shook his head. "Did you just take that baby?"

My brother had the good sense to look ashamed and Rueben quietly said, "That's it. We're done here." He turned to Jake then, saying, "Thanks for the heads up."

"No problem." Jake said, taking Jax from the car seat and handing him to me, calling Sarge to his side, letting him know that everything was fine. Jax stopped crying straight away as Jake continued, "He's been following us for a few days. It took me longer than I liked to get your number." He cut Rueben an annoyed glare.

"Peril of the job, Jake. You should know that. Sometimes there are people trying to get in contact that are really unwelcome."

Jake chuckled, "I've got a school receptionist in the South Island trying to call me."

"What?" I gasped, "You never told me that."

"It's under control." But I could see his worry.

"I'm calling the principal again tomorrow." I assured him. "Did you email the school Board yet?"

"It's on my to do list. We've been a little busy since getting back to Auckland."

Was this what Dahlia was calling about? Or was it to do with the ongoing police issues from the day she was caught with those eggs. Did she want me to change my story, say she didn't snatch my son, convince me smuggling native animals overseas was justifiable? She had a lot to learn about me yet.

"I should've bought Louis in years ago." Jake told Rueben, frowning at me as if reading my thoughts and not liking them. "I almost ruined my life trying to protect him. Don't make the same mistakes. If they say they're almost done, they're not. They stall because they like the lifestyle."

Nodding, Reuben said to Tyler, "Are you coming in easy or am I calling the cops and getting you extradited?" At Tyler's silence he added, "We can work through this, you know I can get you out of the worst of it, but you need to come in now."

Glaring around the room, Tyler said, "Fuck this, I'm done here." He then stormed out the door, arguing with Louis in passing, then silence.

◆ ◆ ◆

Finn called Louis back inside and quickly tidied up the gash on his forehead, offering to do the stitches himself, "I'm a doctor." He said on an evil smile.

"Yeah, do it. I don't want to spend hours waiting at the hospital. Just do a pretty job, I don't mind a scar but not a huge, ugly one." He was still vain.

"Jesus," Finn grumbled, "I was joking. I'm not taking the blame when you don't look after the wound and it gets infected. I've got ninety-nine problems and you ain't one."

This made us all chuckled since Finn and Jay Z were poles apart in the cool game.

As Louis sat there, wincing at Finn's rough treatment, I said, "Louis, you are still unstable and volatile."

"Says the woman who just split my head open."

"I'm sorry about that. I overreacted but you've said that

you liked your undercover lifestyle. I don't want Jax bought up around that."

"What are you trying to say?" He scowled at Finn who stepped away to survey the tape he had used to close the gaping injury.

Everyone gasped as I said, "Let Jake adopt him, he'll be the father you know you can't be."

"No chance." Louis growled. "How could you even say that."

"Then you need to pay child support. You can't expect Jake to cover your share of bringing up your son. That's not fair. My lawyer will send you the amount, and I'm warning you, you won't like it, not when you're paying for Keisha and your pretty apartment too."

He stared at me, thinking hard, "You're not going to give me another shot, are you?"

"Never. But if you pay and get a real job, you are welcome to see him." I didn't want Jax staying with him or Keisha but that was a fight for another day.

"What if Jake dumps you again. Will I have a chance then?"

Shaking my head, embarrassed in front of my sister and Finn, and that Jake was hearing it too. I didn't want him to feel pushed into anything. Not until I got him into bed again anyway.

"Regardless of what happens between Jake and I, me and you are done, Louis. I'm sorry that our history, going right back to when we were kids was so gross and violent, but I can't change it. Be kind and we might be friends again. That's all I can offer you."

Louis looked to Jake, "Will you tell him I'm his real father."

"Of course." Jake instantly said. "But I won't let you fuck him up. It's time for all of us to grow up, Louis."

I expected Louis to be enraged, if it had been anyone else Louis would have gone crazy, but Jake had always been different for Louis. They had been a team for a long time and that relationship had only recently changed. It was up to Louis how much Jake was still involved in his life.

Mulling it over, Louis eventually said to Jake, "If I give him to you will you be easier on me when the court cases start?"

We were all outraged. It was Jenny who said, "He's not a fucking toy. He's a little boy that you can't just give away. Jesus, you really are a fucking idiot."

Calmer, Jake said, "You'll do the right thing. No games. But the choice is yours."

Touching his taped forehead, Louis looked at Jax, then said, "I'll think about it."

Then without a goodbye, he walked out.

He must have made a move to pet Sarge, as Jake calmly said, "He's working. I wouldn't touch him if I were you."

Louis pulled a hand back just as Pothead twisted around his ankles and tripped him up. He fell on a loud cuss that bought the kids and Captain Pugwash rushing down the stairs, yelling like a pack of wild animals.

Pothead moved to Sarge, touching noses, one professional to another, then the cat sauntered back inside with his tail high, doing another walk by of his food bowl.

"There's something wrong with that cat." Jake said, helping Louis back to his feet

Everyone agreed, even Louis.

CHAPTER TWENTY-TWO

Jax was nine months old by the time Jake and I found a lovely home in a nice suburb with good schools. It wasn't a spectacular house but had good bones and Jake assured me he was handy with a hammer. The clinic in Parnell was being finished off and the commute for me wasn't too bad.

You probably want to know how we navigated the whole issue of which bedroom I would be in. It was all sorted out two weeks after we moved into the Auckland apartment. Michelle decided to take Toby to see his grandfather. I followed Jake's unworried lead while ensuring Toby had his phone hidden in his bag, he promised to call if there were any problems. Jake thought Michelle wanted more money out of her wealthy father.

Jax had taken to going to sleep at seven every night and for a whole week had not woken until five. To have all those hours to myself was wonderful and scary. I had a shower as Jake put him to bed, trying to get mashed potato out of my hair before it set hard. When I emerged and padded quietly to check on Jax, Jake entered the shower.

Dressed in only a towel, I bit my lip, wondering what to do. Should I get dressed or follow Jake into the shower? Was he in the mood?

I was ready. Boy was I ready. Jake was still running with Sarge and his body was amazing. Well, I certainly thought so.

Forcing down my concerns, I slipped into the bathroom. Jake had soap in his hair but saw me through the shower door and froze. He was mostly hidden behind the foggy glass but I knew what was hiding there, and so with eyes locked on his I dropped the towel, taking his hand as he held the door open for me, my stomach jumping with fear and excitement.

"You sure?" He husked.

I nodded, leaning in, expecting the kiss, anticipating what came after.

Jake instead held the side of my head, staring at me hard while his warm and wet body pressed me into a cold wall.

"About fucking time, Gristle." He smiled, "This has been fucking torture."

He then took his time to ensure I was certain of what I wanted. It was a long night, a reconnection in a whole different way. Jake had been right, we weren't kids anymore, I felt different but not in a bad way. For the first time I was able to ask for what I wanted and Jake was a willing disciple. As was I. We talked, we laughed, we made love and had raw sex. We had enough emotion and history together to make the experience one I would never forget.

We were on the sofa watching television the next afternoon when Toby returned.

"Are you guys sick?" He asked, anxious eyes dropping to Jax who happily rolled around on the floor in front of us.

"Nope, we just missed you." Jake grinned, hugging his son.

From then on Jake and I shared a room and Toby never mentioned it. When we moved into our new house we bought a king-sized bed to share (mainly because Jake took up a lot of space when he slept and the boys found their way in like magic).

We had only been in the house a few days when someone started leaving notes in our letterbox claiming to be from the neighborhood watch association. Apparently, they had decided as a group that a dog of Sarge's size was not welcome. At first

I was outraged, I became suspicious about this neighborhood watch group when the letters quickly progressed to complaints about Jax's crying (he wasn't a big crier, and certainly not a loud one) and how badly I dressed when out walking (this was possibly true, but rude).

Being proactive, I knocked on a few neighbor's doors, introducing myself and saying which house we had just bought. I then asked about joining the committee and without fail everyone had no idea what I was talking about. When I showed him the letters, one elderly man in a tiny house at the end of a long driveway, suggested I talk to the cops, that he had lived in this area all his life and had never heard of any type of neighborhood group.

He invited me in. His name was Arthur Lynes and he was an ex-military man. He claimed he was still suffering Post Traumatic Stress from the Vietnam war. I politely refused to look at the scars on his back from agent orange. He had a huge tabby cat that I noticed had a weepy eye. Explaining I was a vet I recommended he take her in for a visit. When he gingerly admitted he couldn't afford it, that he had been worried about it for days, I checked the cat over. It looked like there had been a fight, a scratch near the eye looking a little infected. I promised to bring over some drops and help administer them if needed. He was grateful and promised to keep an eye on my letterbox when he was on his daily walk. I went home feeling lighter, remembering there were still nice people in the world.

I was surprised when Arthur knocked on my door later that day. He was holding out his phone to show me a clear photo of a woman posting something in our letterbox.

"Is it someone you recognize from the neighborhood?" I asked.

"In that fancy dress?" He chuckled, "She's an outsider, I'd guess from the *provinces*." He said this exactly like everyone in the provinces said about Auckland and it still made no sense to me.

After zooming in on the photo I gasped and asked him to

send it to me, admiring his pride that he knew how.

When my phone pinged with the message I opened the photo on my larger screen. Nothing had changed, there was Darling Roach dressed in a pretty sundress, hat and sunglasses, dropping another letter in my postbox. I needed to think about what to do with her and talk to Jake. She was a long way from home and was obviously not going to give Jake up without a fight. Jesus, the man hadn't even dated her. How had the Grafton community dealt with her? This was another thing that needed sorting out before I returned to work and life became infinitely busier.

It appeared Grafton would hold on to me for a little longer and I decided to call Dahlia back, to find out what she wanted, and to get her off my back for good.

As far as I knew my brother was still in the country but Uncle Rueben wasn't taking my calls. I didn't know why Tyler was still here, if he was anything like our father he was hiding from the real world and that wasn't a good option.

Louis had once more disappeared and I needed to get him sorted out once and for all and the only way forward was a meeting with all the key players in my life. So I invited Louis over, not mentioning that I had asked Tyler to come too. Jake would be home, Toby at school and Jax was going to my sisters for a few hours. She lived close enough that she picked him up in her double buggy pushchair, claiming it was better than a gym membership.

Without a clue what I had planned Jake was in the shower after a run when Tyler arrived first, Louis not long after. There was a tense standoff when the three men came face to face and I could see the hurt in Jake's eyes that I had not warned him. I had no choice, he would have convinced me it was a bad idea and to let things work themselves out in their own time. We didn't have time, I wanted my old life back, to work with Finn and get back to small animal veterinarian work. I wanted to enjoy my time with Jake and watch our kids grow without the threat of these men turning up whenever they felt like it and ruining everything. I was taking control of the situation.

Each man believed the others had manipulated me into this meeting and it took some fast talking to convince them otherwise.

There was plenty of ranting and empty threats but when we were all seated around the new kitchen table, I said, "I'm not offering you drinks since I don't want them used as weapons."

Jake chuckled while Tyler glared out the patio doors to Sarge as if the dog had offended him.

To Louis, I said, "Your head still looks bad. Did you get a doctor to have a look at it?" This was from the plate I had thrown at him and I felt bad for it.

"It's fine." He said but I could see lines of infection beneath the plaster.

"I'll have a look when we're done here." I added, concerned with how pale he was, certain the idiot wasn't looking after himself at all.

"Did you get the adoption papers?" I asked him.

"I'm not signing them." He growled, "Jax is *my* son and I'm not being kicked out like that." I wasn't surprised, had not expected Louis to walk away but we needed to clarify the situation, and when Louis was hard to find a form in his apartment letterbox was guaranteed to elicit a response.

"Great, thank you, Louis." I glanced at Jake who was stony faced. "That means you need to contribute to his upbringing."

"When I can." Louis growled.

"That's not good enough, Louis." I said, trying hard to remain calm. This wasn't about money, this was about Louis doing the right thing and remembering his responsibilities. He couldn't just be a dad when he felt like it. That wasn't fair on Jake and it wasn't fair on Jax. "We were all bought up in dysfunctional homes."

"I wasn't." Jake assured me. "I had great parents."

My look reminded him that his birth mother was complicated too, and that being bought up by her would have been a different experience.

In reply Jake conceded, "I didn't know my birth parents."

Louis frowned, "You were adopted?"

It was so nice to know something about Jake that other people didn't. I hoped I hadn't force him into admitting he was adopted. I'd make it up to him later.

"What I'm saying," I said, "Is that we don't have to continue the dysfunction. We can do a better job than our parents, that's what I want. Jax's start wasn't ideal but he has the chance for a great life, better than ours." I turned to Louis, "Leaving Jake to do all the hard work is not fair."

"It's fine, Sophie." Jake assured me before saying to Louis, "But you can't undermine me. Tell him I'm an asshole when you turn up once a year with gifts. Be in or get out. Think of someone other than yourself for once. You were a good man once, Louis. What you devolved into . . . I don't want Jax to see that part of you."

Instead of his usual anger, Louis looked thoughtful. He then stunned me by nodding, "I can live with that. I'm not going to be around much since I'm moving down south to study psychology and write a book about what I've been through. A couple of reporters have been in touch and want to do stories on the failings of the police. Might be an easy way to get the public on side and promote my talks." He looked to Tyler then who was quiet. "I suggest you do something similar."

"What choice do I have." Tyler sighed, "I can't go home."

"Why?" I asked, "What about your family?"

"The Australian government have officially deported me. I was born in New Zealand and regardless of what I did for their country, how long I worked for them, paid their taxes, now that I'm implicated criminally they've deported me to my home country."

"That's crazy." I gasped, "What about Ruben?"

"He's fine. Sorted his citizenship out years ago. I hadn't signed one form or some other bureaucratic bullshit. Now he's telling everyone that I was working alone, that he had no idea what I was really doing."

"And did he?" I already knew the answer.

"He masterminded most of the operations I ran. He always had a bigger score, a bigger criminal." My poor brother was caving in on himself, the stress and pressure suddenly right at the surface.

"This is such bullshit. You've given up everything and now you get tossed aside. It's not right. Same with you, Louis."

Seeing my evangelical look, Jake said, "Stop feeding their need for attention, Sophie. They knew exactly what they were getting into and the possible outcomes. We were warned about staying in too long but both you idiots," He pointed from Louis to Tyler, "Thought you knew better. Now you'll face the consequences of all those dumb decisions you made. Regardless if you helped the community or just yourselves, it's over. Find something else. Find people of substance to fill your lives and move the fuck on."

My mouth had dropped open. Jake was a man of few words but when he talked it had an impact.

"I'm trying." Louis said, "I want to see what's next for me, I'm ready now."

Tyler frowned. "But how can you just walk away from all that money? You'll never live that way again."

Louis leaned forward, his clasped hands on the table before him, saying to Tyler, "How many hard guys have you seen get old? What happened to them?"

Rolling his eyes, Tyler said, "You know better than anyone what happens to them. They get taken out, walked over. Stupid old fucks."

"Those stupid old fucks didn't know when to quit." Louis paused, that mean grin letting me know he was about to land a blow. "Just like your father. He got out of prison and tried to return to his old life, to rehash his glory days, but those days were done. He could have had a decent life on your family farm, instead he's back in prison, pretending he can keep up with those young guys who have nothing and nothing to lose. You need to decide who you want to be, the guy that walked away, or the stupid fuck that got taken out."

"But what about my family?" Tyler moaned, rubbing his forehead. "My kids?"

"Have another family, have some more kids."

"Jesus, Louis." Jake groaned, "That's harsh, even for you."

"We're being all honest." He argued, that yellow tinge to his forehead pronounced.

"While you're expecting me to raise your son." Jake growled.

"Yeah, but you knew what you were getting into when you signed up with me, Jake. You were not exactly a soft or easy touch when you were younger. If you can settle down I guess I'm gonna have to follow your lead."

"Shucks." Jake smiled, "You're trying to flatter me." Then to Tyler, he said, "If Louis can claw a life back then you can too. Be better than your father. You can stew on all the times you got slighted, the times you got cheated, how much you've been let down, or you can move on and have a life. Isn't that the best revenge?"

I could feel the admiration the men had for each other, even after all this time and all that had gone on between them.

"Why am I here?" Tyler snapped, "I can fix my own fucking problems."

"You're doing a stellar job." Louis laughed, "Hunting me down, wanting me to fix the world for you. Face up to your past, and do it with a smile, you miserable fucking asshole."

Louis was laughing but Tyler didn't join in, neither did Jake and I decided to move this conversation on before feelings were hurt and punches were thrown.

"I called you three here today because I need this sorted. Jake and I have moved in together and I'm struggling to trust him. I know it's because I don't have the entire picture of how we all ended up in this place."

"We can talk about this privately." Jake said.

"No, Jake. When I ask you things you say you don't remember or I don't need to know. That's not fair."

"All that fucking studying." Tyler sneered, "You've got to know everything."

Shrugging, I said, "That's right. You all know things about me or things that involve me and I need everything clear in my head before I move on to my next disaster."

"What next disaster?" Jake asked.

"Your stalker from Grafton, Darling Roach has followed us here. She's the one posting all that crap about the neighborhood group in our letterbox."

Impressed, Louis said, "You still got it, old man."

"What do you want to know?" Jake asked, not joining in Louis' amusement.

"How did I meet you guys? Right back at the beginning. How do you three know each other and how did I really get involved? I know there's more to the story but I'm not sure where or how I fit in and it's driving me crazy. I come up with scenarios that are sad and scary and stupid. I just want to know how I met Nathan then Jake then Louis and how you both know Tyler."

"I didn't know Tyler." Jake assured me. "I knew his name and that Louis had dealings with him for the trans Tasmanian drug routes, but other than that I was out of the loop. I had no idea he was your brother."

Louis and Tyler looked at each other and I could see years of history running between them. Eventually Tyler said, "It was me. I told Nathan to cause that scene with his dog in front of you. He knew how to find you and was waiting for you that day. I knew you would overreact because you always did when it came to animals. Remember when Mum started breeding guinea pigs for eating. You were like eight, so just before I ran away, you let them all go then smashed the cages, knowing Dad would beat the shit out of you for it. Or what about the time the preschool had its turtle stolen. You biked to every kid's house until you found it. Then you didn't call in an adult, you just stole it back. Remember the fight Dad had on the porch when that idiot turned up to tell him you had stolen his stolen turtle." He laughed but they were not happy memories, they were memories of sad, frightened little kids who didn't deserve what they had been forced to endure.

Like he was unburdening himself, he continued, "What about the time when Dad wanted some breeding cows and took you to the stockyard sales." To Jake and Louis he said, "She saw all the working dogs tied to the backs of every second pickup truck and let them all go. It was fucking mayhem for a couple of hours."

"It was a really hot day."

"Dad gave you a good belting for that one."

"It was worth it." I assured him while remembering the terror I had felt that day. I had not wanted to let them go, I didn't want to face Dad's wrath, knew that one day he would probably go too far and kill me, but I had done it anyway because the thought of living with myself afterward was worse.

"Nothing much has changed." Jake said, but it was quiet and he was looking out the window instead of at me, quiet despair on his handsome face.

Continuing, Tyler said, "Nathan assured me you would take the dog then he would set up a meeting between you and Louis. When I didn't pay him on time he tried to get the dog back sooner."

Jake made a grunt of disgust, saying, "He turned up at the clinic then we had a brawl outside a restaurant." He flexed his hand as if remembering old pain. "I broke my hand on his face and Sophie got hurt, your own sister. All because of what? What did you want, Tyler that you couldn't have just asked for outright?"

Louis spoke then, voice cold and hard, working this out in his head too, "Tyler called and said he had heard about some fight with Nathan Bright and a woman who had information on me and the dog fights." To Tyler he said, "You told me you had evidence that would link me directly to those fights. You knew that would have caused me major problems. I used Nathan as my cover. Even Jake didn't know I was running dogs. I had no intention of carrying it on but they were a simple way to move

217

drugs, neutral ground."

"And animal abuse." I said, jaw bunching tight. It had been a good idea not to have a cup in front of me or Louis would have a matching injury.

Shrugging, like he still didn't care about those dogs, Louis said, "I expected to threaten you and for you to run away like a whipped mutt, with your tail between your legs." He smiled then, as if at a wonderful time of his life, "Instead you threatened me right back, promised to kill me down a dark alleyway."

We stared at each other and I silently prayed that he would not mention anything more about that day, how I had a fake gun pointed at my face, how I had hopped into a strangers car, how we had threatened each other then kissed. I had been injured, worried about Jake and exhausted. Louis had caught me at a vulnerable time.

"You let Nathan beat me up." I said, devastated.

"I told him to stay away from you after that. I had no idea who you were, how I would feel about you. It was the first honest feelings I'd had in a long time. Can you at least admit it surprised you too?"

Glancing at Jake, I shrugged, "It was shitty timing since I had just met Jake." To my brother, I said, "What did you get out of it?"

He laughed then, cold and bitter, "I got fucking nothing out of it. I knew things were changing for Louis, rumors were going wild, everyone saying he was going crazy, was planning to take over the Toa family. I knew better, that he was planning to quit the undercover work or quit the cops for good. It was always harder with Louis because I could never find out who his contact was. I knew it was someone experienced, like Sheppard himself. Was he the puppet master?"

The glare between the two men was complicated. "But you never found out who it was." Louis said as if he had kept at least one secret.

"Nope, I never did." Tyler agreed.

"It was me." Jake baldly stated. "It was always me. From the time Louis went undercover, right through getting me and Sarge almost killed, I stayed with him, to finish what we started."

Tyler was wide eyed. "No fucking way. I thought you two were just old cop mates. You weren't even working in the cops anymore."

"I negotiated to keep track of Louis."

"Or I told Sheppard I was out." Louis added as if he had done Jake a favor.

"Sheppard was a fucking asshole." Tyler snarled, "You think he gave a shit what happened to you? He was brutal and should have been put to pasture long ago.

"Sheppard couldn't touch me, and he didn't care so long as I was getting results. I had Jake and knew I could trust him."

"Until we both met Sophie." Jake sighed.

"Yeah, it got complicated when you tossed your sister between us." Louis agreed.

"I needed intel." Tyler replied, "Sophie's so nosy, always sticking her beak in other people's animal business, and Louis was always such a fucking show pony, I thought she would get Louis talking and he could admit to things I might need to know." He made it all sound so simple and logical yet it had been anything but.

"Why?" Louis asked.

"The fucking Toa's were moving into Australia. Pushing hard and violently for space. I needed something, anything to get a handle on them and Reuben found out that you were boning the Toa's oldest daughter." He grimaced, "Now that's fucking dedication."

"Whatever it takes." Louis chuckled. "She got me in where I wouldn't have had a chance otherwise."

"But, Tyler, you never contacted me." I said, disinterested in who Louis slept with. It was not my concern and never had been. "Not once."

"Your number was constantly changing. Every time I

tried to find you, you slipped away again. Jenny would give me a number and two months later I'd have to contact her again like I was a good brother trying to keep in touch."

"You were a shitty brother." I assured him. "I'm just beginning to realize how shitty. And my number kept changing because I was constantly getting crank and abusive calls. I've been running since I met Jake and Louis." I sighed at his confusion, "You are such an idiot."

"I had to try." Tyler argued, "I was being adaptable and changeable. Right, Louis?"

But Louis had the sense to say nothing, raising his palms like he was staying out of it.

Turning to Jake, I said what worried me the most, "Why were you there, Jake? The day I met you, why did you stop me and Nathan fighting? How did you end up in my path? Please, no more lies or half-truths. This isn't for any purpose other than proving that you guys know how to be honest." I looked at them each in turn, "My brother. The father of my son. My partner. I need to know everything."

Jake shook his head, "No, Gristle. You don't need to know everything, you *want* to know everything and you'll make our lives miserable until then."

"Maybe." I agreed.

"I want to know too." Tyler said.

Jake looked to Louis who shrugged like he didn't care. Jake sighed, rubbed his eyes and said, "Fine. Louis had been becoming erratic. He had stopped calling in as often as he should and I had to track him down every time I got back from overseas. When I did find him he was angry, secretive. Our entire relationship before then had been founded on honesty so I figured he was doing things I wouldn't like, things that would get him pulled in. Then suddenly he went completely dark, I couldn't contact him, couldn't find anyone who would talk or tell me what was happening. Even Sheppard was being cagey." He looked to Louis, "Did Sheppard tell you to go for the Toa's like that?"

"He said it was the final goal." Louis confirmed, not looking at Jake, just staring around the room, eyes returning to me more than I was comfortable with. "That it would eradicate operations both here and in Australia. Sheppard believed there were people over there asleep at the wheel."

Jake was outraged, "He played you. He fucking played us both." He shook his head, taking a breath to calm his anger. "I had dealt with Nathan in the past, had heard he was working for Louis, something to do with dogs, so I started following him when I got back. Not seriously, just when I could, when Toby was at school."

"And when you were on a date." I couldn't help adding, remembering the Barbie clone he was with the day we met.

"I was just hoping to find his trail again, work out what he was planning before deciding if it was time to pull him in." He smiled then, "Instead I find stupid fucking Nathan Bright brawling in the street with this crazy woman who completely ruined my carefully constructed and almost empty life. All I had before I met you, Sophie was work, Louis, Toby and Sarge. Louis knew I wanted you and used it against me, always threatening to take you away if I stepped out of line. I was trapped."

"You could have told me." I argued.

"What could I say without giving us both up? Louis can manipulate any situation. Why do you think he's so good at what he's been doing? It would sound like I was trying to turn you against him and you would have ended up hating me more."

"But you used me to stay close to Louis too." I couldn't look at him, didn't want to have this conversation in front of other people. Suddenly I wanted to be alone with Jake, to discuss this privately.

"I'm sorry." Jake exhaled, "I keep saying that, but I had a job to do with Louis. Something I agreed to do long before I met you, regardless of the cost."

Standing then, pacing the room, Tyler stared out the big window in our new living room. It showed our back garden that was perfect for kids and big enough for a dog as big as Sarge and a few extras. We had gone for a worse house to get the land size. It was raining now, the garden needed the moisture. I would message Jenny soon and let her know I would come and get Jax and not to walk in this weather. I wanted to hang out with my sister. She was teaching me plenty about Jax's continuing progression as a human. As soon as I got on top of one new issue, a brand new one arose. He was crawling now, making the house a minefield of dropped things and sharp corners. Just yesterday he had shocked me by standing, using the coffee table. At my delight he had smiled at me then toppled backward, the lump on the back of his head making me cry in fright. He was too young to attempt walking and Jenny would know how to stop it. I had a sneaking suspicion there was no stopping it and I was again going to have to adjust to the changes.

"Jake fucking Rowland." Tyler said, arms crossed, peering at the rain and Sarge, now sitting in his house. Tyler then suddenly turned, chuckling, "You have been the unexpected variable in everyone's plans the entire way through."

CHAPTER TWENTY-THREE

Our phones were making sounds, the rest of the world attempting to interfere in our meeting. I wanted everyone to put them away but that wasn't fair. We all had kids and other responsibilities.

Jake and Tyler were staring at each other and it was Jake that smiled and said, "Perhaps it was fate that bought me and your sister together."

Unimpressed, Tyler said, "Finding a crazy woman fighting in the street over a dog was fate?"

"Sure, why not. How was anyone to know I would want her, that Louis would want her too. Was it her or was it timing?" He shrugged, "Who knows and it doesn't matter. We're here, Louis is no longer working for the police. If you want to go for the Toa family, do it. You'll get yourself killed. That family have done so well because there are twelve brothers who hate the world more than they hate each other. By yourself, you haven't got a hope of taking them on. They will go after your kids, your sisters, their kids. Is that what you want? Let the Toa's go, let the younger cops hone their skills bringing them down. They'll do it the right way. Our way doesn't work anymore."

Skeptical, Tyler frowned, saying, "It just doesn't feel right. We made all the sacrifices, for what? To be cast aside, pulled through the courts and social media."

No one spoke for a few minutes, then Jake said, "I really did like you from the start, Sophie. I'm not like Louis, I can't act or pretend in a way that you wouldn't see through."

This was a conversation I was not going to have in front of Tyler and Louis who was clenching his fists. Was he even more pale?

"What about Mike?" I asked. Mike had been best friends with Jake back in their police days, I wasn't sure if Louis had been included and Louis detested Mike who had been outed in an affair with Jake's wife. It had all gotten very complicated and messy.

To Louis, Jake said, "I sure never told him you were undercover."

"He only recently found out." Louis agreed. "Michelle knew because I used her to keep tabs on Jake."

"I fucking knew it. Using people is your idea of success." Jake hissed.

Louis was pleased by this, his grin smug and victorious. "You never know when those you trust will stab you in the back. I always told you that Mike was a self-obsessed shithead, were you really surprised that he hooked up with Michelle? He can't keep it in his pants, and she's so fucking needy. You got what you bought when you married her. I can't believe you went through with it after I told you she hit on me before the wedding. It was a disaster waiting to happen and there was no one to blame but yourself."

"I was a fucking idiot." Jake said, studying Louis for a long moment. "We all were. What's that grin? I know that look. What do you know that I don't?"

I turned to Louis as he collected his phone from a pocket and lifted it as if in explanation. "Exhibit A." At our ongoing confusion, he said, "Michelle called me yesterday, said she knew I was in trouble and had a way for me to make some fast money."

"Do I want to know this?" Jake groaned, rubbing his face and leaning back in his chair. My eyes were caught when his shirt rose enough to expose some of that lovely flesh. He still made me jittery. It was nice and stressful in equal measures.

"I taped the conversation." Louis explained, placing the phone directly in front of him like it was fragile. "I'm taping most phone conversations right now because I don't know who to trust. Michelle asked me, no demanded that I eradicate Sophie, or if I couldn't do it that I find a hitman. I gave her Tyler's number." He smiled and this time Tyler chuckled.

"I wondered who that crazy bitch was. I hung up on her. She had no idea that Sophie was my sister, was screaming and ranting."

Me and Jake weren't laughing. Jake was furious. "Send me that recording." He demanded and Louis collected his phone.

"What are you going to do?" Louis queried, "She's your wife."

"That batshit bitch is going back to prison." Jake said through clenched teeth.

"All these women fighting over you, Jake." Louis said, "What's your secret, old man?" He looked to me again, checking to see if he had upset me. I think he wanted to.

"Michelle just wants control. Christ, she's living with Mike." I knew that Jake was thinking about Toby, what the long-term ramifications were of his mother going back to jail.

"When's that ever stopped her." Louis said. "Think of the recording as a parting gift."

"No, Louis." Jake said, "You are going to take it to the police, and not because it has leverage for you, but because it's the right thing to do, and because Sophie is the mother of your son and someone has just threatened her life. You think Michelle will stop? She gets what she wants eventually, her father has enough money to ensure it."

Louis' good mood plummeted like a frightened myotonic goat (you know, one of those fainting ones). "I fucking know that, Jake."

Under my breath, I said, "I hate her. Don't tell Toby. Louis, you take that to the police. I'm taking it to the police too.

Promise me." I demanded.

"I will." He said, rolling his eyes like we were all being unreasonable.

More than willing to agree, I said, "Can we change the subject? Talking about Michelle gives me hives. How do you two know each other?"

This time Tyler brightened and I figured this would be a funny story.

"Remember how I got kicked out of school, when I was like six?"

"No, I would've been four."

"Oh, right. Well, I was a horrible little shit, copying Dad like crazy, wanting him to pay me attention, or show that he loved me, even slightly. I hit some kids and got kicked out of school. I was sent to that better school on the other side of town, Mum was pissed about it and refused to take me. Lazy bitch. I had to bike all that way. I met Louis there on my first day. We were best friends straight away, right?" He asked Louis who nodded while my jaw was somewhere near the floor. I had no idea of this. "He was the one that told me to stop hitting people, that I should play rugby instead. It got most of the aggression out of me. Dad even came and watched a few games, then said I wasn't going to be famous. What a fucking asshole, I was an angry little kid. I told Louis I was running away."

"I didn't believe you." Louis said, "Or I thought the cops would bring you back. Kids were always running away, and they always turned up. It's New Zealand, how far could you get? Anyway, school was way more boring after you left." He smiled but there was real sadness there too. "I didn't even know you had sisters. All I knew was our fathers were friends and then you were gone. For a long time I thought your old man had caught you leaving and had hidden your dead body somewhere. Then I forgot all about you until that meeting in Adelaide."

"Meeting in Adelaide?" Jake asked, perplexed.

"Imports and Exports." Louis winked which I took to mean it was illegal, probably drugs. "I recognized Tyler as soon as we were introduced."

"But how did you know you were both undercover?" I asked, perplexed at the secrets and the links that kept pulling us all back together.

"Why else would we be using fake last names?" Louis said on a shrug.

"You could have changed it for a million different reasons?" I said.

"There were rumors." Louis said, "There's always rumors about anyone who comes in without family history or links."

Fists clenching again, Tyler said to Louis, "Then you stepped up your game." To me he added, "I thought he was going for the Toa's territory. I was relieved, he would push them away from Australia and keep them focused here. Then I hear he's joining them."

"Business was booming." Louis said, eyes squeezing as if his head hurt.

"I expected you to give me up to get more leverage in Australia." Tyler said.

"I did." Louis answered, lifting his hands in surrender, amused when Tyler took several aggressive steps toward him. "Sort of. The new commissioner was pushing me hard, saying Sheppard was going down, that I would have to do jail time to appease the public if my identity got out. I mentioned that I knew about others in Australia and I would name names for time off my sentence."

"I fucking knew it!" Tyler yelled, gaze cutting to Jake who had stood to protect Louis. Reverting to their old roles and scaring the shit out of me. I forget what Jake did sometimes.

"You gave me no choice." Louis assured him. "People were talking. I heard some kid was going to take you out to claim your place. You know how it works."

"So ruining my life actually saved it?" Tyler spat, the clear glint of fear obvious.

"Yes. You can thank me some other time." Louis said. "Your idiot father was talking already, so I knew you were done.

Elias wanted to use you as leverage. Said he had found out his son was undercover and unless he was let out early he would start whispering in ears. You need to work out who had been talking before me. You got a new boyfriend?"

"A husband." Tyler sagged, imagining who had ratted him out and devastated by the obvious person.

"Jesus." I said. "That horrible old goat that we call our father doesn't know when to quit. He would never have forgiven you for being in the police."

Jake was outraged. "Is that why your parents hated you? Because you're a cop?"

Tyler laughed bitterly. "They hated me for as long as I can remember for being gay. I always knew I preferred boys and that was never going to be accepted. I would've changed if I could but I couldn't so I had to find a way out." His gaze flicked to Louis, "Don't worry, I wasn't looking at you or anything."

On a smile, Louis said, "Only because Jake wasn't around to steal my thunder."

"I was a little kid, terrified of being found out, that Dad would shoot me in the head for besmirching his great name. Fuck he is a loser. I got in touch with Uncle Reuben and he paid for my flight and agreed to take me in. He was still stunned when I called him from the airport in Sydney but agreed that our folks would never bother trying to find me, not overseas." He sighed, "I had a decent life over there. I don't quite know how it's all fallen apart so badly."'

"Why did you become a cop?" I asked him.

"To piss the old man off." His smile was sad. "Or maybe not. Probably same reason Louis did, for some stability, a family. When the offer of undercover work came up I knew I'd be good at it. With my upbringing, integrating into groups of nasty fuckers was natural."

"Yeah, being in there's the easy part." Louis agreed, rubbing his eyes that were bloodshot and heavy lidded. He was deathly pale too. "Getting out is what takes balls."

"Are you all right, Louis?" Jake asked, his concern ramping up my own.

"Just feeling a little lightheaded."

I moved around the table to push him back against the dining chair. That he let me manhandle him without a fuss was deeply concerning too. Touching the edges of the tape covering his wound, I said, "This is really infected. You need antibiotics today. Jake, can you take him to a doctor?"

"Sure, if we're finished here?" He looked from me to Louis then to Tyler, all of us nodding. "This is not a dumping ground." He added, pointing a finger at Louis then Tyler in turn. "You two will respect this space. Sophie and I are trying to make a life for your family. You are both welcome here, but you can't just show up when you feel like it. There are routines and plans in place, if you want to come, call ahead."

Someone knocked at the door then and on a frown Jake opened it to Uncle Reuben who took one look at Tyler, let out a long gasp of worry, clutched his chest, saying, "Thank fuck." Then he collapsed, thudding through the door and landing on the mat.

Tyler raced for him, weeping openly by the time he was kneeling at Rueben's side.

Then Louis stood, gasped in shock then dead fainted over the dining room table. I helped him slide to the floor, pushing him into the recovery position while Jake lifted his phone to call an ambulance.

To Tyler, I said, "Is Rueben breathing?"

"Yeah, and pulse is okay, a little erratic."

"I'm on hold." Jake said, his stern working demeanor in place. To Tyler he added, "Just in case, do you know CPR?" Tyler nodded and I sent a quick message to my sister, telling her I would be a little longer and to put a bottle of wine in the fridge. I had so much to tell her.

Jake and I eyed each other as Jake connected to the ambulance service, explaining that there were two men collapsed. As he slipped his phone onto the bench, he said, "Your family sucks."

"Sorry." I said, "Hang on, no I'm not. You married Michelle and have a crazy stalker who is going to need a stern talking to. I think we're equal."

He bent down and helped Louis to sit. "Stay there, pal. Ambulance is coming." Louis tried to argue but after struggling to stand agreed to be propped up in a sofa chair until he was bundled off to the hospital for IV antibiotics and fluids. Apparently he didn't drink water because it was tasteless. What an idiot.

◆ ◆ ◆

L ater that night I knew that Louis had ended up with seven stitches and Uncle Reuben needed a stent for a blocked artery. Tyler was beside himself, claiming he had almost lost the only person that had ever stood by him (he had never given Jenny or me a chance to stand by him, but whatever) and had decided he was going to get out of the police. He even talked about studying with Louis. He was yet to understand that Louis didn't share the limelight and that they both worked solo. They would figure it out.

With all the upheaval and stress it took me a few more days before I had the opportunity to contact the local police over Darling Roach, Jake's newest stalker. There had been a few more notes in the letterbox but my new friend and neighbor, Arthur Lynes had scared her away a few times. I had remembered the eye drops for his cat (I had stolen them out of Finn's storage cupboard in his garage, leaving a note to up his security game. I could imagine his outrage when he found it in the future).

"She is certified batshit." Arthur laughed. "That last time, when I told her I had called the cops, and that stalking wasn't attractive, she gave me the finger like a teenager. I told her the whole neighborhood was watching that letterbox and getting photos for the cops."

"She must be coming at nighttime now." I said, shivering at the idea of a stranger stumbling around in the dark outside our home while the kids slept.

It made me a little more anxious about leaving the house with Jax for a walk but I did it anyway, refusing to be scared by some new nutty person who was trying to push their way into my life. Jake and I deserved to be happy and boring.

Louis had not called to check on his son but was in contact with Jake, I figured they were working on the upcoming court cases.

Jake was busy with school drop off's and running with Sarge. We were fostering dogs for the police who wanted Jake as a trainer but he was in no rush to decide, happy to be around the house as we made alterations, transforming it to fit our needs.

We found out that Louis had given his awful recording to the police when Michelle was arrested and returned to jail for trying to hire someone to kill me. She was undergoing psychological help and I hoped never to see her again. The police had talked to me but there was little I could offer since Michelle had rarely spoken to me. I was just a face, a new barrier to her control over Jake. Her father had called Jake, crying and begging him to find a way to get that taped conversation erased. Jake said there was nothing he could do, that this time Michelle was going to have to face her problems alone. Her father then insisted on paying for therapy costs for Toby, to ensure he was not damaged by his mother. Jake agreed to a few sessions which had surprised me. Toby was enthusiastic, treating them like a holiday since he got a few hours off school.

Mike was devastated that Michelle had ruined their new life together over her ex. He was kicked out of the house by Michelle's father who still owned it, so Mike had moved in with their old police friend Samson. Within a week Mike suffered three broken ribs and a shattered nose after hitting on Samson's wife Abigail. It was sad enough that I didn't find it funny while

Jake thought Mike needed help, that he was purposely destroying every good relationship he had, pushing everyone away to feed some lonely need.

I knew Mike better now, saw past that magnificent face and body to the lost and lonely man beneath. Mike liked beautiful woman, he loved broken ones even more.

Thankfully I was neither and Mike was not ever going to be my problem.

CHAPTER TWENTY-FOUR

I discovered Louis had applied for a divorce from Keisha when she arrived at my door, poised and looking better than ever. She took one look at me and burst into tears, her black mascara ruining the effect she had been attempting to create.

"You can't have him." She said on a heavy breath.

"Who?" I barked, knowing she meant Louis but refusing to be drawn into her drama.

"Louis. He's mine and you need to leave him alone or I'll hurt you. He's a married man, you should be ashamed of yourself."

"Where's Savvy?" I asked rolling my eyes in a way that caused Keisha to frown. Had she had Botox? Her forehead crinkled strangely. I looked behind Keisha for her daughter. "Have you changed her name yet?"

"Her name is Sauvignon and she's with my mother. I give Mum a few bottles of wine and she looks after her for two days while I'm at work." The thought of Brenda Bright looking after a baby gave me hives but people could change, and as much as Keisha was a pain in my butt she was loyal when she chose to be and so far had given no indication that she was a bad mother, just the opposite. Except calling her kid Sauvignon. That was unforgivable and a joke too far. As for Brenda, some shitty parents made great grandparents (my own mother hadn't been) and who was I to judge?

I ushered her inside and made tea while Keisha calmed down and fixed her makeup.

To take her mind of Louis, I said, "One thing has always bothered me. Why do you have a different name from your family?" Keisha and I could have been related by law if I had of gone through with marrying her shitty brother Nathan. That was one bullet I had thankfully dodged.

She tried to stare me down before remembering that I knew her better than that and she sagged, saying, "Fine. I was married when I was eighteen. His name was Justice Monk and he was like seven foot tall. When we met I asked if he played basketball . . ."

"Because what else would a tall person do?" I was being snide but Keisha missed it.

"Exactly."

"And I'm sure he had never heard that one before." I added, certain that this time she would understand what I was trying to say. "About being tall."

"She never cared what other people said or thought. I wished for that level of self-confidence. "Anyway," She said, like she was sick of me interrupting. "He *did* play basketball and said he had just signed a contract with an American team and that if I married him I could live with him over there. Imagine it, away from my family, a new life, all that money."

"Wow, I guess you changed your mind?"

"We had a nice little wedding, he promised me something fancy when he got paid and we moved. But he lied. I thought he was in the NBA, instead we were living on a big campus, me sitting alone all day in a shitty apartment while he went to practice. So after a week I got on a plane and came home. He sent divorce papers years later. I kept his name since I had my passport and a few credit cards in Monk."

"You know it's a big deal to get into the university basketball teams, that the NBA scouts go watch them?"

She shrugged and unable to help myself I Googled Justice Monk, quickly turning my phone off when I saw a photo of a huge, muscly guy, half naked with a basketball and a supermodel on his arm on the cover of some famous sports magazine. That would not help Keisha, but she really was her own worst enemy most of the time.

"How's the new clinic?" I asked instead.

"Better since Finn left. They're easy to organize."

I smiled, desperate to pass this on to Finn who would be delighted to hear that clinic was now under Keisha's maniacal rule.

"Keisha." I said, stern at her anxious pacing. "What's going on?"

"Louis wants a divorce and I know it's because of you."

"Nope, nothing to do with me. He's working with Jake to sort out all his legal problems but he's ignoring me and his son. Leave me out of this. I'm going back to work soon and I live with Jake. If you come between us again I won't be so forgiving."

She was confused and trying to hide it, "I'm pregnant again." She stated.

"Congratulations?" It sounded like a question due to her uncertainty.

"Thanks. I haven't had a chance to tell Louis yet. I thought he must be with you. I forgot about Jake. Rumor has it he's getting rehired by the cops?"

"How do you find all this stuff out?"

"I know people, and I always ask about you."

"Well, stop it. I'm just a regular mother now. I don't want anything to do with your life with Louis. Keep me out of it. He's all yours."

Her glare was cutting but I had years of experience with it to fall back on and just stared in return. Eventually Keisha saw what she needed and changed the subject, her way of saying that she believed me and that she forgave me any slights. "Who's the bitch hanging around outside? Is that Louis' new woman? He always has one."

"What do you mean? What woman?" I was instantly on hyperalert, thinking of Michelle out there, ready to finish me off for taking Jake.

"There's some skank walking up and down your street. I know because I was out there waiting for an hour, hoping to catch Louis sneaking around."

"He'd be here to see Jake, not me." I rubbed sweaty hands on my shorts. The winter was mild so far but I knew that once the rain started properly it wouldn't stop for long weeks. "Do you think its Jake's ex-wife? He picked up a stalker when we were in the South Island too. They both think I'm keeping them apart."

"Fucking crazy bitches. South Island was months ago." Keisha could not see that she was doing the same thing about me and Louis.

"This is escalating." I said, remembering that Michelle was either in jail or a psych unit. It was Darling Roach and she was out in daylight watching the house like a demented Batman, no longer caring that the neighbors might see her.

"I know." Keisha said, "Louis is up to no good."

On a sigh, I said, "This has nothing to do with Louis. I told you I haven't seen him, Keisha. Get your shit together. I'm calling the cops again. Jesus, I'm like a prisoner in this house. Why couldn't I be attracted to an accountant? Why couldn't Darling be attracted to an accountant back in Grafton." Tears were threatening but there was too much to do.

"What's her story?" Keisha asked, waving me to follow her to the front of the house. Without asking she entered my bedroom and peered out the window toward the road.

"Not sure." I said, unwilling to discuss one crazy woman with another. "She's older, about fifty-five, I found out she had affairs back in Grafton, she blackmails her way into men's lives then won't be shifted."

"Is she blackmailing Jake?" Keisha used a nail to hold back the curtain, whispering as if we could be overheard, the gleam in her eye showing she was enjoying this.

"He wouldn't even go on a date with her. She broke into our house almost naked, threatened me, told Jake if he dumped me she would ensure Toby became president of the world or something. She was Toby's school receptionist."

Keisha's pretty button nose curled, "I hate her."

"You and me both."

"If she ruins your relationship with Jake you'll want Louis back." She stated.

"Oh my god, Keisha. I don't want Louis back."

"You say that now. But my life is infinitely easier if your happy with the hunk."

"Yes, okay. Fine. Whatever. Anyway I'm calling the cops and I don't think you want to be here when they arrive. Is there anything else you need?"

Keisha's eyes lit up and I followed her gaze to find a young woman with a tight little body stuffed into activewear stride past the house. Keisha was out the door like a shot as I called, "No, that's not her. Darling has a blond bob."

The woman striding by had long dark hair tied into a loose plait down her back, mirrored aviator sunglasses covering half her face.

I dithered at the doorway as Keisha sprinted up behind the stranger, hauled one of her arms up her back and frog marched the woman to my house. Keisha might be vain and self-obsessed but she was also tough and not to be crossed.

At the door, Keisha said brightly, "Look, Sophie. I found a guest."

I waved them inside, about to apologize to this stranger until Keisha tugged at the dark hair. My apology froze as a wig slid away to show blond hair combed back to a small ponytail at the base of Darling's neck. Before she could speak, Keisha slapped her across the face, the sound reverberating in my head. I just stood there blinking in the hallway like an idiot, hoping Jax remained happy crawling around the living room a little longer. It was getting close to lunch and his routine was not to be trifled with.

Darling reeled from Keisha's unexpected slap and thudded into the wall, holding her face, eyes wide with shock.

"Who are you?" She asked then burst into tears that were as fake as she was.

"Sophie and I are best friends." Keisha said down her nose. We all know that was an outright lie but I still just stood there, numb and confused at how this had escalated so quickly. "You are going to leave Jake alone?" Keisha added.

"I . . . I don't know what you're talking about." Darling stuttered.

On a snort of amusement, Keisha was at her confident and most intimidating best as she growled. "Yeah you do. If I ever see you anywhere near that hunky bastard again I'm going to come down to shitsville Grafton and hunt down every one of your friends and every one of your family and every man you've ever tried to steal off some hardworking woman. I'm going to talk to every one of them and I'll tell them how you're a man, how you're a man and how you got me pregnant."

Both Darling and I dumbly stared at Keisha.

Darling said, "You're supposed to say you're going to kill everyone I love."

Keisha's pretty face pursed like she had bitten into a lemon. "Do I look like I should be in prison? All those women would fight over me, just like those reality shows." Sometimes I really had no idea what went on in Keisha's head. Her next sentence highlighted that. "Prison carbs would ruin my figure and I'll blame you completely, even if you're dead I'll ruin your life, I'll stalk you on Facebook, Insta, Twitter. I'll start a social media storm with photos of you naked from when you were a kid. Those men you've been blackmailing will tell me things about you and I'll fill my blog with what a skank you are. I'll pour sugar in your gas tank, I'll stuff dead fish under your carpet. Trust me, I'll make your life a living hell." She smiled then, friendly and encouraging, "Or you can just leave Jake alone, go back to Smallville in nowhere land and I'll forget I ever saw your face. What say you?"

With her hands on her hips, Keisha waited for the reply.

As the confused silence extended, I whispered to Keisha, "You never did those vindictive things to me."

"You were my boss." She said like I was stupid, not taking her eyes of Darling.

"I thought she was your best friend." Darling gathered herself, brushing back stray wisps of hair from one cheek.

"Shut the fuck up." Keisha growled. "The big girls are talking here." She glanced at her watch, adding, "Actually, we need to wrap this up, I've got to get to work." She then quirked a perfectly sculpted eyebrow at Darling and repeated, "What say you?"

Taking a long breath, Darling pulled herself up to her full height, which wasn't very impressive and said, "I can fuck you over faster, bitch."

Keisha's eyes sparked with delight and she struck out, grabbing Darling by the hair at her temple and dragging her head into a wall.

"Jesus!" I hissed, just as Jax crawled around the corner to join the fun, his little face wide with excitement. There was no way I was letting my son see this, even if he was too young to remember it.

Snatching him off the ground, I returned him to the living room and closed the door while Keisha smacked Darling against the wall a few more times.'

"I don't think you understand what I'm trying to tell you, Miss Clueless." Keisha hissed at the shorter woman. "Probably because you're an uneducated ass-wipe while Sophie and I are educated women." Keisha then asked me. "What does she do?" Jax thumped into the door and started crying, his angry cry, it was fascinating to me that I could tell the difference now.

"She's a primary school receptionist and she more or less ran the rodeos."

"Rodeos." Keisha laughed, "Do you think you're in the American wild west? What the fuck is wrong with you? Don't you know those animals have feelings too? Jesus, I'm amazed Sophie hasn't stabbed you."

"The rodeo got cancelled." I clarified, not wanting Keisha to think I was going soft. "She told everyone it was my fault. That's why me and Jake had to come back. We lost our jobs, and our rental was getting graffitied with blood and stuff."

"You didn't know your place." Darling cried, collapsing to the ground, only looking up when Keisha said, "Smile." And snapped a few photos on her phone.

Jax was really losing his mind now so I opened the door, lifting him off the ground where he looked at the two women with interest, his tears gone.

"Damn, that kid's cute." Keisha said, "Not as cute as Sauvignon. I'm putting her in a modelling agency."

"Naturally." I said. "Maybe I should bring Pothead over? He's like a guard dog that doesn't need walking. Even Sarge is scared of him."

"Yeah." Keisha agreed. "I sure miss that big furry asshole." She sounded wistful. "He'd kill this bitch, especially since she looks like that pot smoking Michelle. You ever met Jake's ex-wife?" Keisha grinned at Darling, "She's pretty and crazy. She will cut your throat just for looking at her ex. Sophie's already living on the edge."

Darling did look like an older, blonder version of Michelle. "Pothead doesn't like living with me." I said, "You should have seen the mess he made of my old apartment. And he's obsessed with my sister Jenny and her kids. Not Finn, he hates Finn and tries to sit on his face when he's asleep."

This made Keisha laugh hard, "I can just picture that. I do kind of miss Finn even though he is a grumpy troll. I don't know why he left that cruisy clinic." I didn't mention that Finn and I were going back into business again, terrified Keisha would say she was coming back to work with us. Instead I said, "What do we do with her?" I pointed at Darling.

"Oh, yeah." Keisha thought for a minute. "Should I call Nathan? He can hide her body in the bush somewhere. Hope you don't mind seeing your ex."

"I'd rather not have Nathan knowing where I live." I felt sick at the idea.

"But my brother loves women like this. These batshit types never know when they aren't wanted."

My mouth was too quick to stop me saying, "Like you and Louis."

"That's different. We're meant to be together." Keisha assured me.

Jiggling Jax, wanting these women gone so I could feed him and put him down for a nap, I said, "Don't call Nathan. I know who to call. The perfect person to sort this out."

Mike arrived ten minutes later since he was nearby. Darling took one look at him and swooned, declaring that she had seen Jesus. Mike really was terrifically handsome and he loved dramatic women, no matter how much he denied it. He was single until Michelle was let out. I was hoping Michelle and Darling would then spend so much time trying to kill each other they would leave me and Jake alone.

Keisha sadly shook her head at Darling and said, "Fucking checkmate, bitch."

CHAPTER
TWENTY-FIVE

Later that afternoon, Toby was home from school, doing homework, sitting across from Jake who was busy emailing at the kitchen table. Jax was wobbling around the living room with me hovering over him in case he got more bruises from falling over.

Jake said, "He's got to learn, Sophie."

"Tomorrow." I assured, smiling at Jax as I stopped him from falling backward and into the coffee table (that was going to be burned), "Tomorrow afternoon to be precise."

"Why?" He cringed like he wasn't sure what I would say.

"The community nurse is coming. I don't want him looking like we all beat him up."

"He's an early walker. Those nurses have seen it all before."

I knew he was right but just couldn't leave Jax to headbutt every pointy thing that passed his cute little head. Toby flicked on the television after saying he had finished his homework, and hearing his voice Jax stared for long enough that Toby pulled him onto the couch beside him and they had a weird babbling conversation. I told Jake I would cook, the living and kitchen an open plan room meaning I could keep an eye on the boys while I worked, until my phone buzzed and I answered without checking the ID. Would I ever learn?

A familiar woman's voice said, "Sophie, please don't hang up."

"Who is this?" I asked, the sharpness of my voice turning Jake's head.

"It's Dahlia Doyle from Grafton." She said then waited as if expecting me to hang up. I should have but something made me hang on the line.

Eventually, I said, "We don't have nothing to say to each other. I left Grafton because no one wanted us there, they would rather believe some crazy woman's lies than admit the rodeo was barbaric bullshit."

"I just wanted you to know that Darling Roach has disappeared." She paused, waiting again but this time I refused to speak, so she added, "She took a shine to your boyfriend and I've discovered a few things about her that I thought you should know."

"You're too late, she followed us here." I sighed, "I've sorted it out." I winked at Jake who had been horrified when I retold the afternoon hijinks with Keisha. I thought it was a whole heap funnier than Jake did who called Mike to ask him what happened. Mike had been cagey which I knew meant he was smitten too. It gave me the shivers.

Dahlia continued, still hesitant but determined. "I want to explain why I did it, the animal smuggling. That you think so badly of me is really playing on my mind. No matter what you think, I did like you. Not for ruining my business but it was going to happen, it was my own stupid fault for getting greedy. Maybe I wanted to get caught."

"Don't forget how you grabbed my son and tried to use him as ransom. I sure can't."

"I panicked." She argued, "I just wanted to get out of there and get on my plane. I would never have hurt your baby. I swear it."

"Look, say what you need to but make it quick. I've got to make dinner." Jake came up behind me and took the wooden spoon from my hand, kissed my head and pushed me toward the dining table. Jax was back on the floor, using the coffee table like a tunnel and smiling at Toby who gave up his cartoon to join in. Sarge peered at them from outside, a silent sentinel beyond the closed French doors, chewing on a giant bone and contemplating the world. It was a nice, normal family scene, exactly what I wanted from my life.

And here was someone from the past coming to haunt me again.

Dahlia began, "My husband Baron died the same day I found out that he had been having an affair. I barely got the chance to yell at him when he curled up and dropped dead right in front of me. I called the ambulance and they discovered later that he had taken a whole heap of his prescription meds all at once. Must have been the knowledge that I wouldn't forgive his betrayal."

There was a pause and I quietly asked, "Did *you* do it? Did *you* give him those pills?"

Another pause then she replied, "Anyway, I stayed in town because I wanted to know who it was, who my Baron had been sleeping with when he didn't even take me out for a meal. Nothing. I could never find out then all this happens with you and me getting caught with the eggs and suddenly Darling has left town. Everyone is talking about her. It's like her evil spell has been broken and I've found out she was blackmailing men, a couple of school principals, a few farmers and councilors. She was a busy woman."

"What's this got to do with me? She wasn't blackmailing Jake because he refused to be alone with her. She was angry and bitter that he wouldn't do what she wanted." I turned to Jake who rolled his eyes. "Do you think she was having the affair with your husband?"

"Possibly, although I can't imagine what she would have been blackmailing him about. Don't get me wrong, I loved my husband but he was a lazy son of a bitch. That he was boning someone else when he couldn't be bothered with me just frizzles my brain."

"She is very inventive and perhaps he never did anything. She broke into our house in her underwear. I'm guessing if Jake wasn't up to the task she would have just taken some photos to make it look like he was. Like you said, she enjoyed a spot of blackmail."

"Then why would my Baron have gobbled all those pills?" There was a hitch to her voice, like she had just heard something she had never thought of. Perhaps Baron knew his wife was not the type to forgive or hear reason.

"Only you can answer that."

"I need time to think about that and it isn't why I'm calling. Those eggs I took, I don't just *take* them somewhere, I bring them back with me too. From the Islands, Samoa, Tonga but mainly from Australia. When Darling took off I knew she had a couple of snakes as pets because I had given her the eggs."

My eyes shut and I knew I was about to hear things that would piss me off. "Don't try and tell me you were worried about those animals. I know plenty of those eggs don't make it to their destination. Most get crushed or the heating goes wrong."

She laughed then, deep and throaty like she had been caught out. "You got me. I know a guy who would buy those snakes in a second. If someone broke into her house it's not my problem. She should've been home instead of chasing some young guy with kids."

"Can you get to the point? I've got a baby here that loses his shit if I'm late with his dinner."

"I'm telling you this because I figure you might be able to let the right people know."

"Know what?" I barked, wanting to get to the point of this conversation.

She continued as if I hadn't spoken. "How can I tell the cops, especially here in Grafton, without admitting I had been there this morning?"

"You broke into her house this morning?" My voice went

up a few octaves.

"How else was I going to steal . . . I mean, save those poor snakes."

"Rumor has it," Her voice was getting irritated now and I knew to keep quiet or she would never admit what was going on in Grafton. "Not that I would know for sure but I heard that the back of her house has big garages that are loaded to the gunnels with pregnant dogs and cats, that there's puppies and kittens of all breeds in there. Even bunnies and rats."

I had discovered where Darling lived before we left Grafton, feeling it was in my interest to know my enemy's territory. "But behind her house is all Department of Conservation land." I said, my skin tingling uncomfortably.

"And her sheds are hidden right at the tree line. I imagine anyone who thought to investigate what those buildings were doing on that land were hounded into the ground until they shut their traps."

"Are you telling me that Darling is running a pet mill?" The world shot into clear focus. I could see Jake, his back muscles flexing through his white tee as he worked at the bench, still making my stomach clench with lust. I could hear the boys giggling and Sarge's bone knocking against the door as he chewed. I could smell spices and feel that my feet were cold, but it was all in the background of my awareness, my full concentration taken up by what Dahlia was telling me, what I didn't want to hear.

"You've seen how she dresses, the fancy cars she drives, all that makeup and those jewels. Where else would she get all that money from? It sure ain't from working at a school, the government pay is shit."

"Were those men paying her to keep quiet?"

"Yeah, there's probably that too. She might be a bitch but she isn't dumb."

"How big are we talking? How many animals?"

Dahlia's chuckle sounded awfully close to being impressed with Darling and made me hate them both all over again. I bit it down for information. I could bury her later.

"Biggest I've ever heard of." Dahlia clicked her tongue, probably frustrated that she hadn't thought of puppy mills. I would have to talk to the SPCA in Grafton. Willow Otto liked to talk but she was kind and obsessed with animals for all the right reasons. She would keep an eye on Dahlia since I was gone.

"That's impossible. Who was helping her?"

"She approached Harley."

"I knew he was bad." I interrupted.

"Jesus, let me finish before you show off your prejudice. Harley told her to get lost, that he wouldn't deliver animals. To be honest, it was probably because he's a little agoraphobic and scared of dogs."

Pushing aside my guilt, I asked, "What should I do?"

"First, go check out her online info." She then gave me a few websites, mostly ones that allowed online animal sales (they would be hearing about this), she also gave me the name of a big pet store chain, claiming that the sheds were lined with cages ready to be filled with pets destined for their stores.

I took a few long breaths, calming my mind, slowly blowing out while I thought. Jake studied me with suspicion and I tried to reassure him with a small smile, but this was bad and I would have to fix it.

"Do you have her physical address? It'll save me time when I call the cops since I can't remember it." As we said our goodbyes, I asked, "What's in this for you?"

"Have some faith in human kindness." At my silence she added, "Alright, when those pedigree pets turn up at the SPCA I might be able to turn a profit."

"Over my dead body." I growled. "I'll get an assurance from the SPCA that you can't have any of them, you're a convicted animal smuggler."

"We'll see. Don't forget everyone here hates you for ruining the rodeo."

"I didn't ruin the pissing rodeo." I hissed, squeezing the phone enough that the plastic creaked. "It was Darling Roach.

She had been trying to screw Rick Mussett, the president, she gave up on him and without her input the rodeo fell apart on its own, because rodeos are shit and people don't even think about why they go."

"You might be right. We just had an animal free event in its place. It was still called a rodeo so the hillbillies didn't get confused. Instead of animals there was blow up castles and mechanical bulls. It was a hit. The rodeo committee made more money than ever in booze sales alone since there wasn't all the overheads."

"That's what I was trying to say. People don't give a crap about the rodeo, they just want an outing. You could have a Tibetan throat singer in a paddock with a PA system, so long as there's a bar it would be busy."

"You're preaching to the converted, bossy britches. I just thought you would like to be in the loop about Darling Roach."

"Have you taken those snakes already?" I asked. "Why would you ring me now?"

"You have no faith in people. That's a real shortcoming."

"There aren't that many people who deserve my faith." I told her, noticing Jake's chuckle of amusement. "Put them back or I'll tell the cops you have them."

"They won't care."

"I'm going to call them now."

"They won't listen to you."

"Yes they will. You're just trying to find out what I'm going to do first. You knew Willow at the SPCA would call me as soon as she found out." I closed my eyes, trying to work out exactly what Dahlia wanted out of me. Did she want me to call the cops so she didn't have to do it? Was she as horrible as I had built her up in my mind? "The cops will listen to me." I assured her, "Or I know someone who will ensure they do." I winked at Jake who smiled, that mouthwatering one that gave me butter-flies in my stomach.

"I liked shifting those eggs. It was easy money."

"Do you understand the damage that is caused by taking

those eggs from the ecosystem? Do you want there to be none left in the wild?"

"Just hatch some more." She sniffed.

"It's not that simple. Think of Kea, they are crazy smart parrots who need their parents to ensure they know how to be a wild bird."

"Oh, I see what you mean. I guess I hadn't thought about it that way."

"Are you going to prison for smuggling those eggs?" I already knew the answer.

"No, home detention. I'm on supervision and not allowed to travel. I had to give my wheelchair back since the doctors could find no reason for me to use it. That means I've lost my disability parking which is a hassle at the supermarket."

"Oh man, I can't even deal with all that right now. Just stay away from animals then we'll never need to deal with each other again. And put those snakes back before the cops get there or I'll come back to Grafton myself and get them off you."

"That's not very nice." I could imagine her pout. "I liked you."

"Do you mean that?"

"Well, you bought stuff off me and I liked that."

"That's not very nice of *you*."

"I'm just trying to earn a living. I'm a woman on my own."

"You run a successful business. Enjoy that."

"But my van costs a lot to run."

"You don't need a van." I was exasperated. "Sell the van and buy a little car."

"I can't stand little cars. They have no point. One more thing." She said and I sighed.

"What?"

"Why did you sell all my stuff back to Concise Consignments?"

"Because they were open after Jake and I were run out of town. The stuff either went to Concise or it went to the dump. You weren't there. You were in jail for smuggling native eggs.

Being loyal to you was not and won't ever be high on my priority list again."

"Oh, I see. Still, it was a little mean."

Frustrated, feeling like I was in the Twilight Zone, I hung up on her, then feeling bad I called back, saying, "You cut out. Thank you for the information about Darling. I've dealt with people like her before. It doesn't end well, so I appreciate that you made the call." I was thinking about my sister's little pug dog Captain Pugwash and the old woman I had taken him off. Years before she had been convicted of animal abuse, for leaving her sweet dog Daisy chained under her house for five weeks while she visited her brother. I had looked after Daisy at the end and finding the woman with Captain Pugwash had ended in me and Jake being pepper sprayed by the supposedly kind old lady.

"I don't want to think of all those little kitty's suffering, not the dogs, I hate dogs. I'm a cat person."

"They all depend on humans for survival. It's what we wanted."

"Keep your pants on. Oh, and don't let the cops tell you that they're busy. They have a retirement party later tonight and every cop in Grafton is decorating the hall, even the ones in uniform and the ones that should be making sure no one speeds. You know how many people die on the roads down here? It's criminal."

"You're more upset about that than the animals, aren't you?"

"People are more important than animals."

"We're all animals." I said on a long groan then quickly said goodbye. Without giving myself time to gather my thoughts I contacted the police in Grafton, crying when they claimed they were unable to attend for a few days. I guess they were factoring in hangovers.

I called the SPCA, speaking to my friend, Willow Otto. She was the senior administrator and one of the few people actually paid to be there.

Willow was happy to hear from me, saying, "Sophie, I

don't care what anyone says, I'm delighted you blew that rodeo apart."

"It really wasn't me. It was Darling Roach, that's who I'm calling about."

"You wouldn't have heard but she disappeared, apparently ran off to Auckland with some ex-police hunk. Didn't you live with that hunky ex-policeman?"

"One and the same guy. She's stalking us."

Willow wasn't even surprised. "She sure is batshit crazy. Everyone's talking about how she was blackmailing people. Never a dull moment. And I've had so many people in saying how glad they are that the rodeo is done. Did you hear about the fair? Roaring success and just between you and me, I bet there are a ton of babies in nine months, if you know what I'm saying."

Like I said, Willow loves to talk and I cut her off by quickly running through the probable pet mill out the back of Darling's property. She was suitably upset and said she needed to talk with the manager and that she would call me back. I reiterated that it was urgent, that the police were trying to wait a few days because of a retirement party. Then I begged her to let me know what was happening, that if things were stalling or they needed a vet to check the animals I could be down there by tomorrow. She assured me they would be fine, that my presence might cause more problems.

So I returned to being a mum, eating, giving Jax a bath, listening to Toby reading a book, but my mind was in Grafton, worrying about those animals.

As I got ready for bed I received a text from Willow saying they had assessed the farm and removed all the animals, calling in most of the community to help foster them all until they could fully assess the situation. Willow was driving to neighboring towns collecting as much pet food as she could get her hands on and the police had put out an arrest warrant for Darling Roach. That little bug was about to be stomped on.

Thankfully Toby was in bed because I burst into tears, showing Jake the message when I couldn't explain it all.

Jake smiled as he hugged me close, "You did it again, Sophie Carter."

CHAPTER TWENTY-SIX

Then life went on, it was busy, hectic, fun with bouts of frustration. Like most lives. I would easily say I had never been happier and living with Jake was natural and easy.

It was a week after Jax's second birthday before I saw Louis again. He turned up unannounced when we were at Jenny and Finn's for dinner, claiming Jake had invited him.

Jake shook his head and asked for my phone, saying to Louis, "Are you tracking both of us or just Sophie?"

Louis shrugged and smiled. He looked different, that nervous edge was gone and he had gained some weight. It suited him.

He was delighted to see Jax but when he tried to hold him, Jax just cried and wanted to run around. Louis looked sad so I tried to take his mind off it.

"How's Keisha and the kids?"

"Good. We're trying to sort it all out."

"Might help if you stop travelling."

"I've got a career, Sophie. How else am I going to pay for these kids?"

"You don't pay for your kids." Jake said.

"And I know you were hiding money from your illicit life

for afterward." I added.

Jake groaned, "Please say that isn't true. You know they are going to hunt through your finances, like," He clicked his fingers, "Soph, give me a good animal metaphor."

"Oh, um, just say ferret through his finances."

"That works." Jake smiled, pleased with the statement.

"Don't you want Jax?" Louis grumbled and I had the urge to punch him.

"That's enough." I snapped.

"You ungrateful asshole." Jenny's shrill voice cut through the tension. "You should be thanking Jake for doing a job you were too hopeless to do yourself."

"I *am* grateful." Louis argued. "Jake knows that."

"How would I know that?" He said, "I don't want your shallow fucking gratitude. Just don't bring your shitty, self-obsessed arrogance around him."

"Alright, I'm sorry. Are you on your period, Jake?"

On an eyeroll, Jenny changed the subject. "How are all the court cases going?"

"Yeah, I wanted to know too." Finn said, sipping wine as Jenny handed Louis a beer.

"Almost there." Louis nodded to Jake.

"Are you still studying?" Jake asked, lifting Jax for a moment when the boy tried to climb him like playground equipment, sharing a quick hug before he put the wriggling boy back on the ground, watching him closely as he ran out the door to be with his cousins.

"Yeah, it's good, interesting." To me and Jenny he added, "Your brother got into the same course but hated Wellington. He moved back to Auckland. I hear his husband divorced him and remarried some millionaire."

"What about their kids?" I asked, feeling sad for the children I would never know.

"Not Tyler's and he didn't want much to do with them. The reason for the divorce."

"Really?" Jenny and I said at the same time, Jenny adding,

"Selfish asshole."

"He's been through enough." Louis said making me gasp, "Who are you?"

He chuckled, "After my media shitstorm I learned a little compassion."

Louis had been outed and dragged through a legal and social media scandal that was still ongoing. Personally, I think he liked it, he was getting speaking engagements, mainly at universities to discuss ethics and what he had been through, why he had gone undercover and what those sacrifices had done to him and his life. Like I said, I'm certain he loved it. Pretty girls and rapt audiences listening to him discuss his favorite topic, himself.

He had a book coming out soon and had sent me and Jake an early reader copy. It had been tricky reading over each other's shoulders so I had taken to reading aloud when we were in bed each night. We laughed more than not at Louis' antics. I was glad I hadn't known most of this stuff and I would keep this copy for Jax to read when he was old enough.

"I've got a favor to ask." Louis said to Jake, still not even looking at me which was stranger than usual for this deeply strange man.

"Depends what the favor is." Jake was wise to be suspicious.

"I need somewhere to crash when I'm in Auckland. The cost of hotels is killing me."

Jake stared at him for an extended beat, holding a hand up when I went to refuse. There was no way I wanted Louis and his crazy energy in our orderly, simple existence.

"No, Louis." Jake was calm but clear. "You have a wife in Auckland and a couple of little kids that could use your presence."

"But Keisha is too difficult to live with. She's great when I'm in Wellington, she comes down some weekends." He gulped his beer and looked around, "Don't judge me."

Finn laughed and after a moment Jenny joined in. "You

are such an idiot, Louis." She said. "I'm so glad my sister picked Jake."

It was tense until Jenny leaned over the table to open the lid on the meal she had prepared and the smell changed everyone's attitudes.

Louis ate like a starving man, soon asking Jake, "Did you hear Sheppard died?"

Jake was shocked. Sheppard had run the program that Jake and Louis had joined to go undercover and had pushed hard for Louis to keep getting information. Louis had taken down plenty of criminals but Sheppard was ruthless and hadn't cared at what cost. He had cared more about his own legacy than the men he was using. Jake had complained that Sheppard had scoffed at modern policing like it was a bad thing.

"I can't believe no one told me." Jake said, "Did you go to the funeral?"

Louis shook his head, still shoveling food in. "Closed funeral. His family said the cops had taken enough and they wouldn't give them anymore."

Jake sighed. "People like him should have been retired long ago."

"People like him forget that we are people too." Louis said, burping behind a fist. He offered to help with the dishes and I followed him into the kitchen. Not even thinking about being in close quarters with him.

He stacked the dishwasher, clearly unaccustomed to being domestic and it made me smile. When we had met he seemed above such trivial things. I guess we had all changed.

Checking we were unobserved, he said, "I miss you, Sophie."

His back was turned and it still sounded weird when he said my real name. He had called me Miss Doctor Doolittle from the beginning and I had grown to like it. A shared joke that spoke of history that wasn't all about fear and violence.

There was nothing to say so I pretended not to hear, turning to leave, deciding it was best if I just left him to finish cleaning alone.

"I'll get a divorce." He quietly added, peering out the window over the sink.

"More pointless words." I hissed, "I never thought I would be this happy. Don't ruin this for me. Keisha loves you more than I ever could. Be loyal for once, stop expecting more than your share. You're getting too old for this shit. Move on and grow up. Jake and Toby are in counseling for the bullshit you and Michelle pulled. Give us all a break and go away."

"You have my son."

"Then be my friend, that is all I can offer you." I frowned, thinking about the situation clearly, saying, "You know what, I don't need you as a friend. Be Jake's friend. He sacrificed for you and you're still trying to outdo him."

"This isn't a game." His voice was emotional and I didn't understand why.

"That's right. This is our lives and I'm telling you to go home to your wife and be a good husband and father." I knew this was hopeless but it reminded me to call Keisha. It was nice keeping in touch, hearing how she was going at her job. She made me laugh and I would tell her Louis had popped in. Secrets festered and I would not keep any for Louis.

Jake and I had made a pact that the only secrets we would keep were the kinky, embarrassing types. They were all ours.

Leaving the dishes, Louis made his excuses and readied to leave, shaking Finn's hand, pecking Jenny on the cheek, distractedly rubbing his son's head, then hugging Jake tight with more back slapping than I thought was necessary.

As I saw him to the door, Louis looked at me, his face creased with confusion. He stupidly said, "Sophie, you look different." He then winked, "Guess all the soft living with Jake is widening you out."

Jake covered his face while Finn hissed, "Do you want her to assassinate you?"

I just stood there with my mouth hanging open at how rude and self-absorbed Louis really was while Jenny barked,

"She's pregnant, you dumb ape."

He was genuinely stunned and I saw a flicker of hurt cross his face, but I might have been imagining that part.

"With twin girls." Jake finished. "She's due in eight weeks." He bit his lip as he looked at me again and I hated the worry that etched his face whenever the babies were mentioned. At first I thought he was worried how fat I would get or was terrified of having not one but two newborns, it sure scared the crap out of me. When I confronted him about it he had cried, big tears of worry that something might happen to me.

I had kissed away his tears, relieved, telling him, "Jake, I'm not going anywhere. After all the effort it took to get here, you think I'd do anything to jeopardize us?"

"You might not have a choice." He had argued. "Giving birth is dangerous."

"Nothing will stop us growing old and saggy together." He had been appeased but the shadow of worry sat on him and I knew it wouldn't go away until after the birth.

He had returned to the police, working with dogs and their trainers. We were enjoying the regular hours and both planned to take maternity leave to stay with the babies when they were born. We would muddle through. We always did.

As I watched Louis walk away I knew he would always be dropping in and out of our lives. Would Jax be okay with that?

Jake came up behind me and hugged me, his big hands rubbing my belly. It was huge, how Louis had missed it just boggled the mind. I thought back to that day I had met Jake, while I was brawling with my ex-fiancé in the street over a poor dog that had been used for human entertainment. Jake had stepped in when no one else would, a big scary ex-cop with a complicated and lonely life. I had wanted him from the moment I set eyes on him and that attraction had forged my way to this new life.

In my ear, he whispered, "He asked you to leave me, didn't he?"

I didn't want to answer that, it didn't matter in the least.

"He doesn't know what he wants. I got the only good thing out of Louis I was ever going to get." Jax ploughed into Jake's leg and he let me go to pick the little boy up.

Man and boy peered at each other and Jake said, "Me too."

EPILOGUE

Two years later.

I was racing from the clinic where I had gossiped for far too long, too worked up and anxious to just go home and face the music. Primrose had tried to usher me out, claiming she had to get to the hairdressers and get her makeup done but I just nattered on, talking about nothing. Finn and I had managed to talk Primrose into coming back to work for us. We had been determined and had moved fast, before Keisha discovered we had reopened and demanded her old job back. There was no chance, but also no stopping Keisha when she wanted something.

Primrose agreed to a meeting with us where we soon discovered she was embarrassed about my treatment by her brother Neil on the farm down south. I assured her there was no hard feelings, it had been a complicated situation. Primrose admitted that her brother had been blackmailed by Darling Roach to get rid of me. He had stupidly had flowers sent to Darling at school a few years ago and she had kept the story for just this type of scenario. Zoe had just found out and Neil's future was up in the air right now. I felt bad for him, that he was idiotic enough to imagine life with Darling would be better than with the lovely Zoe. He was an idiot, but like Primrose said, it was complicated. She agreed to come back to us straight away, was excited about it.

Another complicated relationship was the ongoing saga of Michelle and Mike. Turns out Mike had moved in with Darling who had relocated to Auckland to be with him. She had served a few months in prison for the mess she left behind in Grafton but she took her punishment well and had dropped off the map when she started her life with Mike. Only a few months ago Jake admitted he had heard rumor that Mike was seeing Michelle again. They were back to their favored way of romancing each other, illicitly. Michelle was still on behavior conditions but out of jail. Toby visited every so often but refused to stay there. He had his own bank account that his grandfather had set up without his mother's knowledge. Whenever she demanded money her father flat refused.

Toby was fourteen now, tall and handsome, obsessed with sports and helping Finn and I at the clinic whenever we needed a spare pair of hands. He was very serious about saving for his future, not wanting his grandfather to fund his studies, determined to be a veterinarian on his own terms and I couldn't be prouder of the young man he was growing into. He had adjusted quickly to being a big brother and was a kind and patient force with his siblings.

On an exasperated huff, Primrose collected her handbag and pushed me out the door, locking it firmly behind her, telling me she would see me in a couple of hours. I wanted to puke on her but she scurried away before I could prove how bad this idea was. My acting skills were rubbish anyway.

After my lost and lonely time in Grafton, my life had gone back to a routine that I couldn't be happier with. Jax was four and going to daycare every morning, a whirlwind of energy that Jake maximized with park trips and ball games. He was a happy child, bright and busy. He laughed easily and loved Jake and Toby with his entire being. I wondered how he would be if he had terrible parents, no doubt like Louis, a lost boy that had grown into a fierce man.

The twins were two now. Both girls were obsessed with

pink and dolls, an adjustment the rest of us had to make. They were wild and fun, forcing Jake and Toby into endless dress ups and tea parties. My life with Jake was busy. I worked two days a week with Finn and Jake took those days off to keep the home routines on track. It was like tag team and we fell into bed every night exhausted.

I took the long way home, delaying the inevitable for as long as I could.

Jenny was pacing outside my house when I pulled up and she yelled at me, "Where have you been?"

"Emergency." I said and she just rolled her eyes and dragged me inside, pushing me into the shower, yelling at me to hurry up.

Dressing in the lovely summer dress I had found on a trip to Newmarket with Jenny, I let her do my hair and makeup then followed her through the silent house and to the French doors. Our big back yard was immaculate, so pretty my breath caught.

Finn smiled at me, handing me a tissue when tears threatened while Jenny barked that if I cried she would quit. She then smiled brightly and sauntered toward the back of the property, her own pretty dress in place, her kids trying to contain Captain Pugwash who was on a harness and rolling in the grass in delight, his stocky little body wriggling like a jellybean.

Pothead was perched on a cat shelf that was often used for the strays or fostered animals we looked after for the SPCA. He was peering around in disgust, looking down his nose. It had felt cruel not to include him in today's adventure, and the yard was secure enough to contain him. The bow had been a step too far and he had hissed and kicked until a back paw was trapped in it and Finn had to save him. Pothead really was a big hairy asshole but just looking at him made me feel calmer and I smiled, tears filling my eyes again. This was so uncomfortable.

Thankfully Louis wasn't here but he had sent flowers. He had moved permanently to Wellington and he and Keisha were divorcing since he had impregnated a twenty-year-old student and decided she was the one. I was horrified that he could leave all his kids but he hadn't changed, he was still just like my selfish, greedy father.

Finn hooked my arm through his and tried to tug me to move but I was terrified. Everyone was turning to look and I wanted to run for my life. I hated attention and had not agreed to so many people. Then Jax ran toward me, a jumping ball of excitement, adorable in his little suit. Biting my lip I let my gaze lift to find Jake waiting for me. He was dressed in the same suit as Jax, Toby by his side, Sarge, now grey and riddled with arthritis between them, managing to look proud with a white bowtie around his neck. The twins were rolling around in their pretty dresses while Jenny tried to wrangle them to look at me.

Jake gave me a look like, *what are you doing?* And I smiled and turned to Finn, saying, "Jesus, hurry up."

He laughed and we walked down the aisle, secretly pulling at each other's elbows, always trying to outdo each other.

Jake stared at me hard when I stopped before him, shaking hands with Finn who muttered, "Good fucking luck, mate."

Finn grinned proudly at his wife. He had thought I was joking when I asked him to give me away, then had hugged me tightly and said, "Thank you, I'd be honored so long as no one tries to kill me on the day."

Taking Jake's hands, I noted his were shaking too.

We had agreed to get married for the kids, they deserved the stability. We loved and trusted each other, were dedicated to our life together and made plans for our future, but truth was, we were still terrified of messing it all up.

"No regrets?" I asked him, knowing the past four years contained parts that had been hard for Jake. I was still over-reacting to people about their pets, jumping in when I wasn't wanted and taking animals off hopeless owners. The cops had been called a few times. Each time Jake agreed I was right to step in, then he would worry and get upset, claiming I had bigger things to worry about than an old man's pet ferret (it's a long story but I got the ferret and it now lived with Jenny and Finn). I knew he was scared for me but this was part of the deal, this is who I am and we were both learning to deal with it.

As we agreed to be together till the end we both cried which made the twins start crying too. The noise upset Pothead who leapt from his shelf to attack my brother's new boyfriend who was saved by Keisha, the only person brave enough to take the big cat on (Pothead went deathly still, like a mannequin had come to life and grabbed him. Keisha's perfume obsession rendered her dead to the cat). The rest of the day was a mess and I loved every second of it.

Jake Roland entered my life around the same time my obsession with organized chicken fighting was collapsing and we had fought hard to be together ever since. Against all odds we were creating the kind of life my parents would not recognize, a happy, busy homelife. I had become more than just a veterinarian, much, much more.

The End

ABOUT THE AUTHOR

Casey Campbell

 Casey Campbell writes contemporary and paranormal romance, urban fantasy and short horror. She loves each genre deeply. A librarian who likes the quirky ones, people and books included, she lives with her husband, two sons and a very old cat that runs the house like a drill sergeant at mealtimes.

Find her on:
Instagram: @caseycampbellwrites
Twitter: caseycampbell_1
Facebook: Casey Campbell Author
Caseycampbellwrites@gmailcom

A review is always welcome.

BOOKS IN THIS SERIES

The Pits - Book One in the
Despondent Veterinarian Trilogy

When this vet says she will do anything to stop animal abuse . . . she means anything.

Sophie Carter is a stubborn, determined veterinarian who is certain her nice community hides a nasty secret, a dog fighting ring, and those animal abusing bastards are going down. Her attempts to find evidence soon attracts the attention of three very different men:

An ex-police dog handler who wants to help her.

A career criminal who wants to stop her.

And an ex-fiancée that would happily destroy her.

But how do these seemingly unconnected men know each other?

With no one who they appear, each man holds a piece of the puzzle that could eradicate the barbaric amusement. On a blatant promise and a whispered secret, Sophie finds herself confronted by her worst nightmare, the pits, where she must reveal her own complicated past and, once more, fight for her life. Who needs a man to save you when your jailbird daddy taught you everything he knew?

The Pothead - Book Two In The Despondent Veterinarian Trilogy

With nothing left to lose this vet will let it all burn.

Months after the fight in the pits, veterinarian Sophie Carter is again all alone. Dumped by Jake Rowland, the man who offered her the world, and ignored by Louis Martinez, the man that saved her from the pits.

Without warning, her dull life explodes when an arson attack destroys her clinic, almost killing Pothead, her strangely knowing clinic cat. As if summoned, both men return at the same time her father is finally released from prison.

When her sister goes missing, Sophie needs Louis and Jake's connections to find her, except they have discovered her childhood secret, that once upon a time Sophie had a different name, and that her father made her hurt a man. That man's son has dedicated his life to eradicating human scum, secretly hunting down the family that ruined his. That man is an undercover cop who is lost in the violence. That man is Louis Martinez and he will have his revenge.

Uncertain where to turn, Sophie finds herself back at her family farm with her mother, a deluded animal abuser awaiting her husband, a man determined to return to his old life. With Louis and Jake hunting her down, Sophie will discover if either man is capable of being the person she needs.

And what does the clinic cat, Pothead have to do with the fire that ruined her lovely life.

BOOKS BY THIS AUTHOR

The Pits - Book One In The Despondent Vet Trilogy

When this vet says she will do anything to stop animal abuse . . . she means anything.

Sophie Carter is a stubborn, determined veterinarian who is certain her nice community hides a nasty secret, a dog fighting ring, and those animal abusing bastards are going down. Her attempts to find evidence soon attracts the attention of three very different men:

An ex-police dog handler who wants to help her.

A career criminal who wants to stop her.

And an ex-fiancée that would happily destroy her.

But how do these seemingly unconnected men know each other?

With no one who they appear, each man holds a piece of the puzzle that could eradicate the barbaric amusement. On a blatant promise and a whispered secret, Sophie finds herself confronted by her worst nightmare, the pits, where she must reveal her own complicated past and, once more, fight for her life. Who needs a man to save you when your jailbird daddy taught you everything he knew?

The Pothead - Book Two In The Despondent Vet Trilogy

Months after the fight in the pits, veterinarian Sophie Carter is again all alone. Dumped by Jake Rowland, the man who offered her the world, and ignored by Louis Martinez, the man that saved her from the pits.

Without warning, her dull life explodes when an arson attack destroys her clinic, almost killing Pothead, her strangely knowing clinic cat. As if summoned, both men return at the same time her father is finally released from prison.

When her sister goes missing, Sophie needs Louis and Jake's connections to find her, except they have discovered her childhood secret, that once upon a time Sophie had a different name, and that her father made her hurt a man. That man's son has dedicated his life to eradicating human scum, secretly hunting down the family that ruined his. That man is an undercover cop who is lost in the violence. That man is Louis Martinez and he will have his revenge.

Uncertain where to turn, Sophie finds herself back at her family farm with her mother, a deluded animal abuser awaiting her husband, a man determined to return to his old life. With Louis and Jake hunting her down, Sophie will discover if either man is capable of being the person she needs.

And what does the clinic cat, Pothead have to do with the fire that ruined her lovely life.

The Semaphore - A Stand Alone Las Vegas Novel

When Bailey Hamilton's 'safe' husband dumped her for a younger, girly pink model, Bailey did what any outraged wife would do, she stole the lover's tickets and luggage for two nights of fun in Las Vegas. After that she resolves to return to her home country of New Zealand, secure a divorce and get on with her boring life.

But while in Las Vegas, dressed in Bebe's ridiculous clothes, Bailey is mistaken for a hooker and propositioned by Victor Bonds, ex-army, now part time bodyguard to the owner of the Semaphore, a huge casino that will change the direction of both Bailey and Victor's lonely lives forever.

Rules Of Her Game - A Contemporary Sports Romance

During her final year of high school, rugby prodigy, Dani Maxwell's boyfriend was paralyzed by the sport they both loved. Ever since, Dani has openly despised the game, even as her father rose to England's national coach and her brother the newest recruit.

Dani meets controversial ex-player Cooper Graves, her father's newest co-coach. Once accused of a shocking crime, his perfect life was ruined.

The attraction is instant, but is Cooper the dangerous monster she's heard of or the sweet man she is getting to know? Who gained the most by bringing him so low?

Amid the upheaval, Dani is offered an unprecedented opportunity. A natural talent in a male dominated sport, does she have what it takes to uncover Cooper's past while forcing open the doors of an elitist sport that has never wanted women as players, referees and especially as coaches?

Sick Gifts - A Novella

At the peak of his career, Detective Drysdal Weir tracked notorious serial killer, Victor Grains. Both men reveled in the publicity, cat and mouse, good versus evil, each playing their role. Then Victor changed the rules and murdered Drysdal's wife. After that he gave himself up, forfeiting his life. He never said why.

Victor was quickly put to death and the media circus moved on while Drysdal's career and remaining family were destroyed. With few options and unable to leave the town where he failed his wife, Drysdal became sheriff and sunk into a miserable half-life of regret.

Ten years pass and a copycat has surfaced. But something feels off, even if the target is exactly Victor's type, a pretty woman desperate enough to buy a dead man's house. Can a home hold the evil Drysdal senses, or has Victor found a way back?

Small and sweet, Michelle Grady loves her new home. Beset with phobias since childhood she rarely leaves the property, thankfully her best friend and boyfriend ensure she is never lonely. Now someone has sent her a gift, a teddy bear stuffed with rotting meat. Has her boyfriend discovered she cheated? She just needs a chance to explain she was protecting her friend. But her friend has disappeared and Michelle now has the local sheriff invading her privacy.

Can Sheriff Weir put the past behind him to save another woman from a monster?

And what is the link between Michelle and the dark specter that hovers, filling her home with dark need?

www.ingramcontent.com/pod-product-compliance
Lightning Source LLC
Chambersburg PA
CBHW052038240626
47153CB00006B/2139